Neicy

Neicy

A Novel

Akasha Hull

AURELIA
WORKS

Although characters and events may have real life inspiration, this is a work of fiction. The persons, incidents, and dialogue are products of the author's imagination and are not to be construed as real.

Song Lyrics:
"Kansas City" written by Jerry Leiber and Mike Stoller, as recorded by Wilbert Harrison, 1959; "Wonderful World" written by Sam Cooke with Lou Adler and Herb Alpert, as recorded by Sam Cooke, 1959; "Disco Inferno" written by Ron Kersey with Leroy Green, as recorded by The Trammps, 1976; "Pledging My Love" written by Ferdinand Washington and Don Robey, as recorded by Johnny Ace, 1954.

For information contact:
AureliaWorks, PO Box 7385, Little Rock, AR 72217
or www.akashahull.com.
ISBN 978-0-9883607-0-9

Credits:
Author photograph – Ebony Blevins
Internal design and layout – Byron Taylor
Cover design – Denise Borel Billups

for all of my angels,
helpers, and friends —
with love and appreciation

Neicy

March, 1950
Little Rock, Arkansas

CHAPTER 1

Two-year-old Neicy is playing alone on the scarred tile floor of the women's workhouse bathroom in Little Rock, Arkansas. She runs her tiny sharp nails through the grimy buildup between the blocks, watching these grayish shavings add their pattern to the streaks in the faded brown squares. She tires and looks around. Her gaze wavers in the early morning light, then bounces off the bleak green walls and dissolves through the window pane dappled with dirt, its top half turned down just enough to blow in a cup of cold air. She shivers and her hungry stomach begins to growl.

"Mama," she calls.

Mama doesn't answer, only mumbles something to the man standing next to her on the other side of the narrow stall door.

"Maa-ma, Maa-ma." This time a bit louder, a bit more importunate.

"Mama's coming, sweetie." The rushed words promise comfort and love. "Hold your horses."

Her mother's feet in flat brown oxfords slide further apart, the toes pointing slightly outward. The tall man's black work boots move in to fill the space. The backs of his shoes are visible, scuff marks on the heels and threads beginning to fray at the leather seam center. He grunts like a pig and her mama makes a noise she has never heard before.

Just as she decides to crawl under the door to find the hem of her mother's uniform so she can pull it, the stall begins to shake and rattle and the tall man grunts louder like a pig and wheezes. Her mama's sounds are too jumbled to reach her and stay there in the stall, right next to the man.

She crawls a few more steps until she bumps against the crookneck cold of the toilet in the adjacent stall. She could stand up if she wanted, but there are more things to see on the floor than from two and a half feet above it. Like a bubble of old stuff, which she brings to her mouth, scratching and tasting, squizzling and eating as she sits back on her thin, strong haunches.

"Neicy. Neicy, baby. Where are you?"

She had forgot her mama had forgotten about her until her mama's name-calling voice hit the back of her busy head.

Her mother's big dark eyes rolled around the long, narrow room. The tall man bends over behind her shaking out the cuffs of his pants and tying his shoe.

"There she is," he says, standing up and pointing his finger.

Her mother jumped like she had been shot and lifts her child up off the floor, folding her to her breast.

"What's that you into, sweetie?" Her voice lost its blurred edges and her eyes got focused. She moved real fast toward the water faucet, digging in her pocket for the cloth she had just finished wiping her own self with screwing a lousy bastard to get little Neicy some extra milk. The man spat, "Niggers!" – then turned and walked away. At the door, he looked over his shoulder and said, "Git on back to your room before I make the rounds."

"You slimy motherfucker," she breathed, cursing the air he left behind.

Neicy found herself in this workhouse with her mother only one more time. The day the officials released them, another tall white man in light grey slacks cinched by a silver belt buckle slammed in to the prison office. He was mad as a wet hen, his voice booming all the way back to the laundry area where the women with three of their children were wringing out sheets and towels. Neicy witnessed it all, her four-year-old self alert as an electrified fence.

"What y'all doing with Virginia locked up in this place?! Let her outta here. Damn. My wife's at home about to have a baby and I ain't even had my breakfast."

He was yelling at the other two men in the office like they were cheap labor and waving around his hands, fingers full of gold diamond rings.

"Ginny," he called to his Negro maid as if he knew that she and the other females were trying to peep through the door at the back of the room.

The supervisor popped out of his office. He was about half the size of the big, loud-talking man but tried to act like he had the law of Arkansas on his back to uphold. He opened his mouth – "Mr. Gideon, sir" – but footfalls, shuffling and cussing drowned out the rest. Mr. Gideon pulled two pieces of money from his billfold and slapped them down hard on the brown wooden desk. When the supervisor told him he had to sign some documents because he was responsible now, he said, "Where they at?" – looking around the room, maybe for the papers, maybe for the property he was signing out.

Virginia jumped from behind the door dragging Neicy by the hand.

"Mr. Gideon!"

"Miss Mary's at home looking for you, Virginia. Where you been?"

"They put me in here cause I cut LeeGus. But I didn't kill him. How's Miss Mary doing?"

"You know she tired and fretful and craving one of your lemon meringue pies."

"Yes, sir. I'm'a make her one soon as you take me out of here."

With his shiny fountain pen, Mr. Gideon drew curves and a long wavy line on the papers, then marched back through the door he had come in, Neicy and her mama scooting along behind. The little supervisor raised his voice. "Virginia Johnson, I don't want to see you back in here, you hear?" Virginia kept scooting. The bloody red dress she wore when she arrived, and her big pocketbook where she hid the butcher knife so LeeGus wouldn't know she had it til she walked up on him never crossed their minds. Virginia pulled Neicy down next to her on the back seat of Mr. Gideon's Chrysler sedan and said, "Thank you, sweet Jesus!"

All that day Virginia kept rolling her eyes up in the air and repeating "thank you Jesus!" like Jesus was plastered in the top wallpaper seams and looking down special at her from the ceiling corners. That didn't stop her, though, from cleaning Miss Mary's bedroom, and baking coconut cake and lemon meringue pie, and ironing Mr. Gideon four starched white shirts. Keeping out of the way in the kitchen and the back yard got tiresome to Neicy. There wasn't much to do except eat the crumblings that her mama gave her and pull the heads off Miss Mary's flowers boasting up the walls along the blue and white house.

It was dust dark when they finally stepped from the trolley on Linear Street, Virginia holding Neicy's hand in one hand and a bulging shopping bag full of old stuff Miss Mary no longer wanted in the other.

"I'm about to drop, Neicy. Run cross the ditch and tell Beulah we back."

The stretch through the grocery store alley to where they called home with her mama's old woman friend Beulah was a familiar sprint for Neicy. But before she could get a good running start, a black pickup truck slowed up beside them and the man driving it leaned carefully out the window. He looked a lot like the mean white men in the crazy prison workhouse but her mama had taught her that this one wasn't a real white man. "Just call him Mr. Riley," her mama said.

"Riley," Virginia said herself now, all the life filtered out of her drooping voice so that even Neicy, tuned keen as a fork to her mother's moods, couldn't read it.

Mr. Riley was looking at Virginia like he was also trying to find out something.

"You alright, Virginia?"

"I'm alright." She was holding herself up straight, but she wasn't moving, and she didn't say anything else as the darkness came down another couple degrees.

"LeeGus telling people you still his wife and he gon take you back."

"I ain't lawfully married to nobody."

"If you don't want to get back with him, I been dying to have you come and live with me. Now's a good time to make a move. Miz Forbes'll let us rent the vacant rooms in her house. I talked to her on my way to work this morning."

The part of Virginia that was strong enough stood next to the ditch and considered. Riley Washington was nineteen years older than she, a good man but not a thrilling companion. He was not burning sweet to her like Neicy's father, David Walker, who was long-gone to Chicago where he could make bigger book and charge city-high jitney fares. She never used to think about sex, didn't even know what the excitement around being with a man was about until she met David. What her gangly husband had done to her in their backwoods cabin when she was a young bride just turned sixteen right after her grandmother died had not amounted to much. So she decided that the best way to use what she had was to sit on it until some man gave her enough or did enough for her to make getting up off it worthwhile, not counting those times when what was supposed to be hers had been coerced or taken from her.

David Walker had been enticing — hard drinking, good-timing, easy-loving, sporty — flashy with money and generous to her when he had it. She had learned to love liquor. And parties. And playing cards. But some strain of righteous morality her big mama instilled in her unsuited her for the fast, gaming life. She believed that two people shacking up or even just taking up were supposed to be true to each other. And see where that had gotten her! On the women's farm twice with her baby, doing whatever she needed to survive.

Now, here Riley Washington was offering her an easier way of life. She would have to be quieter and drink beer instead of whiskey most of the time. She would have to settle down. But Neicy was getting too big to be dragged from pillar to post, and, Lord knows, she herself could use some steady support that didn't bring fussing and fighting along with it. Maybe reining in her fun-loving spirit wouldn't be so bad.

Mr. Riley and Neicy were quietly looking at her – nut-brown skin smooth over her pretty face except where it wrinkled tired around the red lipstick she had smeared on her mouth before they left Miss Mary's, medium breasts, slim ankles, coarse black hair peaking into her forehead and pulled back in a bun.

"Riley, I'm sick'a shit," is what came out of her mouth.

"No need to worry, Virginia. I'm gon treat you and your baby girl right."

He jumped around to where they were standing in the gravel and took the heavy bag out of her hand, then lifted her other, weightier human package onto the truck seat.

"You comfortable, Neicy?"

With the gearstick poking her ribs, she nodded "yes."

When they got to Miz Forbes's and she finally lay down to sleep on the rollaway bed, still in her checkered dress with the torn lace collar, she felt like she had been up for at least three days.

Living with her mama and Mr. Riley daddy was much better than living in the room at Beulah's with her mama and LeeGus. Even from across the hall with Beulah where she sometimes went at night, she had heard her mother and LeeGus talking loud.

"Naw, I wasn't," he would say.

"Yes, you did," Virginia hollered back. "Don't you try to play me cheap."

She could tell by the bumping noises that her mama was moving around the room like a captured bird, her dress tail flying as she circled the space at the foot of the bed and took a sip from the heavy glass setting on the edge of the dresser.

"I don't know why you accuse me of that woman. She couldn't give me the time of day."

"Day time, no time, I'm telling you, LeeGus Mitchell, don't think 'cause I'm from the country, you can take me for a fool."

One night, her mother got so mad Beulah had to go and help LeeGus keep her from tearing out of the house. She was screaming, "I'm 'a kill you and that heifer both." LeeGus had his arms around her trying to hold her still and Beulah was saying, "I'll go with you, Ginny. Just bide your time." Between the two of them, they calmed her down.

Nothing like this happened after they started living with Mr. Riley. Every Saturday, he gave Miz Forbes folded up money, and those Saturdays were her favorite times. A lot of food in the house. Mr. Riley daddy and her mama laughing and drinking. Music on the radio. Everybody looking at her happy. She could eat saltine crackers and swallow orange Nehi pop until dinner was ready.

During the day, she stayed at Beulah's house, which was still just around the corner, while her mother cleaned and cooked for Miss Mary and Mr. Riley did carpentry work. Old Beulah kept her mind more on beer than on watching her and the other three children whose mamas left them while they went to their jobs – Maryann, Darlene, and Darlene's little brother, Chuck. Chuckie was the one that Mr. Isaac, Beulah's bright-skinned beer-drinking partner, messed with the most. After he and Beulah finished off the fat brown bottles and Beulah fell dead asleep on the kitchen table, a drool of snuff dripping from the corner of her mouth, her head rag sliding just enough to reveal a plait of short gray hair, he came into the stuffy front room where they played on the worn linoleum.

He picked up Chuck, whose face looked even more like a rat when he got scared and silent. Mr. Isaac sat down in the rocking chair that had no arms and unhitched one side of his paint-stained overhauls, then pulled Chuckie backwards on his lap, unfastened Chuckie's pants, and started squeezing and twisting his little boy ding-a-ling.

He batted it around until he put Chuckie down and came for one of the girls. Whenever it was her turn, Neicy hung on the floor, holding the red and blue blocks her mama had brought from Miss Mary's and her new Christmas wee-wee doll. Still pulling away, she got turned backwards on his lap the same as Chuck, only before Mr. Isaac did that, he took his big thing from the placard of his overhauls, then slid down her panties so he could rubboard her back and forth, back and forth on it. As she tried to squirm away, he squeezed her harder to his chest. "Hold on, little sister. I'll be finished tee-rectly." His beer breath mashed against her ear and his hands smelled sour like the dirty clothes basket.

One time she dropped her baby doll and sprang out of his arms so fast she made it to the floor. Mr. Isaac looked mad, but all of a sudden he grinned and fished a nickel from his pocket. "Come'ere, sugar." When she didn't move, he grabbed her up on to his thing and then let her go, popping her white cotton panties back around her waist where they belonged, trying to act playful rocking and shaking her narrow girl hips. Then he caught hold of himself, finished what he was doing, and left out the kitchen door.

Beulah trundled to the room in time to give them cold baloney and some bread from the wax paper loaf with colored balloons just before Darlene and Chuck's mama came. She worked at the new veterans hospital and got off early. Chuckie was sick to his stomach, throwing up pieces of dark pink baloney and mushy white bread swimming in milk and strawberry kool-aid. Miz Anna said to Beulah, "I told you he was too delicate to eat that much cold lunch meat. It won't kill you to take down a skillet and fry it 'til the edges crisp up."

Beulah said, "Sho nuff," and nodded goodbye as the breeze from the open door blew through the house, outlining her tough stringy body. After that, the kids had white bread and mayonnaise sandwiches, jelly and biscuits, leftover cabbage and hotwater cornbread. When baloney came back around, Neicy thought Beulah must've forgot about frying the meat. They ate it cold and Chuckie got sick again.

Mr. Riley daddy was pulling her down the tall high steps of their house in one of the cardboard boxes he had just brought home and unpacked. Every Saturday, he made groceries at Mr. Antonio's store and when the boxes were empty, gave her thrilling rides in them. After three sliding trips down the steep stairs, he walked up into the house and left her "bump" at the bottom, her five-year-old head racing and wavy, hiccupping and catching her breath. She climbed out of the box and sat on a step, reclining on both of her elbows, feeling the hot air caught between her shoulders and the ruffles of her pinafore. It was almost dark. A mosquito ninged next to her ear, lightening bugs flickered off and on around her.

As she raised her body and turned around, preparing to go inside, she found herself smack face to face with another little girl on the back side of the steps who was quietly getting up from a squat. The girl's big eyes held steady into hers while she pulled up her panties. Neicy jumped to the ground as the strange girl finished letting her dress fall haphazardly into place. There was a big gap at the waist where the skirt had been torn and was coming ungathered. The girl's face was dirty and her hair hadn't been combed. She looked wild and funny, her light skin faintly glowing. The two of them stared at one another.

"I had to pee." The girl's voice was loud and definite.

"You're supposed to pee in the toilet," Neicy answered.

"My mama told me not to come back home."

Having said that, she sat down right where she had just finished peeing and gazed out at the dry side yard and dusty street, like this was what she normally did when she couldn't go home. Neicy remembered many nights when she had left her mama inside with grownups and wandered out beyond the shine of house lights. But she could always run in anytime she wanted and pile on somebody's bed or cot or next to her mother's legs underneath a table, the slap of cards and drink glasses clinking putting her to sleep on the gritty floor, totally forgotten until Virginia shifted her foot, surprised that she'd almost mashed her.

"Ain't you scared?" she asked the girl.

"Naw," the girl answered, without moving anything but her lips. "It's okay if I have some newspaper and something to eat." She picked for a moment in her dress front pocket. When her hand came out, it was still empty.

Neicy thought about the catfish and hush puppies she was about to eat until her stomach felt like bursting. Then she thought how her mama told her not to get mixed up with the little bad children. This girl looked like one of them.

"What's your name?" she asked. Maybe knowing her name would make the badness better.

"Erma Jean." She looked Neicy straight in the eye. "Tell your daddy I said to please give me a piece of his bread." She said it like she knew they kept bread in a metal tray on top of the icebox in the kitchen.

Neicy was sure that Mr. Riley daddy had never heard of this girl, Erma Jean, but she told her anyway, "We got fish and hush puppies tonight."

"Yum-yum, gimme some." Erma Jean rolled her eyes and rubbed her stomach and then laughed like she was making fun of somebody.

Neicy didn't like it. "My mama says you're not supposed to beg."

"I don't beg. I just stand in front of people til they give me what I want."

"My mama wouldn't let you do that."

"Tell your daddy." There the girl went again, sounding like she knew her daddy.

"Wait a minute." Neicy ran up the steps to report her.

When the screen door didn't catch on her heels after she yanked it open and let it fly, Neicy jumped to find the girl right behind her. Her mama was turned toward the stove singing with the radio, and Mr. Riley daddy sat at the table counting out dollar bills.

"I told you to wait," Neicy yelled, thoroughly put out with the girl and her boldness.

Her mother turned around and both grownups froze staring at Erma Jean, who had walked a little ahead and off to the side. She looked even worse in the bright kitchen light, picking strands of frizzy orange hair off her cheek and rubbing the back of one leg with the other. Erma Jean and her daddy Riley looked alike. They had skin almost the color of white people, wide round faces, and good hair. And they acted like they could win a fight with anybody. The man on the radio was singing, "Set 'em up, Joe" and la-da-da hum-humming. Her mama liked that song, but Neicy didn't think anybody was listening to it right now except her.

Daddy Riley's eyes widened when he saw the girl. Neicy thought he was about to say something, but he didn't. Without minding what he was doing, he folded the money he'd been counting into a wad and squeezed it in his hands. His eyes were shiny, his forehead was sweaty and shining, the kitchen was hot.

Riley Washington was having the strangest sensation of his outside life and his home and family bleeding into one another. Himself as a child and the adult present collided at the back of his mind. He knew that this raggedy girl with eyes that solicited without asking was the same one who had taken to sitting next to his tree-shaded truck as he broke for lunch on the new job he had just picked up. But flashing on her face so unexpectedly felt like he was staring at his own boy self forty years ago, his skin a little lighter, more country red dust rimming his ankles, the same stubborn spirit that made him push himself forward when everyone around him was beating him back. It wasn't his fault that his sharecropping mother had been forced to give up her body to the man who still practically owned her, her husband, and their children – with his white-looking child self as the too-visible result.

The girl moved closer to the chipped metal table and spoke directly to him. "I want some more of your bread." She must have been remembering the cold cornbread crumbs he had mixed with cheese and fresh garden tomatoes and given her earlier today. But how had she ended up in his kitchen a whole neighborhood distant, and so late in the evening?

He could feel Virginia's quick suspicion rising like another kind of heat from the stove.

"Whose child is this?" she asked.

Little Neicy, careful and thorough as usual in the face of her mother's quick moods, began to spew out her side of the story – "Mama, I was playing on the steps, and this bad girl name Erma Jean peed behind me. Her mama told her not to come home, and she started begging..." – but Riley could tell Virginia's patience wouldn't last through that. She had already dropped the long-handled fork on the spoon drip and come up behind him. With the girl in front of him and Virginia at his back, he felt trapped. So he stood up.

The chair thrusting backward caught Virginia's bare feet. "Ouch," she cried and shoved it forward again into his legs, then bent over to examine her toe.

He resented how quickly Virginia made him uneasy with her cantankerous temper. She was as sweet inside as warm bread pudding but as jealous as a woman could be. All he had done was share some of his lunch with this silent, hungry girl. He didn't know her mother, whoever that was, if she had one.

Neicy stood looking, fussing to herself. All this trouble was Erma Jean's fault. She should have left her outside on the ground.

"Go home, bad girl," she shouted.

Erma Jean didn't move, didn't blink even one of her round, cat-colored eyes.

"Go home, I said." This time, Neicy rushed up and shoved her in the chest. "Get out of my house." She pushed her again. Then Erma Jean raised both of her arms and counter-shoved her so hard she slammed into the table.

Before Neicy could steady herself to push again, Virginia grabbed Erma Jean's shoulder and began to shake her. "You little bitch. What do you think you're doing, pushing on my baby?"

"Wait, hold on now," Mr. Riley daddy was coaxing but forceful as he took a step forward. "She's just a little girl, too."

"So why are you taking up for her? Both of your asses can go when the wagon comes. She don't have no business barging in here and fighting Neicy." Erma Jean was trying to pull away, while Virginia held on, twisting her shoulder harder.

"Mother, please." He called Virginia "mother" as a last resort.

Neicy moved in closer. She wanted peace and quiet. She wanted her dinner. And it seemed like Mr. Riley daddy did, too.

He lifted her mother's hand off the girl, who was still the calmest of the bunch. "Finish frying the fish and let's sit down and eat. There's enough for her to have some."

"I'm not starting to feed every stray child on the block..."

"Just this one time," Daddy Riley interrupted. "Then I'll take her home." He turned to Erma Jean. "Where do you live?"

Erma Jean shrugged.

"I said, where do you live?"

She still didn't answer.

Neicy could tell her mama was about to get mad again. Virginia grabbed the girl's arm and said, "Look, gal. You better answer when we ask you a question." And she knuckled her hard, up side the head.

Erma Jean yelped. "I can't go home. My mama told me not to come back home."

"What kind of shit is that?" Virginia cursed. "You too young to be out on the streets by yourself."

"Don't worry," Riley liked the way she was getting involved, but thought she was handling the girl too rough. "I'll find out where to take her." He sniffed, wrinkling his nose through the air. "The fish needs taking up out of the pan. Come on, let's us sit down and eat."

It was the strangest dinner Neicy could remember. She and her mama and Mr. Riley daddy kept their eyes on Erma Jean, who concentrated on her plate. When all the fish and hush puppies were finished, Daddy Riley took off with her, safely, somewhere in the night. She never wanted to see that "little bitch" again.

CHAPTER 2

Neicy knew that Mamie Brown, their excitable, gold-toothed neighbor, only picked her up on Saturday. Sitting broad in the driver's seat of her husband's green two-toned Pontiac, Mamie roared up and yelled.

Neicy bolted to the front of the house. "Come ride with me," Mamie called.

Virginia opened the screen door. "Mamie, gal, where you going?"

"Over to the base. I came to get my girl." She didn't have any children.

Quickly, Neicy exchanged her old tan shorts for a newer pair of red ones and slipped on a clean white blouse. Virginia freshened up her daughter's hair, brushing in the straying edges and tightening her day-old braids. Feeling pretty special, Neicy dashed down the wooden steps, one sandal coming unbuckled around her narrow heel. Mamie leaned over and fastened it, kissing her on the lips and forehead, and they sped off.

On the other side of town, Mamie turned into a cluster of streets mama and Mr. Riley daddy never entered. The houses resembled those in the alleys around Mr. Antonio's store, but they sat up on concrete blocks in a dab of yard. Mamie parked her Pontiac. "Come, Neicy. I gotta make a little stop by here." Mamie hustled her out of the car, over a broken glass bottle, and in through the door.

A man and woman Neicy had never seen – him in his ribbed tank undershirt and her wearing a mu-mu house robe – lounged in a big bed.

"Hey, gal. Go in the kitchen and get you a glass," the man greeted Mamie and reached for a bottle on the bedside table. "Have a taste."

"No, thanks," Mamie smiled, her eyes turned toward the woman who was propped up on her elbow, smiling back at Mamie, her robe sliding open in front. "I'm on a run. I thought I'd pop by and see if Queen had sumpen good for me in the mail today." She was staring at the woman on the bed, who slowly rolled further forward until one of her breasts came loose. Mamie's eyes got bigger. Neicy saw that the woman's titty was larger than her mama's but not as big as Mamie's, and colored creamy brown.

"Im'a have to look." Queen's voice was low. She sat up and laid her cigarette in a cut glass ashtray. "Baby, reach me that house shoe."

Neicy sprang forward from where she was standing alongside Mamie's thigh, but felt Mamie catch her arm and pull her back just as the man leaned over his side of the bed and came up with a man's house shoe walked down at the heel. Queen slipped it on her foot, and then rifled through a stack of envelopes on top of the chest of drawers, not actually looking at the letters but really at Mamie as the man poured himself another drink.

"I don't see nothing here, but could be Mozelle misplaced it." She winked quickly at Mamie. "Maybe you better check a little later."

Mamie glanced at the man, who was still concentrating on his drink, then nodded her head real fast, twice, to the woman. "Me and Neicy are headed over to the base. If Sergeant Brown lets me keep the car, we'll stop back by."

The woman double shrugged her shoulders, jiggling her creamy breasts, and took a long drag off her cigarette. When she looked at Neicy and smiled, Neicy didn't know whether she should return the smile or not, but the woman let her smile travel upward to Mamie – who was intently watching her – and said, slowly, "I'll probably still be around."

Mamie shifted. "Y'all take it easy," she said in a louder voice as she reached for Neicy's hand. "Leave Mr. Beam one leg to stand on."

The grownups laughed, the man's "Mamie, you a mess" ushering the two visitors out the door. Mamie was breathing hard, her chest and talcumed neck heaving. Before they pulled off, she said, "Baby, the baby she was talking about was that big ole nigger laying up in the bed with her — not you." Then she yanked the vehicle in drive and turned sharply round the corner, sliding Neicy, who was still confused, across the seat.

Neicy could tell that Mamie wasn't mad at her, but something she wanted wasn't going just right. It was like being down at Mr. Antonio's store with her mama, knowing that she'd better not ask for anything, but hanging around the candy jar anyway wishing Virginia would notice and treat her to a piece.

Mamie's mood improved as they neared the base, which was buzzing as usual on a nice weather Saturday. She drove past the offices and one set of barracks to the place behind the PX where the black service people hung out. It was filling up fast, as more and more soldiers knocked off from their duties and more and more women and girlfriends drifted in from outside.

"What you want, baby?"

"What you want, baby?"

"Baby, what you want?"

Now, the dark faces and smiling teeth were talking to her. Folks liked to see Mamie coming and gravitated toward her, always treating her little girlfriend.

"I want a hamburger, some cheetos, and a grape pop." She had figured this out before they crossed the bridge to the base.

"Make this pretty little lady a hamburger," one man yelled back to the kitchen as Neicy shook off his heavy arm. Another one pulled a bag of cheetos off the rack on the counter, while the man with the scar standing closest to Mamie went over and returned with a cold grape soda and beading Falstaff beer.

When her hamburger came, Neicy bit into it and immediately started sniffling, what her mama and them called "tuning up." Mamie twirled toward her, touching her troubled chin.

"What's the matter, Neicy? Sumpen wrong with your hamburger?"

Silently, Neicy let it slide in her grip, let a slew of greasy fried onions slip off the bun onto the thick white plate.

"Oh, sugar. I forgot to tell Dancy to hold the onions."

That was the consolation she wanted. Mamie swept aside the fried oniony mass and put the hamburger back together.

"Here, sweetheart. See how you like this."

"Thank you," Neicy said, politely accepting the made-over hamburger from her hands.

Neicy ate as Mamie rested her eyes on her, occasionally lifting a slick of onion from the plate and dropping it into her mouth. Bereft of Mamie's company, the three men had started arguing about which boxer was going to win tonight's fight.

Nothing had been settled when Sgt. Frank Brown muscled his way into the crowded room, as forceful here as he was whipping around a platoon of recruits on the dry practice field. He and Mamie were about the same size, but he was harder and blacker and took up more space.

"Hey, Frank."

"Sgt. Brown. Come buy me a cold one."

Sergeant Brown kept walking through the voices back to where his wife and little neighbor sat at the bar. He slapped Mamie around her waist and greeted Neicy, "Hey, baby sister. You saved me some of that hamburger?"

"Uh uh." She shook her head "no."

"Frank, do you need the car? I want to do some shopping with Neicy. If you gotta work, I can come back and get you." Mamie sounded casual, but she was talking kind of fast and fiddling with the plate.

"I'm off for the day, but I need to stick around," Sgt. Brown answered. "I'm 'a drop y'all by the house, then come back over. You know I don't want you driving around by yo'self at night." He gazed off at the corner of the room.

Mamie jumped in with her reply. "We could leave right now, and then come fast back for you."

"Naw. I wanna go home and freshen up."

Mamie had been half looking up at Sergeant Brown, and half down at Neicy's plate. Now the plate got all her attention while her voice raised up. "Aww, Frank.

"Mamie, you can run around with Neicy any time. Right, Neicy?"

She didn't say anything. She could tell from the tone of their voices that he wasn't really speaking to her. All the grownups today were definitely talking around her, even more so than usual.

Sergeant Brown turned toward the door. Neicy took the last bite of her hamburger as Mamie got up off her stool and held out her hand. She scrambled down and followed them through the center of the room. Again, voices and arms reached out. "Bye, little lady." "Come back and see me next Sat'day." Knuckles brushed her side, a palm patted her on the booty of her red shorts as she scampered out of the way. Sgt. Frank and Mamie didn't have much more to say to each other or to her during the ride back home.

After Sgt. Brown freshened himself and left – full of the pork chops and gravy he had made Mamie fix for him and smelling like aftershave lotion – Neicy hovered around the table, where Mamie still sat in her chair. Virginia had said she could stay the night since Mr. Riley daddy wasn't at home, yelling a "Be sweet, baby" over the heads of Beulah, Miz Sophie and Miz Ella's other husband when she, Mamie, and Frank blew by the house.

Neicy stood next to Mamie's chair and looked at the meat grease congeal on the plates, wondering if this was going to be a night when everything stayed on the table or were they going to fill up the sink with warm soapy water and wash the dishes. If they did, she would get to turn hot water on and off. Cold was the only kind that ran out of their faucet at home. She was dragging the stepstool to the sink when Mamie said, "Neicy, come here." Mamie put her arms around her, looking thoughtful and sad, then led her to the bedroom.

"Whew, it's hot in here." Mamie pulled cords on the venetian blinds, trying to block out the evening sun, which was making long lines on the pink chenille bedspread as it slanted behind the fence.

"Neicy, unbutton me." Mamie always got her to unfasten her blouses that closed in the back. She was a big girl when she did that, one who could handle things right. When she finished, Mamie dropped the straps of her brassiere down over her shoulders, turned it around and unhooked it, and rubbed the welt marks under her breasts. Neicy helped with the welt marks, too. Now all Mamie had on were her white nylon step-in's, their shine contrasting sharply with the dark moon creases under her broad behind.

"Come ride me, Neicy," she said, as she threw the step-in's on the pile of her other clothes.

Neicy got up on the bed where Mamie lay on her stomach and clambered on top of her, leaning forward but tall like she was driving the car. Mamie's flesh rolled underneath — the soft stretch-marked upper arms reaching under her ample body, the cushy fat butt, firm legs and thighs. Whenever they did this, Mamie kept both eyes closed.

Neicy bumped and bounced up and down Mamie's back, and, on her knees, rocked forwards and backwards all over Mamie's giving body. She jiggled and tickled her with her small girl hands. Looking along the side of Mamie's face, she saw the tight round curls in her short black hair slowly coming undone.

"Lay down on me, honey," Mamie said huskily. "Go faster." Neicy stretched out doing what Mamie had taught her, feeling the sweat and the soft sides of her titties as she continued to rock and glide. All of Mamie was moving now, and Neicy experienced the thrill of the ride, more fun than the hobby horses at the fair on colored day. She thought of the man in the room who didn't mean her when he said "baby" and of Mamie smiling at the woman's pretty breasts. She rode harder and faster and Mamie said "baby" too.

When it was over, Mamie flipped on her back. She put Neicy's two hands over her chest full of chenille pattern lines and then laid her on her stomach. In that position, Neicy felt Mamie begin a gentle snoring. She crept up in Mamie's arms, snuggling happy and warm, as they both fell sound asleep.

In the fall, Neicy started school. She loved it. And she loved her kindergarten classroom. On the window sill, geranium flowers glowed red as blood in the clear open light and soft yellow sunshine streaming in through the squeaky clean panes. Other things also lined the sill, but it was the flowers coloring the pristine light that always caught her eye. The white walls, the blue and yellow, and green and brown crayon pictures on rough lined Big Chief paper was just so much muted background. On this September Monday morning, she was one with the red and the light, absently daydreaming in the rhythm of rubbing her bare bottom back and forth, steadily back and forth on the coiled jump rope beneath her.

The next thing she knew, Sister Mary Frances had jerked her off the bench, the nun's ugly pink face stippled with red, beady eyes tight, narrow lips a pale harsh line.

"You horrible child, you horrible little nasty girl! What in the name of the Father are you doing?" She was half dragging Neicy by one of her skinny arms as she lifted the hem of her jumper.

"Where are your underpants? What did you do with your undergarments?"

Yanked from the pretty light and the familiar soothing motion, Neicy didn't know what had hit her until Sister Mary Frances dropped the hem of her uniform and slapped the side of her face.

"Answer me, you little devil. What are you doing? Where are the rest of your clothes?"

Neicy couldn't fathom why in the world the nun was so upset. She had come out of the house the way Beulah sent her. Sometimes she laid out panties for her to put on, sometimes she didn't. And when Jeanette came by, the two of them walked to school. Our Lady of the Blessed Sacrament was the closest elementary, but it was still too far for her to navigate by herself. Jeanette was a big girl in third grade. She knew which of the rutted clay streets to turn up or down on and how to get past the barking dogs. Her mama had said, "God knows, I don't like Catholic, but it'll give Neicy a good start 'til she can go to South Bend by herself."

When Virginia worried about how to get her ready for school in the morning, Beulah said, "Ginny, I'm not Neicy's grandmother or nothing, but you know you can count on me." So her mama went to work at Miss Mary's after Mr. Riley daddy left, and Beulah, already figuring how to get her first drink of beer, troddled around to the house. Mr. Riley daddy didn't think this was a good idea. Neicy heard him raise his voice to Virginia about it. "Mother, you can't just leave Neicy with anybody." But that's how it went anyway.

Now Sister Mary Frances was hurting her arm and yelling at her. She told the other children, "Class, stay in your seats," and dragged her out the dark wooden door to the principal's office.

"That's what's wrong with these children and the people they come from," the principal said. "What else can you expect?"

To Neicy's dismay, he and Sister Mary Frances kept looking under her uniform like that was going to answer their questions. When he came at her again, she started flailing him away and screaming as Sister Mary Frances jumped to restrain her.

"I didn't know this one had a temper. Where's my paddle?" he asked. "I'll give you something for Christ's sake to scream about."

With the sister helping, he swatted her with the thick polished wood until her outstretched palm mottled beet-red.

When the day was over, Jeanette dropped her at home and gave the note the principal wrote to Beulah, who passed it on to Virginia when she came from work.

"What's this, Neicy? What do those teachers want to see me for?"

"I don't know." Neicy started to cry.

"Then, what are you crying about?"

"They paddled me."

"Paddled you? What you talking about?"

"Sister Mary Frances and the principal gave me a whupping in my hand. See?" There was nothing there to see except Neicy's hurt, and she couldn't sense whether her mama's tired eyes were getting that or not. Virginia caught the palm turned up in front of her and firmly rubbed it.

"Neicy, what did you do?"

"I don't know."

"But you must've done something. They don't whup you unless you do something wrong. I told you to behave yourself, Neicy. What did you do?"

"I didn't do nothing, mama," and she started to sniffle again.

"Stop that. Never mind. It looks like I'm gon have to come over there myself and see about this."

Virginia stood in the middle room floor like one of the frightened backyard chickens considering which way to run. They had moved from Mrs. Forbes's to their own house down the street, with their own front room, middle room, and kitchen lined up in a row and the indoor toilet that Mr. Mackey, the landlord, had built on the other side of the kitchen door. Virginia walked out of the always-dusky room and started fixing dinner, her head still cocked like she was listening for a guiding sound, her brown eyes wide, her hands moving fast like Uncle Buddy shuffling cards.

Next morning, Virginia got Miz Ella to use Jeanette's 'em phone and tell Miss Mary she was sick and couldn't come to work today, and then she walked with Neicy to school. Virginia had on a beige church dress and a nice pair of wedge-heeled shoes. Glancing over at her, Neicy thought she was looking good, but not as good as when she went out to enjoy herself and put on dark red rouge and lipstick and shiny earrings. Neicy chattered about the dogs and the bad boys and which ladies stopped them and which ones spoke to her and how often Jeanette had money to buy rubboard cookies at the store. Her mother was listening, but not talking much. All she wanted to know, again, was did Neicy do anything. "Naw, mama." And then, "I don't know."

Virginia left Neicy in her classroom and went over to the principal's office. When she returned, she broke into the room and snatched her daughter out of her seat. "Come on, Neicy. You going back home with me." She hardly gave her time to pack up her tablet and her book and pencils. A funny kind of mad sad shamefaced look crossed over her as they passed two of the sisters in their black and white habits standing by the door. On the way out the gate, she glanced over at the house by the church where all the nuns lived and said, "Kiss my ass. You baldheaded bitches. You can kiss my beautiful black ass."

When her mother was that mad, Neicy had to run to keep up with her. A couple blocks from the school, she slowed down enough for her to catch her breath and pull up alongside. Virginia peered down with a puzzled look that made Neicy think for a minute she was going to ask her something. But then she didn't. She just wet her middle finger on the tip of her tongue and groomed both of her eyebrows smooth – Neicy liked it when she did that to her – and then started up walking again, now not so fast. They swung into Mr. Antonio's store and bought two quarts of beer on credit. When Neicy asked, Virginia opened up her pouchy leather change purse and gave her a penny for one jawbreaker that she could suck for a long long time as it went from red, to pink, to white.

Well into the second bottle of beer, Neicy's mama and Beulah's voices rose louder from the kitchen. Up in the front room where she used to play with Darlene and Chuck, Neicy couldn't make out what they were saying – something about panties and tail and between the legs. Her mama sounded angry and anxious, and Beulah cussed a lot.

When they walked into the room, Neicy continued writing her full name cursive between the solid lines in her penmanship book. Beulah said, "You just send her back there, Ginny, and don't worry 'bout nothing. I'll fix her up. They may be Catholics, but they ain't gon hurt her." Virginia looked at her down on the floor with her lesson book open.

"Neicy, I thought I told you to go play somewhere. You mind Beulah, you hear, and do what those white teachers tell you."

"Yes, m'am." Her "Neicy" that she wrote was perfect, but she was having trouble making the hump of the "h" and the "n" in her last name, "Johnson," appear as two separate letters.

"What's that you practicing?" her mama wanted to know.

When she told her what she was having trouble with, Virginia borrowed her pencil and showed her how to do it, then watched as she wrote her whole name – "A" quality – three more times. She was indeed "Neicy Johnson," perfect.

The next day, she went to school the same as usual with Jeanette. For about a week, Sister Mary Frances checked under her dress. All she found was her holding her bottom still in clean cotton panties. No more nakedness, no more rocking on thickly coiled rope. After a few months, she got skipped to second grade because she was "smart" and always knew her lessons.

She was paddled only one more time when a lemon-faced boy named Jerome bumped into her at the holy water as they were dipping their way back into the classroom after lunch. The whole fount fell off on the floor. Poor Jerome got whipped so much she decided to take the blame even though it wasn't her fault. She just squeezed her eyes tight and counted the licks, then went to her seat on the far right side of the room and looked at the saints and holy family up high on all four of the walls. When she got into third grade at South Bend elementary, in a plain wooden room tacked on with some others like an outhouse trailer, she was still saying "I believe in God the Father almighty, Creator of heaven and earth" and still seeing the red heart of Mary, red wound of Christ. And her mama never could break her up from making the sign of the cross.

CHAPTER 3

Nobody asked her whether she wanted to be in the fifth grade oratorical contest or not. The teachers just put her in it because they knew she could memorize. The speech Miss Williams assigned her was entitled "Amazing Grace" and contained five stanzas about God saving a woman at different times in her troubled life. What she liked most was that, at the beginning of each part, she had to sing some lines from the hymn, such as "Amazing grace, how sweet the sound, that saved a wretch like me," or "Amazing grace, so great the love that sets all captives free." In this piece, she got to do a solo and a dramatic reading.

Because her mother wanted her to win the contest, she made her practice at home.

"But, mama, I can say every word without a stumble."

Knowing all the words wasn't nearly enough.

"You have to put some life in it, Neicy!" Her mother sprang to the middle of the floor, rolled up her eyes, opened her mouth, and waved her hands real slow and wide through the air as she repeated the words, raising her voice and primping her lips like every sound was real important. Miss Williams was teaching "classic elocutionary style," but she liked even better how her mama did it. Taking Virginia's place in the center of the room, she imitated her way of delivering the speech. When she widened her foxy eyes and snapped her cute bow mouth and stood sort of lopsided in one hip, she felt churchified and sassy all at the same time.

The teachers were patting themselves on the back for giving her a speech. They said getting up and performing in front of people was "bringing her out." According to them, she had been "too quiet" and now she was blossoming. If they had paid close attention, they would have seen that she was still quiet. But up on the platform, she could let loose and be as loud and important as she wanted.

At school on Thursday before the Friday contest, Miss Williams had a very long practice and then they rearranged and cleaned up the room. She got home late, but her mama said she still needed to have one last "dress rehearsal."

"But mama" – she was talking back – "I already can do my piece perfect. I just wanna rest."

"Rest from what?! You too young to be tired. You don't know what tired is. When you work everyday cleaning and cooking for Miss Ann like I do, then you can talk to me about tired." One minute, Virginia was cursing out the Miss Ann's and Mr. White Men's of the world. The next minute, she was acting like they were better than the colored and she should be on her best behavior so they would like her.

Virginia kept yanking three straight-backed chairs into a raggedy semi-circle. The only problem was that, at this time of the evening, she couldn't find anybody else to come sit in the other two.

"Mama, I can't say my speech just to you. One person can't be no audience."

"I can be your audience," Virginia said, clapping down in the middle chair and folding her arms. She was just like all the other adults – willing to give her time when she was doing what they wanted, but being too busy otherwise.

Virginia was looking at her and waiting and she was staring sullenly offside at the floor calculating how far she could take her rebellion when Mr. Riley daddy, who she mostly called "Daddy" now because her mother told her to, got up off the pallet on the porch, walked into the room and said, "I'll be the audience, too."

You could've knocked her over with a feather. Her mama also looked surprised. Not that Mr. Riley daddy wasn't nice, since he helped take care of them. He paid Mrs. Forbes the rent and brought home groceries every Saturday. She knew he wasn't her real daddy though because Virginia had told her. Some kids had been teasing and she'd bust out crying. She wanted to have a real daddy, too. Her mama made her dry up. "Half a loaf is better than none. I'm not crying over spilled milk and ain't no sense in you bawling either." But she'd stooped down, kissed her teary cheek, and said, "I haven't had a grandmother, mother, or daddy since I was fifteen and been taking care of you without your daddy every since you were born. You're always gonna be my Neicy baby. Stop sorrowing about what you don't have."

Still, Mr. Riley daddy no longer played with her like he used to when she was little. He didn't pull her down the steps any more in the discarded grocery store boxes when he and Virginia drank beer on Fridays and Virginia fried big bone buffalo fish. She was probably too old for that. But he also didn't let her stand on top of his paint-crusted brogans anymore either, holding her hands while they danced. She never did learn how to strike up a conversation with him or how to get him to notice her when she wanted. So she gave up and stayed mostly out of his way.

Mr. Riley daddy knew what tired was, though, because he drove his black truck home every evening after doing carpentry work and lay right down on the pallet. One time she asked her mama, wasn't the floor too hard. Her mama told her to stop being disrespectful. Mr. Riley daddy, her daddy now, had hurt his back on the railroad and sleeping on the hard floor made it feel better. She had gotten used to him looking like a white man and his silence, and she knew he didn't go to church with them because being in rooms full of people like with all the hypocrites at New Bethel, he said, gave him shortness of breath. When she asked her mother what hypocrites were, Virginia told her, "folks who say one thing and then do something different."

"Oh, you mean, like when you promised I could cut me some bangs after I turned ten years old and then told me now I need to wait until I'm eleven. Or like the time we were supposed to go to the colored branch library for Saturday session but you changed your mind and stayed over at Beulah's drinking beer."

Her mama looked at her so hard and long, she started thinking about getting away.

"No, miss smarty pants. I mean, like when Deacon Falwell gets the deacon board to turn Cynthia Ann out of church because she got pregnant and, come to find out, he's messing around with Cynthia's mama behind his wife's back. Or like when Rev. Sanders stands up in the pulpit and preaches against gambling but he still bets money when he plays coon-can over at the barber shop."

She didn't see the difference. But whatever it was, Daddy Riley didn't like hypocrites – they were next on his list after white people, who he said could do some really bad things – and he didn't like going into church. The only program he ever attended was a Girl Scout camp evening they had when she was in fourth grade. Little Mrs. Sweet was so glad some parents had come, she asked "Mr. Washington" to give a few remarks. Her daddy made a speech. It had a lot of "er-rur's" and throat clearing in it and he moved from one foot to the other with his hands in his pockets like Miss Williams said you're not supposed to, but she had still been impressed. She had never heard him say so many words all at the same time. He actually looked sort of happy out standing amongst the trees. He seemed taller and even more handsome than the rare times he dressed up to go out with Virginia, and she detected something like a twinkle in him.

Now, she couldn't imagine what made Mr. Riley daddy decide to get up off his pallet and be the audience for her oration. He plomped down in the chair on Virginia's right, planted his feet, and crossed his arms. Like Virginia, he sat expectant and solemn, but his sweat-stained undershirt and calloused leather suspenders took off some of the edge. She looked at her daddy looking at her with slightly reddish eyes and felt like she was seeing him or he was seeing her for the very first time. She could have been, as Virginia liked to say, naked as a jaybird in the wind.

Pausing, she took a deep breath and started "Amazing Grace." They were pin-dropping quiet, and she felt shaky, like the contest was taking place right that minute and not waiting for another day. But her singing voice and her speaking voice stayed strong as she took her time, made all of her gestures, and finished the first two stanzas. Her daddy shifted his back and shoulders, her mama's face softened a bit. She kept on going. The woman's mother died, then she fell sick, and then her children left her. And at the end of every affliction, God was there to buoy her up.

Next to the last stanza, her daddy started crying. Not out-and-out boo-hoo tears, but his eyes got redder and crinkled around the edges and even though she couldn't see where the water came from, little wet tracks appeared by the side of his nose. He kept looking at her out of his light face with his deep black eyes until she finished and then went back on the porch.

"Did you see your daddy? Did you see your daddy?" Her mama twisted around in her chair.

She acted like she didn't hear. This performing speeches was causing more things to happen than she would have ever imagined.

"He was proud of you, Neicy. Did you see that? He cares for you like you were his own. That was pure love in his eyes. Didn't you see it?"

She couldn't see anything but Daddy Riley's chair and was feeling a lot of confusion. Didn't you have to belong to somebody before they could be proud about you, especially proud enough to cry? Why was daddy crying? Did he wish she was his real little daughter? And why was she still standing here on the brink of tears?

Her mama left her there and went back into the kitchen. She finally polished her saddle oxfords and got in the rollaway bed.

The next day at school, everybody clapped the loudest and longest when she finished her speech. Her oration was the best. But she didn't win the contest. The panel of judges declared Rowena Spreckles the winner. Rowena's mother ran the Jack and Jill's and her daddy was the A.M.E. church pastor. They gave her second place. For that, Miss Williams and Principal Blackburn presented her with a small gold pin shaped like a hunched up frog hanging from a Grecian scroll. Every time she glanced down at it resting on its cushion of cotton, she saw her daddy in the straight-backed chair looking wet-eyed at her.

She got home, took the frog pin out of the box, and hid it underneath the paper in the drawer where they kept her good panties and her Sunday socks. No matter how often Virginia said the judges were jealous, low-down niggers who discriminated against her just because she didn't come from one of their high muck-de-muck families, or called Principal Blackburn an old, ass-licking bastard and the teachers hankty, stank-pussy bitches, it didn't make her win the contest.

She was good and ready for fifth grade to be over, could hardly wait for the big block numbers on the Rexall calendar to go from black to red three in a row at the end of May. Then all the houses with veterans would fly their American flags and summer vacation could begin in earnest.

Her mother said it was time for her to sit on the mourners bench at the June revival. But she didn't want to, even after Virginia reminded her that she should have done it the summer before. She had walked up Laura Street hill to New Bethel almost every night, but begged her mama not to make her go on the bench at the front of the church where the visiting preacher running the revival could look sinners dead in the eye and point his finger, and where all the deacons on the left side and deaconesses on the other could come stand right over them when they prayed, like they were sick or had done something wrong.

"But, Neicy," her mama reasoned with her, "You're ten years old now. Don't you want to give yourself to the Lord?"

She didn't know the answer to that question. It was fine to sing in the junior choir, and learn about Jonah and Job and the psalms and "suffer the little children" in Sunday School, say Easter speeches and welcome addresses, and play in the basement with the other kids when service was done. But she wasn't sure about "joining" the church and hated all the yelling and excitement that happened when someone gave themselves to God – the preacher crying and sinners stumbling, desperate singing splitting the air, and loud amen's jumping out of every corner.

So, she begged and pleaded, but to no avail. Her mother made her sit with four other children on the mourners bench, first pew, left side of the aisle.

In the old days, revival used to last two weeks, now they had cut it down to one. On the first night, nobody joined the church, but that was okay. The minister was just getting warmed up. On the second night, a big doofus-looking, country boy in blue jean overalls that everybody called June Bug gave his hand in fellowship. That broke the ice. Wednesday night, the preacher was hot. It was raining outside and, inside, everything was so loud and steamy she could hardly breathe. A set of twins from Mississippi who were staying with their aunt over the summer were pushed up to the pulpit on a big wave of shouting and song. That left her and Bobby Drayfus on the bench Thursday night. With the other three gone, she felt like they were two lost dummies nailed on a plank of wood.

As her mama had walked her into the sanctuary, folks patted her shoulder. "Neicy, you're going to be a great woman someday." The church leaders generally boosted her up, but tonight, they were pouring it on.

"I know the Lord's laying his hands on you, Neicy. Ain't you feeling the spirit?"

"You'se a good girl, Neicy. I told Rev. Sanders last Sunday when you gave the young people's address that Christ had a faithful little servant in you."

Old Sister Jethro even put her arm around her and said, "We's praying hard for you, child. Let the Lord work his way with you."

Virginia edged the two of them through the crowd of bodies with a sanctimonious look on her face, the same look she put on whenever people complimented her for being a good mother after her "little Neicy" did something well. The pressure was building.

When the reverend finished his sermon, she and Bobby were still sitting on the mourners bench. He stepped down out of the pulpit and walked over to them, the deacons gathering by his side. They kneeled her and Bobby on the floor, their faces pressed into the seat. Unbeknownst to anybody, she made a hasty sign of the cross. The congregation hummed and moaned as the preacher prayed.

Lord God, what now? Nervous thoughts were racing through her. "Am I really your child? Do all those other children who run up to the altar belong to you? How do they know, Jesus, what kind of signal do you give them? Maybe they don't get a signal. Maybe they suddenly get tired of kneeling. Maybe the deacon or sister praying over them is shouting way too loud. Maybe they just want to make their grandmother happy. Maybe they were afraid they'd be the last one left. Maybe... God, don't strike me dead... but maybe they saw that nothing really happened, so they just went ahead and did what everybody believed they were supposed to anyway."

Crouched face down in the bench and ringed by the army of God's helpers determined to bring them through, she was frantically thinking her way around these thickets. The church had broken into a hymn and the hardcore pleading had begun. The air in the crook of her arm was hot. She thought she smelled gum and Mum deodorant and something else that reminded her of how her mama smelled when she got out of bed with Mr. Riley daddy at night. But, at this point, she was totally relieved to sit back upright on the pew, although her face still felt like she was sweating but, in the middle of her last blasphemous thought, she realized, no, her cheeks were covered with tears. When she wasn't looking, somehow God must have touched her. "Oh, oh, oh, it must have been the hand of the Lord."

"Thank you, Master!" "Bless Jesus!" "Praise the Lord!" Joy rang out as she walked up to the pastor, gave him her hand and her life to God. When she stepped out into the vestibule of the New Bethel Missionary Baptist Church, the night breeze on her face was wondrous and cool as a peppermint kiss. She looked at her hands, and they looked new. She looked at her feet, and they did, too. On them, she started the short journey with her satisfied mother down the unpaved hill.

For a fact, nobody forced her to raise her hand in Miss Valentine's sixth-grade class in the hot afternoon and excuse herself to the girls' toilet at the end of the hall. Then, to keep walking and creep around the back of the building into the woods where Ezra was waiting for her. She had promised that she would meet him so they could "do it." He had asked and tickled "gimme some" in the palm of her hand.

They stood under a young, low-limbed oak tree in the dry bright shade, with the branches now and again snagging her thick pony tail. Lifting the skirt of her dress, she dropped her panties. He took his thing out of the slightly soiled placard of his white cotton briefs. He was dark dark-skinned next to her sun-bronzed yellow. The dusty leaves on the trees had still, whispery spaces between them.

Ezra put both of his arms around her, rotated his booty, and wiggled his thing against her front. She paid real close attention because she wanted to learn once and for all what doing it was about. Ezra kept jerking around, his soft meat pressing on her. She kept waiting and watching.

After a while, he pulled apart and started fixing his clothes back together with a yum-yum grin on his face.

"Did we do it?" she asked him. "Are we finished?"

"Yeah," he said, "ummm, ummm. You wait a little and then come back to the room. I'm going now."

She pulled up her day-of-the-week, pastel-colored panties and smoothed down her burgundy-striped dress. But she didn't think to run her hands over her napped-up hair. When she walked back into Miss Valentine's classroom, she felt thirty pairs of eyes staring at her, all fixed on the tree twig sticking out from her head. Of course the kids started talking about her and Ezra opened his big mouth and bragged to his friends.

But she didn't think they had actually "done it." What they did was like playing mama and daddy under the high porch of doodlebugs and old peeling lumber with Eugene and Billy Ray from across the street, except, playing house, they all laughed and giggled like they were having fun. "Doing it" was serious. More serious even than playing doctor with Jeanette on her back steps where they started poking under each other's armpits until they sneaky-fingered their way to brushing the sides of titties and feeling nipples. They could pretend that nothing was happening as they switched from doctor to patient, patient to doctor, and then went back to beating each other at fiddlesticks or chinese checkers.

"Doing it" was what grownups fought about and tried to keep quiet at night, joked about when they got drunk, and put in their blues songs. It was what made the men guffaw sitting under the trees, what the women went "shush" about when kids ran into the kitchen. It hung everywhere. Ezra had said he knew how to do it, but he didn't.

Macarthur did. He lived one street over, was real cute, with tight muscles and black curly hair. He was thirteen and still at Our Lady of the Blessed Sacrament because his folks were Catholic. She was in seventh grade at McKenzie Junior High.

When she and Macarthur finally did it, they were on the strip of grass between her piano teacher's garage and backyard fence. Virginia let her stay at Miz Hedgeman's and play with the other students when her lessons were over. Sometimes she even spent the night to keep Miz Hedgeman company since her postman husband died from sugar diabetes. Miz Hedgeman practiced fancy show tunes while she sat contentedly in the brocaded armchair by the stained glass lamp drinking cocoa or chocolate milk.

The evening she and Macarthur got together still felt like summer. The kids were using Miz Hedgeman's steps to play hide-and-go-seek as dusk turned to dark and night descended. Right at the end of the last round, she and Macarthur hid in the same place. They panted against the garage with the fence in front of them.

"Shh," Macarthur whispered.

"You shh, I'm not talking."

"I don't want anybody to find us," he said.

He leaned over and pressed his lips to hers. Like she had practiced with Jeanette, she opened her mouth, tasting his sweat. His small teeth rubbed against her tongue, which she slipped into his mouth so he could suck it. He gave his tongue back to her, his saliva as clean and warm as his lips.

They kept kissing and hugging. She could feel the back of her eyelids go dim and her heart thump excited. New nerves in her body she had never been aware of were jumping and getting scared.

"Neicy," Macarthur called her name like a question. His breath on her cheek was raggedy. She couldn't make her voice say anything, but wanted him to know she liked him and liked what they were doing. So she placed her lips back on his mouth and kissed him again. It felt as if he liked her, too. He was hugging her tight and touching her, which made her feel special and precious.

By the time they laid down on the stiff, scratchy grass and he ran his fingers under the crotch of her panties, she was eager for them to do it and knew this would be different. It hurt just enough to make her flinch and go "ohh," but was gentle and sweet. Yes, Macarthur must really like her. She forgot about the prickly grass and marveled at the purple night.

She was still marveling when she rushed, perspiring and flushed, through Miz Hedgeman's front door. Her piano teacher wasn't like her mama and couldn't see through her, but she was still glad when Miz Hedgeman only glanced up from the stove and told her to go take her bath.

On the way to the bathroom, she felt wetness in her panties that turned out to be a spot and a smear of blood. She knew that meant she was not a virgin anymore. As she soaked and splashed in the tepid bath water, she wasn't calming down or cooling off and her head began to ache. If she had been one of the ailing white children in the school magazine pictures, she would have been pink with tiny red sick dots on her face.

She got out of the tub, still feeling funny. When she saw more blood on the towel as she was drying off, she began to get worried. Losing your virginity was not supposed to make you ill. She rinsed out the towel with cold water, folded toilet tissue into her panties, and put on her clean set of clothes, then strolled as nonchalantly as she could down the hall to the kitchen.

"Miz Hedgeman," she said to her piano teacher as they ate their turkey wings and spaghetti. "I'm not feeling too good."

Miz Hedgeman put down her fork neat and proper, like when they got ready to talk instead of eat, and dabbed her napkin to her mouth with the points of her fingers. Following her teacher's lead, she, too, had been practicing her manners – chewing and swallowing extra slow, dabbing and pointing so that the both of them would finish at about the same time.

"What's the matter, Neicy? You look fine to me, just a little worn out from playing so hard."

"Yes, m'am. I think I played too hard. I think I'm getting a fever. Maybe I better go home tonight."

She squirmed in the dinette chair on the cushion of toilet paper between her legs. She didn't exactly know what she would do at home and she sure wasn't going to tell her mama about Macarthur either, but maybe her mother would do something Miz Hedgeman couldn't, since mama had a child, her, and Miz Hedgeman was what Rev. Sanders called "barren." And, besides, her mama was her mama, regardless.

"Neicy! What you doing back at home?"

"I don't feel good, mama."

"What's wrong with you?" Virginia walked up to her, peering so hard at her flustered face that she started worrying that her mother might see what she'd done with Macarthur. But, fortunately, Virginia's mind was off somewhere else. The card table in the middle of the room with ashtrays setting in two corners meant she was using her being at Miz Hedgeman's for a grown-up night. Daddy Riley was away helping his friend Mr. Dawson paint Mr. Dawson's brother's house in the country, so she and Beulah could have a ball.

There was no use beating around the bush. "Mama, look." She pulled down her clothes, gapped open her legs, and showed the bloody tissue. Her mama let out a laugh and gave her a hug.

"So... you're a young lady now," she said, dragging out the words like a dramatic recital.

"What?"

"Neicy, you got your period. You've started menstruating."

Then, and only then, did she remember the "so you're a young lady now" pamphlet that her mother had given her to read. She had believed it a little bit more than the story a girl told her about blood streaming down her leg, but all that writing about eggs and tubes and sloughing off womb lining was almost as bad. Neither one had told her what she needed to know in order to see that she was having her very first period — and on the day that she first had intercourse, too!

"It's alright," her mama continued. "You remember we put you a sanitary belt in the bottom drawer, and let me show you where I keep the kotex." She was bustling toward the back of the house. "So... you're a young lady now."

Why did Virginia keep saying that? It sounded real stupid. But she followed her to the small chest of drawers, got out the belt contraption, and anchored a sanitary napkin between her thighs. It was way too big.

"We'll have to get you some regular's," her mother said. "These large ones are super's."

"I'm not going down to Mr. Antonio's store and ask for no sanitary napkins."

"It's alright, baby," her mama said, good humoring her. "You don't have to worry 'bout that. Here, come have a cup of sweet lemon tea. After you drink it, you'll feel better and I can walk you back 'round to Miz Hedgeman's. Did you tell her what happened?"

"Naw. Naw, I didn't. I thought you weren't supposed to talk about your period business."

"No, not to just anybody. But since you were over her house, I just thought maybe."

"Naw," she said again. Boy, this bleeding thing was making her touchy. She needed to stop dealing with people and be by herself. She had new experiences to mull over. It would be good to get back to Miz Hedgeman's where she could snuggle up in the quiet bedroom wallpapered with cornflowers that was hers for as long as she stayed in it.

CHAPTER 4

"Neicy." "Hold up." Francine and Karen, the two buddies she had made since coming to ninth grade, were calling from the open gym door as she cut across the field to Kinland Street. She wanted to wait for them since they were the only girls in her class who seemed to like being friends. The rest thought they were better than she was or that she was stuck-up, too yellow, too cute, too smart, or too fast. But she didn't feel like stopping. The new thespian club advisor had kicked her out of rehearsal. If Darlene hadn't kept trying to make her mess up her lines because she was still mad about getting beat out for the lead, she would never have exploded and called Darlene an ugly black bitch. Quiet and peaceful unless she got really upset, she had been taught by her mama not to take shit from anybody.

Miss Brown told them both to go home and cool off or neither of them would be in the play. No way. Before she would let that happen, she would murder Darlene in her bed. Being in plays and oratorical contests was the reason she came to school. This life of hers that her mama liked to call "young and sweet" hadn't been all that sweet. As she rummaged her mind for memories, her earliest flickers were red color, white nuns with black habits, and ropes on her bottom, plus a lot of treading up and down streets as hilly as the one she was walking now.

When she asked her mother what kind of baby she had been, Virginia said, "You were the darlingest thing. Everybody wanted to keep you. I could get dressed up and go out and just leave you with anybody — even after you got bigger. Do you remember Mamie Brown?" No, she didn't. "Mamie adored you." And she couldn't recall, either, that she'd spent her days at Beulah's house before going to school.

She remembered running to Virginia when she was in fourth grade and asking was she beautiful. "You're cute, sweetie." Her mama told her she looked like her pretty but dark-skinned grandmother and had the same thick head of hair, hair that she and daddy Riley still hadn't let her cut. She thought of Rowena Spreckles, the girl the teachers made win the fifth grade oratorical contest. The one time she had been to Rowena's house for Rowena's ten-year-old birthday party, none of the kids she played with were there and Rowena's mother kept watching everything she did in their uncomfortable living room. She and Rowena would never have been friends in a hundred thousand years, even if she hadn't told them about going to see what it meant to pick cotton with her daddy at his friend, Mr. Dawson's place, or helping her mama clean up at one of the Miss Ann's houses when Virginia had the flu. They acted like she had confessed to having lice. Virginia lectured her afterwards. "Baby, don't you let what evil-hearted Negroes think about you make you lose one blink of sleep."

She remembered being called on so she could show off for the white assistant superintendent when he visited their class her last year at South Bend elementary. How she got into trouble for daydreaming too much. What it felt like to be the sting end of the long, speeding line when they played pop-the-whip during recess. How everybody plus God made her join church and, because she was a good little sister and delivered speeches, how she got to go in the back by the pastor's study where the deacons counted the money and they gave her nickels and dimes when they hugged her. She knew not to talk about that even when they didn't wink. She gathered the hugging was wrong and it made her uneasy, but it still felt good, better even than having the spending change she didn't need to ask anybody for. She wondered what happened to Christine, the girl she had sat on the peeling sill with when she first left Our Lady of the Blessed Sacrament, who had spit out the window and it landed on a lean, serious boy hurrying home to his widowed grandfather.

"Neicy." "Neicy." She hadn't known Francine and Karen were trailing behind until they caught up with her.

"Come over to my house," Francine invited.

She knew that meant practicing their dance moves to 45's on the record player, gossiping about other girls, and if some boys they liked came along, fooling around with them. She had an hour to spare before she needed to be home to help take care of her mother, who had just gotten back from the hospital, so she might as well give herself a break.

Before they made it into Francine's, three guys from eleventh grade strolled by and came in after them. One boy, Hal, had been trying to get her attention. He was as tall as she was and sharp as a tack with a light, delicate moustache. She had wondered if he knew how to work it when it came to kissing and stuff. She'd probably get her chance to find out.

Pushed down beside him in a corner of the couch, she tongued him 'til they both got hot. They had necked the couch cover to the floor and Hal was trying to get under her blouse. Breaking the "good girl" rules like this was definitely exciting. The pleasure in her body and the emotional thrill was just as they wrote in "True Romances." But the best part was being, at this heated moment, the most important thing in the world.

"Baby, let me," he was moving her blocking palm. "Can't you see I need you?" He tried to place her hand on his crotch. "What you want me to do with all this?"

She liked it when they begged. But, then, that was a problem. She always felt sorry for the hardness that seemed to be hurting them until it got satisfied and felt like it was her job to do so. But if she gave in too fast, they called her a whore and dropped her. This was too fast.

"Do you really like me?" she asked as she lifted up and slowly backed him off, straightening her blouse and trying to catch Francine's eye who, right on cue, came over from the record player and yelled, laughing, "Hey, you two, my mama don't allow that in her house. I bought this new Sam Cooke. Get up and dance."

A couple of cha-cha's later – no slow drags – she left Hal at the door, telling him she'd catch him again soon, she had to get home now. Would he find out her number from Francine and call her later? Was some other girl trying to get him? Would he send her a note?

Daddy Riley never talked to her about boys and stuff even when they were together in his truck as he gave her an occasional ride to school. But he said things to Virginia. He didn't like it when she wore tight skirts and lipstick or when older guys walked her home and hung around the house. If he had asked what she was doing, she had no idea what she would have told him. She just did what she did and did what the boys wanted, and it got her holding, appreciation, and love.

When she entered the house and tiptoed to the head of Virginia's bed, checking on her, her mama was fast asleep. She hovered there, lingering around the pillow. Suddenly, silently, Virginia opened her eyes and reached for her hand with fingers that were bony and gray, she'd lost so much weight in the last six weeks. Surprised by the movement and the clammy touch, she jumped like she had been grabbed by a Halloween skeleton even though she was gazing directly into her mother's eyes. They were sunken and ravaged, exactly as she imagined Catherine looked without Heathcliff in Wuthering Heights. When she became a famous actress, she planned to be Catherine in a fabulous Broadway play.

"Mama, I thought you were asleep."

Her mother didn't answer, just smiled and squeezed the part of her hand that she had managed to capture, trembled a little and started to shake, then leaned over the side of the bed. Nothing came up.

She wiped her mama's face with the threads-thin washcloth and bent to give her a clean sip of water. Virginia refused it, closing her lips and turning her head. Oh, heavens. She wanted to be a good nurse to her ailing mother and was trying so hard to do what the grown women did. But it obviously didn't help. She felt like crying.

"It's alright, baby," her mama said. "I'm not gon be round here sick much longer."

Then she did burst into tears.

"Go on cry. When the only mama you ever gon have in the world is about to leave you, it's alright to cry."

Nobody was at home this warm October afternoon but the two of them. Daddy Riley was still at work, the neighbor ladies were seeing about their children and their dinner, and Beulah was taking a break, maybe having a beer at Miss Celeste's house.

She was holding down the fort and not doing a very good job. What could she really manage when she'd just turned fourteen and her one and only mama was dying, right before her eyes? When the young white doctors and the gray white doctors had sent "Virginia Johnson, colored" home from the Negro women's ward of the Charity Hospital with a bottle of medicine and a prescription for tablets, saying they had done all they could, and given some other body a turn in the chipped metal bed. When no one else knew anything to do, and her mama still deathly sick here amongst them, sadness creeping around the laughing and into the quiet. When the grownups kept on living, kept on going, they packed her back to school. Nobody else's mother had ever died. She didn't know what to do. She hardly knew how to feel. Was her mama really going to die and leave her, just like that, right before her very eyes?

Virginia took a deep breath and raised herself from the soft, lumpy mattress. "Neicy," she ordered, sounding almost like her regular old self, "help me up."

"But, mama..."

"Help me out of this bed." She continued to struggle up. "I got something I want to show you while I'm still in my right mind."

There was nothing she could do but help her, so she put her arm around her mama's shoulders and scooted her to the edge, then thrust her thin arms into the sleeves of her fancy pink quilted house robe, pushed her house shoes onto her feet, and supported her standing beside the bed.

"What you got to show me?" Her mother's unexpected action had halted both thoughts and tears.

She didn't believe there was anything around their three-room shotgun house she hadn't seen, either because they all knew about it or because she had sneaked and looked when she got the chance – even the playing cards backed with nasty white women with their legs cocked up and their breasts and pussy hairs showing, or the pearl-handled pistol in the bottom of the box at the rear of the middle-room closet.

"Mama, what..."

"Be quiet, Neicy. I need to preserve my strength."

Leaning on her, Virginia walked slowly to the kitchen. At the corner pantry, she eased down into one of the two chairs that still had backs. The sun was dropping, a few stray rays hitting the rusty screen door.

"Neicy," her mama's voice sounded out weak but clear, "just listen good and do what I tell you so I don't have to keep repeating myself."

Turned partly toward her mother and partly toward the pantry, she still couldn't imagine what there was to discover in the kitchen.

"See there, in the pantry, that last, low down bottom shelf – pull it out."

"But how I'm gon pull out a shelf," she started to protest, but caught herself and kneeled down on the planked pantry floor in front of the red-and-white oil-cloth-covered boards suspended at irregular intervals. They went deeper than it looked at first glance, from the general dimness of the pantry into darker gloom. She had never given the whole area too much notice, just reached for the items they commonly used from the front of the shelves and not bothered with the jars, bottles, tin cans and canisters lined up behind.

Now, on her knees in front of the lowest outcropping, she could see that what looked like a shelf way down at the bottom was some kind of wide, broad something draped by the checkered oilcloth.

"Pull that out," her mama told her again.

It was a stout, beat-up trunk – and heavy. But she dragged it into the room, trailing dust, dead bugs and spiders.

"It's been a while since I went in that trunk," Virginia mused, looking intently at it. "Well, go head," she said. "Open it up."

Turning it around so that the front faced her on the floor, she undid the big buckled clasps. When she raised the cover, all she saw was a lot of old newspaper and a few pots and pans dented and stained with brown grease.

"Lift all of that out." Her mama ordered.

The paper looked okay, no insects floating on it, so she pulled out the rumpled newssheets and piled the other stuff carefully, one piece at a time, on the far side of the trunk.

"What do you see down at the bottom?" Virginia asked.

There was a spread of things. But what caught her attention was a dark circle in the near-left corner that she picked up, then immediately let go of, then gingerly picked up again. It felt like animal hide but was really a coil of heavy black hair caught up in a strip of brown leather.

"That came from my grandmother."

Her mother's grandmother? She tried to visualize that grandmother and her head of hair, wondering who cut it, who saved it, and how come her mama still had it in this trunk.

"You heard me say she was half-Indian, remember? Before she came home and settled down with my grandfather, Charley Wims, she lived wild like an Indian with a Indian man. That's his hair."

What to say, what to ask? Her mind was a slate of questions she didn't know how to put into words.

Virginia finished the story. "That's all she brought back of him. And she never talked much about him."

With a shiver, she turned away from her mother and put the heavy lock down. Next to it was a queer pin cushion, six little big-headed chinamen with their twelve arms stretched around a faded red sphere.

"Give me that." Her mama began rearranging frayed threads and re-knotting the tiny pigtails.

"Did your grandmother really use that for a pin cushion?"

"Yes, she did." Her answer sounded like what kind of idiot would even ask the question. "Her – and mama, too. It stayed on the front edge of the sewing machine, the one that I sat under and worked the treadle."

Indian hair, funny pin cushions, and out-of-fashion sewing machines. People who had died way before she was thought of. Places so far away her mama had to lean back and close her eyes to remember. Why were they digging in this old trunk?

"Neicy, these things may mean something to you one of these days."

She doubted it.

"When I'm dead and gone..."

"Oh, mama..." Virginia was harping on that dreadful subject again.

"Oh, mama, nothing. Did I think my grandmama was going to leave me when she died? And after that, did I know I was going to be a motherless child at fifteen? The Lord giveth and the Lord taketh away."

She couldn't say, "Blessed be the name of the Lord." She was back to feeling like crying.

But her mama didn't let up. "For instance, those two dresses in that trunk." One of the dresses was black and one was white.

"Those belonged to my sweet little mother." Virginia sounded like she was both a big woman taking care of her sweet little mother and like a spoiled baby girl. "Lay that black one here across my lap."

Whoever wore this dress was really a skinny lady. She was having trouble thinking of this mama's mama as her own grandmother. The dress was narrow as a pencil, fancy-made in crepe material with a big flat shiny bow draped low at the waist.

"Mama walked the back of the benches at St. Mark's in that dress when she got happy. Boy, howdee, could she dance!"

Suddenly, she could see this small brown woman in her beautiful black dress shouting on a country Sunday morning. Her slim expressive hips went up and down on either side of the satin ribbon as her bowlegs pumped and her fingers waved high in the hymn-filled air. She got lost in the picture playing behind her eyes until she found her mama staring at her.

"Neicy, that was your grandmother. Her name was Velma." She paused a while. "She lay down with men, but never found fulfillment. She worked away from home and lived with us when she could."

Her mama had never told her anything like that before.

"Did Vel..." she stumbled, "did grandmother Velma make this dress?"

"Naw, honey. Can't you see this was one of her store bought ones? Some she bought, a lot of them they made. She never finished that white eyelet. That's the one she was working on just before she took sick."

Sickness and dying. Dead mamas and grandmothers hanging like smoke everywhere. Her head was aching so bad she wanted to rest it on top of the dress in her mother's lap.

"There ought to be one more dress in there, Neicy. It's what I came out here to give you."

She didn't move. She didn't know if she wanted any more of these gifts. Not only was her head hurting like crazy, but her chest was breathing thin. She had been on the edge of crying far too long. She didn't want to look at another something or hear one more story. She wanted to go and lie down across her bed.

"Neicy, I'm too weak to come there on the floor. Baby, reach in and get it."

"Mama, I don't see no dress in here."

"Look good. I know it's in there."

"I'm looking, and I don't see..." But, then, it jumped out at her, folded up in a lopsided rectangle. Not a lady's dress, that's why she didn't recognize it, but a garment that would fit a little girl maybe six or seven years old.

It was a peach-colored chemise, really old-timey — square cut, dropped waist, and big wide pleats. There were faded streaks and a couple of places where the fabric was so worn you could almost see through it, and a moth hole here and there.

"My dear mother made me that dress, every stitch sewed by her hand." The stitches were visible, especially along the waist and collar, even and strong, and so neat they looked like an illustration in a home economics book.

"Mama combed my hair in two long plaits swinging down my back and put me on that jumper. Bow ribbons the same color. I was the best dressed of all the girls. They really fixed me up pretty."

So, her mother was spoiled and petted and was sitting here remembering how good it felt to be loved. Two mamas sewing for her and dolling her up. Virginia hugged the peach chemise with a sad and shiny, faraway look in her eyes.

"Mama," she burst out louder than she intended, so she surprised both her mother and herself. "Mama," now she was almost shouting, "why you never made me a dress?"

Crying, she snatched the little chemise away from her stunned mama and held it, so upset she didn't know what she was saying or doing. "Where's my dress? What I'm gon have to keep at the bottom of my trunk?"

"Oh, baby, you're my precious – and this dress is precious to me. It's me – and your grandmother – and your great-grandmother. I wanted to tell you about them and give it to you."

"I want a dress you made me. What am I gon have to hold on to whenever you're gone?" She finally let herself know that her mama was up and leaving her, going wherever dead mothers and grandmothers go. What would she have when she didn't have her?

"I'm gonna die, Neicy baby. But I'm never gon leave you..."

"Mama, where's my dress?" She was still crying, still shouting, her head splitting like fire.

"Neicy... Neicy..." Virginia dropped down on the floor and hugged her. They were sobbing in each other's necks, both of their bodies shaking. "Neicy, listen. I never learned to be a first-class seamstress like they were. I ran wild like a tomboy and they never made me sit still. You remember that green and white polka dot dress I sewed for you and you called it ugly and wouldn't wear it." Her mama caught her breath. "I tried to make you a dress."

They were holding on to each other, crushing the peach frock between them as she strained to remember what happened to the polka dot dress. Virginia had really started to shiver and shake. She shouldnt've been down on the kitchen floor. She shouldn't even have been out of her bed.

"Mama, come on, mama." Her mother was hot as a furnace and damp with sweat. She got her back in the bed, wiped off her face, and gave her a drink of water. Virginia's stomach was heaving, but otherwise she was quiet. Like a long dry hum, she herself was still crying. She squeezed her mother's little girl dress to her breasts and stretched out at the foot of the bed, gradually calming down.

When her mama finally died two weeks later, she was in that same position, curled up on the lower half of the bed, clutching the precious peach dress. From the day of the trunk until her mother left her, she felt like her heart was about to be sick to its stomach and the only thing she could do was hold still so it wouldn't spill out. Then she cried and she cried, oozing big beads of tears and nobody could console her. Not Daddy Riley, or Beulah, or her chaperone, Miss Cherry from church. As the mortician's men threw dirt on the lowered coffin, all the moisture inside her dried up, congealed like a pond in frozen winter, under unmelting snow.

May, 1982
Philadelphia, Pennsylvania

CHAPTER 5

When she awakened the morning of her thirty-fifth birthday, it was not the sun burning through her sheer purple curtains that roused her. It was the recurring dream of her dead mother dragging scene after scene of baffling images she couldn't understand. Virginia had been coming at her hard ever since she left Baltimore for Philadelphia to take the only acceptable job she could find with Philly's Penn Theater Two – later for being a starving artist waiting tables in New York.

This dream felt as important as the first time her mama communicated through the spiritual world. Her ovaries remembered and then ached as she lengthened her stretch in the bed. She had been fifteen, pregnant and scared, with a six-week fetus in her belly she didn't know which boy to blame for or how to uproot.

She had heard Miss Celeste and Beulah or Miss Sophie and her mother or whoever say that some "gal" had "gotten rid of" a baby or had "th'owed" a baby away in tones so loaded that she could never figure if they admired or condemned the girls. Something merited their judgment, but whether it was the girls getting the baby in the first place or their disposing of it or the world itself where babies were made and discarded, she couldn't tell.

No way was she ever going to let Daddy Riley find out she had gotten herself in trouble. She could talk back to him loud as she wanted and tell him he couldn't tell her what to do since he wasn't her real daddy. She could pretend to ignore the worried looks in his eyes when she came sneaking in from cheap supper clubs and hourly motels smelling like liquor and sex. After Virginia died, she went wild, and there was nothing he or anyone else could do about it since she still went to church on Sunday, starred in school plays, and made "A's" in most of her classes.

But when the days of no-period clean panties started racking up one after the other, she got worried. That's when her mother started to come to her in her dreams. Virginia walked into her room and led her up Laura Street hill to the bus stop in front of the drugstore. There she would push her into the bus and point down the street. Over and over. Through the door, into the room, then up the hill and on the bus, Virginia's set face determined and her arrow-stern arm and finger piercing down the street.

The dream started on Monday just before she woke up and went on through Friday. Saturday morning, she put on a blouse and some neat pedal pushers and left the house, telling Daddy Riley as she strolled out the screen door cracking a jawbreaker that she was going to the Rec. She walked down the splintery steps past the cape jasmine bush through the stubby little yard and on up the long, steep hill. By the time she got to the drugstore, she was winded and the bus was one stop away.

She sat at the back, ignoring the young dressed-up woman — probably a Seventh Day Adventist on her way to Saturday services — and two middle-aged men laughing with each other. She was going to ride this Kinland Street bus to the end of the line — past her church and the three-room houses with lopsided concrete steps, the branch library and proud new high school, then the houses that got bigger and better after Weingarten Street. She eyed the green lawns, white shutters, trim red and pink bricks and flashed on the saditty principals with their stuck-up daughters who thought they were hot shit because they lived in homes like these.

When the driver turned the bus around and put on his brake, she stepped down to the sidewalk. More of the self-satisfied lawns and smug houses. Why did her mother want to bring her out here? Instantly, her eyes lit on a sign swinging next to the mailbox of the smallest house: Dr. H. W. Matthews, M.D. A doctor's office, a medical doctor. She started walking on a quick diagonal to that door, so intent on her destination she failed to see the car backing out of the driveway.

The driver slammed on brakes as she jumped out of the way, tripping on a huge tuft of grass. "Watch where you're walking, young lady," he yelled in a smooth, commanding voice. He came alongside the car, assessing the black Cadillac's tail fin and then her.

She was righting herself from her grassy stumble. "You're supposed to be watching, too."

The man was about 5'8" or 9", way shorter than Daddy Riley, decked out in a shiny suit. His almost gray hair was waved back with pomade from his face, the skin of which in texture and color resembled a brown paper bag. A little on the round side, he moved with quiet force. She was an inch or two shorter than he was, but felt the strength of her own wide-shouldered, firm-hipped body.

"Are you alright?" he asked.

She thought for a second. "No. I'm not."

"Well, you'll have to come back some other time. I keep a short day on Saturday — my nurse doesn't even come in. I'm on my way to Westside for an insurance board meeting." He ran his hand in his pocket and glanced at a gleaming gold watch.

She decided to do an Erma Jean on him. She planted her feet and silently stood in front of him, staring him in the face, fixed to the spot. Everything about her said she would stay so forever or until he reopened his office, whichever came first.

With a shake and a rousing shiver, Dr. Matthews pulled out his watch again. "Okay, I guess I can give you a few minutes."

In the living room turned reception room, she sat down on the flowered couch. Dr. Matthews took the edge of his nurse's straight chair. Before he could ask any questions, she blurted, "Mr. Doctor, I think I'm pregnant."

"That's what wrong with three-quarters of the girls and women who walk through that door."

"Oh." She tried to process the implications of that statement. "I don't want to have a baby."

"Yes," Dr. Matthews replied, "I understand that. I can help you out, but you need three hundred dollars. Can you get that from your boyfriend? Who sent you here?"

"My mother."

"Your mother?" He sounded like that wasn't how it usually happened.

"Mrs. Virginia Washington." She gave her mama's married name.

"Virginia Washington," he repeated, slowly and thoughtfully. "I don't believe I know anyone by that name."

"Virginia Johnson," she revised, and then he brightened.

"You're Virginia Johnson's daughter?" And then his countenance dropped. "Didn't she die sometime last year? Didn't you say she sent you?"

"I was only kidding."

Dr. Matthews didn't know what to do with that. "Well, so, you're Virginia's daughter. Does your stepdaddy know you're here?"

"Nobody knows I'm here and I don't want you to tell them. Please. I don't want anybody to find out I'm pregnant. Can you give me some pills to stop it?"

"How far along are you?" He was trying to see the size of her belly in the green-and-white pants.

"I only missed one period."

"Pills work sometime. Most times they don't. And in the meanwhile you're just getting further and further along, which makes the next thing that much harder."

Should she still ask for the pills? Should she skip the pills and do the next thing, but what was the next thing and why was it harder?

Before she could form a coherent question, Dr. Matthews suddenly stood up and said, "Let's take a look at you," in a friendly doctor, impersonal voice. Obviously he had decided somewhere along the way that he could miss his meeting. She definitely started to feel shaky. Riding to the end of the bus line to see what her mama wanted was one thing. Proceeding on the spot with this doctor-baby business was something else.

But she followed Dr. Matthews into the next room, her heart beating faster and faster as her nervous vision blurred over the objects around her — wood and cottony things in various glass containers, a long pair of fluorescent lights, a black leather examination table with a round stool and steel lamp at the bottom, cabinet drawers, a sink, and a cluttered desk in the corner.

"Take off your pants and step-in's and lie down on the table. There's a sheet at the foot you can cover yourself with." She hadn't noticed the sheet.

Dr. Matthews half-looked at her as she undressed, half-minded the motions of taking off his suit coat, washing his hands, and putting on his white medical jacket.

When she was situated on the table, he placed her feet in the stirrups, rolled back the sheet and opened her knees. She could see his head and shoulders as he adjusted the lamp and pulled a tray of instruments closer. She was so scared her knees started to quiver.

Dr. Matthews gently rubbed her calf. "You just take it easy. We need to see what's up here."

She felt cold metal, and rubber-gloved fingers, and her insides being pried apart. Then something needling around inside her. And then a sharp pinch so excruciating her body jumped.

"You got to lie still," Dr. Matthews admonished, "or you could make me hurt you. I'm almost there."

There, where? And what would happen when he arrived? What he was doing now pained even worse than before. It felt like he had caught a thread of something deep inside her and by pulling slowly on it was turning her bowels inside out. Nothing had ever hurt so bad in her entire life.

While she inwardly flinched and flailed and gritted her teeth, squeezing her eyes tight as tears oozed out of the corners, tensing and willing her muscles and flesh to be still, Dr. Matthews was utterly concentrating, every now and then talking, almost to himself.

"Ah, yes, I can see it... Hold on, we almost got it... Yes, you're small-built, just like your mother... Hard to work with, hard to work with... Nice and small-built, like your mother."

Just as she felt her groans becoming a scream and her taut stillness start to break away from him no matter if it killed her since this pain felt like death anyway, Dr. Matthews said, "Look. You did it. See. Here's what had to come out."

She opened her sweaty eyes, lifted her head as high as she could manage, and tried to focus on what he was holding up. On the metal something in his hand that resembled long-handled tweezers, she saw a slimy string of pink, red, and clear mucus, a little globule at one end.

The agony in her lower back, way down in her intestines was still more than she could handle, even though it was going now from unbearable pain to a barely bearable ache.

"Is that the baby?" she asked, incredulous.

"Yes, that's it," he said, and she started crying, somewhere between fear and relief.

"Now, you just keep lying quiet. You really did well."

She protested. "Ain't you done?"

"Almost. Just a few more scrapes. I have to make sure I got everything out. Otherwise you might get infected."

Then he scraped and swabbed a bit longer, stopping once to hold up a ball of bloody cotton for her to see. Blood. She understood blood. That looked to her like a period. Relief set in and she began to relax. And then to sink a bit further, not into sleep, but furry enough that Dr. Matthews's cleaning up faded into the background.

Suddenly, she became aware of him standing beside her where she lay on the examination table, and then his smooth palm rubbing the softness of her arm close to her breast.

"How do you feel?" he asked.

"I'm doing fine." She was great compared to how bad she was hurting just a little while before.

"Let me help get you up. I have a bed in the next room. Let's you and I go back there."

Swinging her legs to the side, she sat up, then stood up, the sheet slipping to the floor beside her. Before she could rescue it, Dr. Matthews caught one end and secured it around her waist. He pressed himself slightly against her and patted her butt when he finished.

"You're a fine little girl," he pronounced. "If you had been coming to see me instead of your boyfriend, you wouldn't have gotten into trouble."

"What?" She was trying hard to keep up with what was happening.

"I would have seen to it that you never got pregnant. That's what I'm talking about."

She tugged at the sheet, trying to untangle her feet. Slowly, Dr. Matthews led her into the adjoining back room. It was small and felt dusty and except for a bed centered under the blind-covered windows seemed mostly unused.

Depositing her on the edge of the mattress, Dr. Matthews stood in front of a bureau and began giving himself a shot. He took off his shirt and then completed the procedure, expertly injecting the fluid from the hypodermic into his arm. With her eyes adjusting now to the dimness, she could see that his arms were flabby. Then, as he removed his undershirt and his pants, she saw that everything else sagged, too, from the skin of his breasts, to his dry underbelly, to the loose flesh of his lower thighs. She had never seen anybody look so spiffy in their clothes and so bad when they took them off.

Dr. Matthews walked toward the bed, pulling on the front of himself through the fabric of his boxer shorts. He sat down next to her and said, "Give me a little kiss."

When she recoiled, he leaned further into her. "Don't you think what I just did for you deserves a kiss?" Saying that, he twisted her around and put his wet mouth on her lips, which she automatically opened before she could catch herself. She endured his stifling breath and wobbly tongue.

Dr. Matthews pushed her down on the bed, dropped his shorts, and climbed up astride her. His penis and balls sagged, too. He spit in his hands and pulled on the penis. "See, it's coming. I just took the shot. See. It's getting up."

It was difficult for her to focus – everything that was happening stunned her.

Dr. Matthews grabbed her hand, "Here, you rub it." She remembered milking a cow in the country on Mr. Dawson's brother's farm. The heavy fat of Dr. Matthews's penis hardened into gristle. He slopped more saliva on it and pushed it inside, then started twisting and grunting. "Good," he said. "Small built and nice. Come on, put your arms around me."

She obeyed, and when he slapped her on her hip a few times, she rotated her bottom against him. Spit drooled out the corner of his mouth and, with one final jab and a wiggle, he got through.

"Sweet girl, sweet girl," he kept saying, "nice, sweet girl," until he rolled over and stretched out on his back, breathing hard.

She just lay there. She didn't know what else to do.

After a few minutes, Dr. Matthews got up and went into the half-bathroom. She heard the water running. He came back in an old terrycloth robe and handed her a warm towel. "Here, you can wipe off with this."

She did, then looked around for her pedal pushers, which he went to the examination room and brought to her, along with her underpants and a large kotex napkin.

Carefully placing the sanitary pad in her panties and noting the red spot that bloomed on its soft white surface, she got dressed as decently as she could. Dr. Matthews walked her to the living room turned reception room and gave her a peck on the cheek.

"When you can, bring me a hundred and fifty dollars. And take one of these pills every day for infection, there're five of them here." He reached in the pocket of his robe and handed the small box to her.

"Take care of yourself," he said and opened the front door.

In the twenty years since that horrible experience, she never again let herself be raped. And never again was she so crassly used. She made sure of that. Adults sucked, no doubt about it. But she learned that she was every bit as smart as they were, maybe smarter because she could get from them what she needed and keep them believing whatever nice stuff she wanted about her. Yes, she could take care of herself and that was a good thing because she had to. Who else was there to call on, confide in, depend upon? She kept her business to herself, kept herself to herself, and kept on trucking. But what if Dr. Matthews had put her pregnant little ass in his Cadillac and hauled her back home to Daddy Riley and they'd gotten Miss Cherry or one of her women teachers involved? Who she became and her outlook on life would probably be completely different. Or maybe not. When it came to sex, all of them were pretty fucked up.

She stayed away from doctors and was super-conscientious about birth control even as she knew that accidentally becoming pregnant didn't have to spell the end of the world. Maybe she should have sworn off sex, but she didn't. Just kept right on doing it.

She still hadn't told a soul this whole sad story. Not the fast girl in high school who got in trouble, too, and came crying for help. Not her dorm mates in college and definitely not the sorority sisters. Never the young men who told her they loved and wanted to marry her. Nobody she studied or protested with during graduate school in Madison, or the actors who were her only family in Baltimore. All of it now was water under the bridge, old old water. She didn't have any more time this morning for poring over ancient history even if it was her own. Wherever this resided inside her, it could keep staying right there. Rushing out of the shower, she glanced in the mirror at her healthy, shapely body, then looked down at the flat, smooth belly. No one would ever imagine what life had rooted there.

In the '81 Celica she depleted her savings to buy, she zipped the few miles to Vivian's Germantown neighborhood of two-story duplexes and small, humped yards. The full sunny day in a week of cool May weather had brought out the children for Saturday play. Before she could gather her things and slide from the car, three of them had her surrounded.

"Miss Deneicy!" "Hey, Miss Deneicy!"

Just like the kids in her after school drama classes at the community center, these mangled her name with her nickname. She had given up trying to correct them. Besides, she was still adjusting herself to changing from "Johnson" to "Jones." The new Jones she had chosen was every bit as common as Johnson, but the ring of it had more pizazz. Deneice Jones. Miss Neicy Jones. She liked it. It could partner with exotic or homely characters and look good on a theater marquee.

"Miss Deneice, where's our play? Did you all finish it yet?"

Ralph was thirteen, tall for his age and slender. He was eager because she had promised he could do a monologue about hating his social studies assignments. Before she could answer Ralph, Rachel jumped up on her. Her plump eight-year-old body was too heavy to carry, but she always greeted her this way. A loud smacking kiss to Rachel's forehead and then she turned to Ralph.

"We're almost done. Margo and I are working on it now with Vivian." Margo's brown Rabbit was parked at the curb. "I'd better get on in." When they finished, they were going to have ice cream and cake for her birthday.

She dropped Rachel and stooped to hug five-year-old Benjamin whose round face behind owlish glasses broke into instant sunshine.

"Where's your mama?" His bright green trousers and plush yellow sweatshirt were dazzling. Diane religiously dressed him in kid versions of the latest styles.

"In the house." He pointed across the street.

"Can you tell her I'll be by to see you all later on?" She made it her business to look in on him and his mama. Diane was as good a parent as she could make herself be, a high-spirited twenty-year-old whose adolescence had been abruptly arrested.

She gave him another squeeze, closing her eyes to bask in the warmth, then stood and waved them all off. She was really feeling them today. They fired her enthusiasm for the Juneteenth pageant. The city refused to appropriate money for it this year, saying that whatever celebration black people needed could be folded into the Fourth of July. Yeah, right. Incensed, she took it on without pay. Vivian and Margo, community center board members, agreed to help and director Dorothy came up with a small pot of production money.

Walking up the weedy sidewalk, she spotted Margo and Vivian looking out of the picture window. The three of them had spent a lot of volunteer time together. She slid right into the tight friendship they already had. They were rough with their teasing and long on sisterly love. She was lucky to have hooked up with them. When she told them that after one margarita too many at the end of a planning dinner, they didn't know what she meant until she confessed that she felt as if most people, black sisters included, didn't like her.

"It's not that folks don't like you, Neicy. You're just not that easy to know." Vivian always spoke the truth as she saw it.

"Yeah," Margo added, "you come across as a little standoffish. Not exactly stuck-up or anything, but kind of in yourself, to yourself."

"But that's not how I want to be perceived. I want people to like me. It feels as if they're being standoffish with me."

"What I think, Neicy" – Vivian touched her softly on the shoulder – "is that you just need to loosen up a bit. Let yourself be yourself and bring that forward."

"I try. But what I do doesn't seem to come off right. I don't know how to be like how people are in the world. I don't get it right, I can tell. Somebody else can come along and say something and then the person or the whole situation just opens up, while I was there talking and dealing and that never happened for me. It feels like I don't belong here."

"You mean in Philly?" Vivian was trying to understand what she was struggling to say.

"In Philly. In Wisconsin, Arkansas, Trinidad. Mexico, Canada. Anywhere. Everywhere. On the planet."

They didn't know how to answer that.

Finally, Margo leaned over and consoled, totally out of character, "Don't worry about it, Deneice. You're alright with us."

She hoped that she was.

Standing at the window tall and commanding in a splashy print caftan, Vivian was adjusting the blinds. Margo, rounder and shorter with dancing green eyes that camouflaged her racial militancy, munched on something in her hand. If they had been a trio of sisters, she, sister Neicy, would be the one in the middle – her thick hair slightly relaxed and brushing her shoulders, her skin the color that some people liked to call butterscotch, some people liked to call honey. Even though many of her parts were individually slim – like her waist and arms – the overall impression people had of her was not thinness. She looked like a woman with body if not a full-bodied woman – 5'8 1/2", around 140 pounds, the exact weight depending on how hard she was hitting her jazzercise classes and laying off the potato chips.

As soon as she entered the house, Margo and Vivian skipped

over, sing-songing "Ma-ma Deneicy! Ma-ma Deneicy!" circling her in mock imitation of the children.

She tried to maneuver past them into the living room. Normally, their antics didn't bother her, but she didn't feel like any teasing today.

"Cut that out!"

"Ma-ma Deneicy!"

"Didn't you all hear me? I said cut it out! Do I look like anybody's mama?"

"Well, if you really want to hear the truth," Vivian shot back, "you sure as hell did."

"Yeah," Margo chimed in, "all your bosoms were full! The only somebody I know who's that into children is my cousin who can't have any!"

Caught between wanting to slap Margo and wanting to cry, she burst out crying.

"Neicy, what's the matter with you?!" Vivian took her arm and led her to the couch.

"I could have had me three babies right now if I wanted to." She dropped on the couch. "There's nothing wrong with me. I could have had babies. Three of them." She held up the long middle fingers on her left hand like a drunken salute and then slumped, still crying, on the pillows. Her past barreled down on her, unexpectedly exploding in the present. From a place she hadn't known needed release, she told them about her unborn children.

The first one was the glob of mucus on Dr. Matthews's tongs. She recounted that story, still so fresh in her mind. And then she dredged up the second abortion, the one she had the summer after graduation when Richard's condom broke. They were at a six-week workshop in Michigan, immediately and strongly attracted to each other, but without any long-term commitment as they headed to promising futures on opposite sides of the world. Going with him to the nurse he found was the only possible decision and she was grateful that she had the choice.

She thought about the third time and threw the nearest pillow. That instance was really unfair. The damn IUD she was using for supposedly fail-safe protection had failed. Before her arrogant gynecologist would undo the damage, he made her go through the legality of getting a psychiatrist to certify she was mentally unfit to bear a child. "I'm not unfit," she had challenged, "I'm just not ready. This faulty birth control offered up to women is what needs to be examined." The psychiatrist had called her a feminist and, for a very healthy fee, signed the papers.

That memory glaring, she started crying again. "I love children. It's just that I couldn't have these."

"Neicy, it's alright. Nobody's blaming you. We've all been through bad shit like that." Margo was trying to comfort her.

"I know what I did was right. But I'm feeling so sad. I don't know why I'm feeling so sad." Never had it occurred to her that she needed to mourn these children.

Her voice sank to a deeper register and an even more faraway place. "I know that first baby would have been a girl. I was fifteen, she'd be twenty now. And doing what? In her junior year in college? Learning how to teach, or be a singer, or maybe an astronaut? She'd be fine, I bet you, and just as sharp as me."

"Neicy, stop this," Vivian shook her. "You're just making yourself feel worse."

Vivian's shake was as easy to ignore as a gnat fanning past her shoulder. "And that second one, good Lord. I don't have a clue about that one. Come and gone as fast as the summer we made it. Poof, here a minute. Poof-poof, long gone."

Margo and Vivian quit trying to counter the painful journey something in her seemed determined to make. They sat sorrowing and imagining with her. A twenty-year-old young woman stepping out on the brink of life, ready to storm the world. And then a flash of nothing and something, a snuffed beam of light, too ephemeral to make much of an impression but enough to say something has been here and gone.

"When I fought with that psychiatrist and that prick of a doctor five years ago, I almost changed my mind. I could handle a little boy, I told myself, even without a husband to help me, even as I launched my professional career. He'd be five years old now. I'd have him with me and he'd be outside playing with Benjamin and Ralph. I would have named him Nelson and called him LeStar."

"Wait a minute, Neicy." Vivian snapped to. "How old did you say those three kids would be right now?"

She looked at Vivian, her conscious self kicking in. "Twenty, and then – let's see – 1969 – that would be thirteen, and then five. Twenty, thirteen, and five."

"Diane, Ralph, and Benjamin," Vivian said.

"What?" She and Margo inquired together.

"That's the same ages as Diane, Ralph, and Benjamin," Vivian reiterated.

"What happened to Rachel?" Margo asked, so seriously drawn into what was happening that she didn't notice the strangeness.

"What are you all talking about?"

"Neicy, don't you think it's something that those kids, including Diane, are the same ages your children would be? That's too much of a coincidence! 'Everything that's denied must somehow, sooner or later, find expression.' I just read that in this new book I'm studying."

What Vivian said hit her with a jolt of inspiration. She sprang up off the couch. "Get me some candles. Bring me some candles, you all." She tore over to the kitchen, pulling open cabinet drawers. She didn't rationally grasp what Vivian quoted, but on some other level, it made absolute sense. Something was supposed to happen. Lighting candles was what struck her.

Margo came back from the bathroom with a thick lavender candle meant for a relaxing hot bath. Vivian had found two red tapers in her bedside table.

"No," she shouted, "white."

In front of a kitchen cabinet, she yanked out a box of tealights next to a forgotten fondue pot and held them up like they were the prize find of an afternoon scavenger hunt.

Running back into the living room, she knelt at the coffee table and shoved everything aside, then looked around, trying to see what she wanted. She picked up the pillow she had thrown and stripped off the gold and black cloth. Margo touched the scarf around her neck and said emphatically, "Use that, too." Yes, her favorite scarf was very beautiful – a flowing crimson rectangle handmade in India, shot through with threads of bright gold.

She positioned the cloth and scarf. Then took three of the small white candles and lined them in a row – twenty-year-old girl, thirteen-year-old, five-year-old boy.

Margo retrieved the box and thrust a fourth candle at her.

"Is that for me or for you?" she asked Margo.

"Maybe for both of us."

Taking the new candle, she made space for it between the last two candles. Vivian rescued her philodendron from the carpet and placed it back on the table, then handed her the matches. She carefully lit all four candles. The tacky little tealights glowed as resplendently as gigantic blessed pillars at a high holy mass. She didn't know whether she was praying or going batty, but what she was doing on her knees in front of these burning candles felt perfectly right. She stayed in that position and her two friends sat there with her for a good, long time.

Shriven, her mind said. Shriven? Where did that archaic-ass, Catholic school word come from? But, blessedly, she was now past questioning her unfamiliar voices. She laid herself on the couch, bone spent, energy exhausted, the tears drying on her cheeks.

CHAPTER 6

No matter how many times she replayed the scene, she was still amazed that she'd broken and spilled her deep stuff to Margo and Vivian. They hadn't reviled her, hadn't treated her like a monster. In fact, her opening up seemed to have made them let her further in. But the long-term effects might be different. The last thing she wanted was to mess up her new life. She was taking hold here, not moving unmoored and fancy-free as she'd done all through college and grad school. Her job at Penn Two, her side gig at the community center, the chances to act, the various communities of folks who seemed to like her were more solid than what she'd found in Baltimore, not to mention her boyfriend, Curtis. Maybe she was growing up. There was structure now, the smell of stability, although inside she still felt scattered and floppy.

Lazing around the house recuperating had used up the cloudy Sunday. No problem. When there was not a matinee in her life, it was the day she kept for herself. So Curtis ringing from downstairs in the early evening was a real surprise. There was an unfamiliarity about him. Or maybe she was the one who was different and that made him feel unfamiliar.

"Hey, gal," he teased.

"Hey, guy, to you."

"See, I haven't even tipped my hand yet, and there you go, calling up the guy in my pants."

"Oh, you and your pants and your guy! What did they tell you boys? Keep your thing down and your trousers up?"

"Well, in that Reading, Pennsylvania foster home I grew up in, you know they didn't come out with very much. But whatever it was they told us, I must not have heard it."

"You can say that again. But, really, what the hell kind of sense were we supposed to make out of that stupid nonsense they handed us about sex? And not one word, not a single word about love!"

"What about love?"

"Love," she repeated, emphatically.

"Well, what about love?" Curtis asked again.

"I'm asking you."

"You didn't ask me. You just said our folks never talked to us about love."

"And then you raised the question," she countered.

"I wasn't raising a question, I was only repeating what you said."

"Well, I hadn't said anything."

"Yes, you had. You started the whole thing when you made that remark about..."

"What the heck, Curtis? Why are we going back and forth about who raised what and who said what, first or second? What is this exchange about anyway?"

"Love," he answered.

The word fell from his lips like a bomb, the reverberations pushing her over to the kitchen counter where she dropped onto one of the stools, spreading her long arms and torso across the formica top.

"I don't think I've ever heard you mouth that word."

"I don't think I've ever heard you use it either." His quick retort was defensive.

She drew herself up. "Why haven't I ever heard you say the word love? Don't you think that's odd?"

"Actually, I don't, to tell you the truth. When would I have a reason to be talking about love?"

She immediately thought of an occasion when he or she or the both of them could have been talking about love. It was also an early evening. She had leaned lightly on her half-open door before completely admitting him, admiring the padded set of his shoulders in his favorite black leather jacket.

"He-ey," his smile dented the corners of his full, blooded lips.

"Hey to you," she had greeted in return. "You're right on time."

"Neither rain nor snow nor..."

"Yeah, I know. You're more punctual than the mailman, making your rounds."

The dark brown vee of his throat glistened tongue-licking hollow, framed by the jagged edge of a tee ripped rimless for scrubby chic comfort. She took in that triangle of flesh and the striking face above it then dropped her gaze to the handsome front of his pants. Whether they were slacks, pleated and creased, or a pair of gray running sweats, he would always be hard enough for her to see immediately what she was letting in. Although she'd shared him from the beginning with Cynthia and Mavis, whenever he came knocking at her door, everything he brought with him was hers. She could stop fretting about why he liked her or wondering how she stacked up next to his other two women. "Have faith in me, lady," he'd said to her soon after they began sleeping together. "I'm not out to do you harm." She struggled to believe him, even though everything he did tested her trust.

As she curved away from the entrance, he poured through, shutting the door behind him with one hand and pulling her to him with the other. The front of him that she had relished with her eyes now rooted for a groove against her. Besides the good feel of him, her heightened senses drank in his scent, which was so distinctly blended that she called it just "him." She picked out a haunting of Drakkar cologne, a sharp masculine soap, and a hint of some faintly citrus and wood aftershave lotion.

It was one of those nights when they went straight to the bedroom and fell into each other. He may not have belonged to her, but his body, the him in his body right now was hers, from the richness near the back of her throat, to his elongating penis, to the hairy calves of his legs.

"Are you like this with all the girls?" What she had up until now stopped herself from asking slipped out of her mouth.

"Don't even go there," he checked her, gently pulling away.

"Well, if you're going to have a harem, you don't need to be evil about it. I really don't care."

Curtis sat up next to the pillow, his slitted eyes burning, back as straight as when she first saw him giving expert sociological testimony at Little Willy's trial.

"You promised me you'd be honest with me and with yourself, Deneice. You wouldn't have said that if you didn't have feelings."

"It just crossed my mind, that's all."

"Oh, Neicy, come here baby." He gathered her up again, fitted his warm body back next to hers, and took up where they'd left off, kissing, touching, stoking the fire that flamed so effortlessly between them.

Yet, no matter how much she desired him, no matter how exciting his maleness was to her, at the moment when he needed to enter, her body began closing up. That had never happened with any other man, but it often did with him.

"You're locking me out, baby."

"But I'm not trying to."

Although something about Curtis's seriousness, respect, the way she felt about him made him different from the guys she'd known, she didn't see why screwing him should be any more complicated. The good news, though, was that he had figured out ways of getting her to open up. Then the sex was scorching sweet.

"Let me, Neicy, baby... baby girl... open. Let me..." He moved in, wanted more, faster and further. Legs flung wide, round bottom up and thrusting, she always stretched to capacity, taking him in.

During the past ten months they had known each other, there were times of intense connection when Curtis could have been talking, or at least thinking, about love. Yet here he was asking what reason did he have to do so. And then he queried her.

"Well, when did we ever hear you, Madame Deneicy, talking about love?"

"Curtis, please, don't be flip."

"I'm sorry." He took the stool next to hers. "The long and short of it is, I don't use the word."

"Apparently I don't either."

"What's your excuse?" He asked before she could question him.

"I don't know what it means. I guess I don't know what love is."

"And me," Curtis volunteered, "whatever it's supposed to mean doesn't mean that for me. So I say, hey, and just let it fly."

"But here we are, two people who have shared all we've done with each other and we've never even mentioned love."

"If you had, depending on how you did it, I just might have split."

"And if you had, it would've been fine with me as long as we didn't have to do our relationship any different." That was her side of the equation.

"But what I don't understand," Curtis said, "is what's got you..." – she gave him a look – "okay, what's got us talking about it now."

"I don't know." She dropped her head. Love was not a topic she usually dwelled upon.

"Aren't you curious about why I'm in your neighborhood?" Curtis changed the subject.

"I guess I was so thrown off when I saw you I forgot to ask." Slapping him on the shoulder lightened her tone.

"I swung by my supervisor's house to pick up the file of this kid

I keep thinking about. They're trying to railroad him into juvenile, but I think I can get him off."

Curtis took care of his job as a county social worker with skill and dedication, working hard when he was working and apparently forgetting it the rest of the time. But she knew that he really cared about his charges, which was one of the things she admired about him. If this case was bugging him, it had to be important. She let him talk while she listened.

"Sounds bad, yes. But it also sounds like you might be able to do something. We have a couple kids in my teen drama program who are there as part of their treatment. If you wanted me to, I could help you get this boy in."

"Why didn't I think of that? Maybe this one reminds me a little of myself, not so much how I was, but how I would have been if I were coming along now, motherless, fatherless, emotions I couldn't deal with. I learned how to repress and sublimate and also how to work injustice and buck the odds. Now everything comes out of them angry and violent."

"True. But therapeutic drama really can help problem kids. I don't know what would have become of me if it hadn't been for our rinky-dink little high school thespian society."

"You never told me that." Curtis sounded like here was something about her he was supposed to know but didn't.

"I told you I was a troubled kid after my mother died and you know I started acting in high school. Anyway, I'll talk to my boss Dorothy tomorrow and have her give you a call."

"Perfect. Thank you so much."

"Not a problem. Anything I can do to keep the blue children out of the system, you know you can count on me."

"I'm glad you understand. Come on, I knocked on your door to see if you wanted to walk over to the deli."

"Great idea." She rolled and clipped the potato chip bag between her knees and started plotting what she would get. A roast beef sandwich with purple cole slaw and lots of Dijon mustard.

Figuring out what she wanted to eat was one of her favorite pastimes. She took so long deciding what to order in restaurants that friends got impatient. "Just choose something. It's only food, just one meal." "But food's very important," she protested. She had felt that way for as long as she could remember. Curtis was the only person she'd ever known who could totally relate. Skinny and underfed as a kid, now he lifted weights in the morning, absorbed a lot of news, read his "industry" magazines, and attended to his work and women. In between it all, just like she did, he made time to have good food.

On the way back from the deli, they took the long route home, meandering through the short West Philly blocks.

"I know you need to go in," Curtis said, "but what did you mean when you said talking about love would have been fine with you as long as it didn't make things any different?"

She couldn't imagine why she sighed.

"Okay, okay." Curtis heard the sigh. "You don't have to go there."

"I don't mind going there, but I think I'd better save it for another time. I'm too tired to tackle that biggee right now. And I'd want to hear what you meant about running away."

"I didn't say, 'run away,' I said 'split.'"

"Same difference."

"No, they're not the same. I should know."

She couldn't fight him about it. It was his remark.

Arms waisted around each other under their light spring jackets, they walked the remaining way home to her apartment building.

"You're a beautiful woman, Ms. Jones."

"You're a fine man, Mr. Lockhart."

They never said, "I'll call you," or "I'll see you," or any 'til-the-next-time leave-taking formulas. So why was she noticing that now? She bussed him goodnight and opened the outside door. She certainly wasn't trying to tie this brother man down. And, besides, how many different kinds of fool would she be to seriously love a man who was involved with two other women?! Yet Curtis had definitely established himself in her life. No matter how flittish or skittish or ambivalent she was, he stayed the same, a point of constancy and solidity, always pleasant, welcoming, accepting. No, they hadn't talked about love, but maybe Curtis was an instance of actions speaking louder than words.

As she shelved away deli cold cuts, straightened the Sunday paper, undressed and washed up, she kept thinking about the ways he made a big deal out of them even as he kept things easy. That time, for instance, when she met him for lunch and the wannabee glamorous white woman he worked with had been all over him, flaunting eyelashes and cheek until she got pissed off. Curtis had laughed and asked didn't she ever consider giving the white brothers a chance. But he quickly stopped joking when she didn't join in with him and said, "I can like Wendy and work with her and whatever, but a white woman, no matter how cool or beautiful, could never be my other half. I'm into sisters. Actually, I'm into you. Do you mind?" He was challenging, fishing. She had taken the bait and soon after that, the two of them became lovers.

His saying white brothers had thrust Richard into her mind. She hadn't mentioned to Vivian and Margo during her breakdown that the father of the fleet and fleeing middle baby was white, a boy whom everybody except her had called Dana, from some town in Connecticut she had never heard of noted for its rivers and manufacturing of freighter parts. They had stayed in touch for a while then lost track of each other when she got to seriously considering marriage with Tyrone her senior year.

Damn! Every sex and relationship ghost in her closet was trying to wake up and rattle her chains! She placed her toothbrush in its frosted blue glass on the bathroom counter. Get to bed, gal, she ordered. Let sleeping dogs lie and don't start the present to barking.

She stepped through her door at five-thirty from a day of getting out press releases at Penn Two and hard back-to-back community center classes wishing for a chunk of time to herself. But right on her heels, Vivian came in sharp and focused, threw her satchel on the couch, sat down next to it and pulled out their Juneteenth pageant draft. Having had a break after school, Margo sauntered around in visiting mode. Both of them wanted to know what was brewing in the kitchen.

"Nothing but hot water, girls. Wouldn't you like some tea?"

"How about a glass of wine?" Margo was checking bottles in the small counter rack.

"Help yourself."

"Tea for me," Vivian called from the living room as she shed hose and loosened her bra. "And you'd better order us a pizza."

"I was thinking of that."

"You? Settling for pizza? It must've been a hell of a day." Margo paused with a bottle in her hand.

"It could have been worse. I'm just a little on the tired side."

"Uh-uh, sister," Vivian drifted toward the counter, "that sounds like too much Curtis too late."

Margo spun around. "You're not still seeing him, are you?"

Margo instantly pissed her off. People knew that she was seeing Curtis and that she wasn't his only woman. She never bitched or moaned about it and never talked about her private life. If she was okay hanging with Curtis and his other sweethearts, nobody else should jump indignant about it – and certainly not Margo, who went from man to man so fast they might as well have been one-night stands.

"Yes, we still see each other." Period. She decided to do what she'd been doing all day with her unusually sensitive feelings – vault over them and get on with the business at hand.

"I can't say that I blame you," Margo persisted, "he's one fine brother."

"And a decent one, too." Maybe if she stayed easy with Curtis as subject but lifted the conversation out of the trash, Margo would leave it alone.

"You think y'all could squeeze another good sister into the bed? I'm not occupied right now. Or maybe you want a replacement? You don't sound very enthusiastic."

"Margo!" Vivian reprimanded just in the nick of time.

The idea of Curtis, her boyfriend, with Margo or any woman she personally knew was violently upsetting.

Vivian kept talking. "There's a multitude of reasons why Neicy might want to keep hanging with Curtis. Men can be more trouble than they're worth. This way she doesn't have all that to deal. Right, Neicy? Doesn't have to be too responsible, doesn't have to make a commitment, doesn't have to give too much..."

"Can we just please drop the topic?" Margo was a bitch. But Vivian didn't need to be playing shrink either. Sure, she had her own set of insecurities about Curtis and this harem thing she was doing with him. But she wasn't about to let them turn her into some dysfunction to be analyzed. She'd revealed enough on Saturday. Vivian wasn't spilling her guts about how it felt to be man-less.

"Look, it's six-thirty and counting. We'd better order this pizza and get our asses to work." She was supposed to be running the show. This pageant was the first big project Dorothy had given her and she wanted to get it right.

Pizza ordered, she sat down in her armchair next to Vivian on the couch while Margo grabbed a pillow and got comfortable on the floor. "Okay, Vivian, refresh our memories."

"African-American Freedom: The Unclaimed Legacy — Juneteenth Then and Now." Vivian began reading her summary.

"That sounds great to me," Margo burst out as soon as she finished. "We've done more than I remembered."

"Yeah," Vivian agreed. "But we still don't have the speeches or a grand finale. Every pageant needs that."

"True, Vivian, but not too much script." Getting up from her armchair to answer the intercom, she threw in that caution. "As one of my professors used to say, a pageant's nothing mostly except concept and costume. We're already pushing the limit."

"But we should," Vivian argued. "Otherwise this'll look like a minstrel show and no one will end up educated or politicized."

"You know I'm not advocating that." She didn't need to be lectured. Hours of study and experience had taught her about educating audiences and about pageants. She ran down for the pizza.

On the way back up the stairs, she caught the image of herself in her living room with Margo and Vivian, a little protective of her authority, fretful about the outcome of the event, uneasy about how she was coming across with these two black women whom she wanted to like her. Relax, Deneice. Wasn't that what they had told her? She could try.

They dug into the pizza.

"Hey, good women, I'm sorry if I'm being kinda uptight. I'm feeling real responsible for pulling this over the top."

"No problem." Vivian felt sincere. "We understand."

"Yeah," Margo added, "don't sweat it. Let's see. Who do we need speeches for?"

Vivian looked at her notes. "The master, mistress, ex-slave woman, ex-slave man, and the general."

"You know, it would be poetic justice if we made laughing stocks out of every one of those white characters. Payback for generations of white people turning our folks into coons and buffoons."

"So, whaddya mean, Neicy?" Margo started following her drift. "Have the general ride up on a broken-down mule with a sign on its butt saying, Take Me to Forty Acres."

"And you know the general has to be drunk." She herself was warming up. "A pint of whiskey in his pocket that he drops when he bends over to retrieve the executive order."

Vivian joined in, laughing. "Which he cannot read." She grabbed a page of notes: "The people of dis honorable state of Texus are ear-by hen-formed that in ack-cord-dance wid a proclamashun from de Exec15tary of dese United States, h'alla yawl slaves is free."

The three of them were cracking up.

"Naw, Vivian, he's from the North, so he can talk good." She was practically falling out of her chair. "And, on second thought, no whiskey either. That's too stereotypical. Let him be drunk from hogging down the Southerners' strawberry soda pop."

Vivian leaned over to hit her. "Soda pop hadn't been invented yet."

"Okay," she conceded. "Give him a wide slice of red-red watermelon, too big to put in his mouth but he's trying anyway." She picked up the largest wedge of pizza in the box and mock-stretched her jaws.

"Will you women quit?" Margo hooted. "The general's got to keep his cool so he can represent the Union. But we can let the massa and missus cut a little jig to cheer themselves up after they finish crying tears about the belly rubs and sweet stuff they won't be getting from their coloreds anymore."

They laughed and slapped at each other until all three of them straightened up.

"I wish we could do a scene like that."

"Too bad, Neicy, but we can't." Margo sounded sensible. "It sure would give all of us a good laugh, though."

"I actually don't see why we can't. Like I said, they've done it to us for generations. Why not?" Maybe she didn't feel as secure with the black community as she would like, but she was absolutely clear about racism in the world and her active opposition to it. Fighting for African American studies at Wisconsin in a 'fro as big as Angela's, seeing colored folks struggle everywhere she'd traveled had helped school her. A little reparations segment of humor would be in divine right order.

"No, I don't think so, Neicy." Vivian sided with Margo. "There's a chance that even the liberals in the crowd wouldn't dig it. We've never had the power to make any of our white stereotypes the norm or make the whole white race suffer because of them. Still, we'd probably get criticized for doing to them what we don't want them to do to us."

"Crock 'a shit."

"I'm with you there, girlfriend," Vivian conceded. "And the sad part is that we're still recovering from all this slavery trauma — especially those undercover parts that ole massa and missus loved."

"Ain't that the truth!" Margo seconded.

"Okay," she reluctantly got back on track, feeling tiredness like the weight of an x-ray apron in the dentist's office. "How about each of us choosing the one we'd like to do and then running them by each other?" The thought of trying to collectively compose script was sending her over the edge.

Vivian scrutinized her face. "Yes, girl, you look like you need to shoo us out and get some sleep."

"Zzz's at this point would be nice. I'll write the speeches for the two slaves," she claimed her assignment.

"I'll do General Granger," Vivian chose for herself.

"And I'm fine with the master and mistress. Neicy, is it okay if I write one speech and have the two of them speak it together?"

"Cool idea, Margo! That'll play wonderfully." Her compliment made Margo smile. "Well, women, we did it. Somebody take this leftover pizza," she called as she walked to the kitchen.

"Not me," Margo refused. "I already eat too much of the stuff."

"I'll take it," said Vivian. "It can be breakfast and that'll give me some extra time for running."

Dead on her feet at the counter, she wrapped the pizza in foil and ushered her two comrades through the door. She was so exhausted she couldn't even post-mortem the evening to see if she'd played it right.

Scene two of the pageant began as quickly as she could get the gleeful amateurs off and then back onto the outdoors stage. The turnout at the park was excellent this sunny Juneteenth Saturday. The audience crowded around the platform and booed the master and mistress, then hissed at the General when he confessed how federal troops waited for Texas slave owners to reap one last cotton harvest before breaking the news of emancipation. From behind the makeshift curtain, her attention heightened when her fugitive male slave came forward. The deejay who played him reminded her of Daddy Riley.

"I carried my freedom with me like a bright banner inside my soul. Escaped from Roanoke Ferry, but got dragged in again. Now I'm headed back to Virginia, looking for a gal named June. Her memory, sweet as ripe peaches, keeps summertime alive in my heart."

A tall man in work clothes near the stage lifted his cap and yelled, "Right on, brother." She shivered. Then the female slave, played by a petite soloist from the Methodist church choir, came alongside and sang slowly, "I'm running on, to see where the spirit's leading me, I'm running on," while stepping in gracefully widening arcs. Conjuring up these two slave ancestors had really gotten to her. That vibratory past was as alive in her blood as Indian sunsets and cypress swamp knees beckoning.

Ralph got the crowd going with a litany of "Why don't they teach us that in school?" as he corrected a string of omissions about black history. After the final item, he said, with a different voice and intonation, "I see myself in the future doing handstands with my mind on a beam of light." Their light, everything they were creating would bounce back to the planet in who knew what form billions of years from now.

Shaking out of Ralph's mood, she had to rush forward, taking the stage herself to fill in at the last minute for the act that was stranded across town on a broken-down bus. The piece was supposed to be a historical parade and all she'd had time to do was situate a few key moments in her head and grab some suggestive props.

She rocked and swam herself through the Middle Passage, curled like a tortured spoon at the edge of the stage. A rope tied around her waist linked her to a chained coffle trudging to the auction block. Guns she could mime as the Civil War raged and the Underground Railroad pulled intrepid seekers north, sleeping on snaky ground, peering around trees, stuffing the babies with laudanum rags. She held up a pageant poster, singing "We Shall Overcome," and everyone knew what that meant as readily as her shouting "1957" and spitting contemptuously recalled Central High. She became the patteroller, the president, the heroes and villains on every side of the human drama. By the time she'd killed off Malcolm and raised her fist in a final Panther salute, the stage was so thronged with energy she could feel it. The audience began applauding and kept on applauding, sending her off and ushering on Felicia from her teen program, who surprised everyone with her finale.

Felicia sat on the stage and dragged her butt across it, her dark face pained and determined. "I'm trying to flatten my big black ass. I'm trying to flatten my booty. My dance teacher says I can't be a professional because my behind is too large." Then she sprang up and shouted, "But I say my teacher is a big white lie," and broke into a kicking, leaping, high-energy east African dance. Everybody went wild with appreciation. The drummers held the beat as all the participants returned to the stage, cheering with their families and friends.

She joined them. Yes, onstage was where she felt most alive, most comfortable, most herself, most empowered, where she could turn off her worrisome mind and drop self-consciousness, just being totally into what she was doing – like when she had sex. Acting was home, or as close as she'd gotten to what she imagined people meant when they reverently used that word. She beckoned up Vivian and Margo and the three of them skipped around, beaming at everyone.

Circling, she saw Curtis smiling at her and hopped down. He squeezed her to him, his lips lightly brushing her ear.

"Great job, Neicy, you women did a terrific job. And you? You were fantastic. Why didn't you tell me you had a part?"

"I didn't have one. That was a last-ditch improv to fill in."

"You were magnificent!"

Other folks jammed between them, giving her nice words and hugs until Curtis reclaimed her, delight shining in his clear almond eyes. She wondered, though, who might be observing this unusual display of their intimacy. Normally, they were not so spontaneous out in the world.

Dorothy came up, as overflowing as Curtis had been with congratulations.

"Gracious, Deneice, I don't think I've ever seen such phenomenal stage presence. I have a friend at the Philadelphia Repertory Company I'd like to meet you. He's actually the artistic director. Here, I've written his name on the back of my card. I'll let him know you're coming."

"Oh, thank you, Ms. Dorothy." She could hardly contain herself until Dorothy walked away.

"Yes!" She jumped up and down. "Curtis, this could be the break I told you I was hoping for. Penn Two is fine and I'm grateful for it. But if I get a couple of fat parts at the Philadelphia Rep, I could be on my way to New York."

Curtis squeezed her again. "Even more cause for celebration."

Good vibes popping all around them, they slowly wound their way through booths and food tables, running into Benjamin and his young mom. Out socializing, Diane was in an excellent mood as she hailed them loudly, a sleepy Benjamin straddling her hip, about to be deposited for a nap with one of her friends selling Tibetan and African jewelry.

Strolling together, she and Curtis were in no particular hurry. They were headed to a small resort in the Poconos for the next two days and easing into vacation rhythms. Curtis had a knack for getting away as often as he could and thoroughly relaxing when he did so and she really liked that about him. As he unlocked her side of the car, a dark red Corvette roared up. Mavis, his flamboyant girlfriend, leaned out the window. It was eighty-five degrees, but Mavis was dressed in black leather pants that looked as if they had been hot waxed onto her and a tight nylon shell the exact shade of red as her car.

"Hey, guys," she glanced from one of them to the other. "What's going on?"

"Just heading out of town," Curtis replied.

"Oh," Mavis said, "I forgot. This is your weekend away. Have a good time." She shifted into first and sped off.

Curtis didn't say anything and she promptly decided not to give the woman another thought. But every time they passed a red automobile on the highway, uneasiness about how he could be with her and also with someone as different as Mavis attacked her mind.

When they got there, "The Pines" looked exactly as Curtis had described it – a homey black bourgeois retreat whose patronage had thinned after years of desegregation. Surveying the wide open-beamed room with its aging kitchen at one end and tucked-away bathroom, she unpacked her duffel bag. Curtis feigned shock as she lifted out pair after pair of shoes.

"Oh, cut it out. I notice you didn't say anything about all these pairs of panties." She had more of those also than she would need. Curtis used to tease her about never going without underpants. But he stopped talking when she went out and bought a whole new wardrobe of them, mostly red and black lace in a few places with space and gaps everywhere else.

After dinner, they sat quietly on the patio with a pitcher of sangria under the diamond stars.

"Neicy," Curtis's smooth voice interrupted her thoughts. "Just so you know. You're the first woman I've brought here in a very long while."

He must have been reading her mind. "What do you call 'a very long while'?"

"Four or five years, since shortly after I discovered the place. Pretty soon, I started going south to Rehoboth and the Bahamas" — he didn't say, "when I vacationed with my girlfriends," but she added that — "and kept this place for my own getaway, now that there's no entertainment and the clientele has gotten grayer."

"I don't mind that at all."

"I didn't think that you would."

Something about the knowing way he said it felt as precious as a kiss. She reached over and pulled him into her chair. They looked at the sky and drifted until Curtis finally roused them to their cabin.

Dropping into slumber, she felt him pressing against her body.

"Why do you try to make love with me before day in the morning and late late at night?"

"'Cause," he whispered, "I'm trying to catch you when your guard is down. You don't block me when you're half asleep."

"Oh," her soggy brain boggled. "I'm all sleep now. Catch me in the morning."

CHAPTER 7

On a blanket with Curtis after breakfast some distance from the main grounds, she decided to make good on her nighttime promise. As they took off their clothes, one strip-teasing piece at a time, she got looser and looser and even more excited – blue heaven above, clean clear air, and the singing of birds for backdrop. Reaching behind her back, she unhooked her bra, cupped her breasts and offered them to him, then slid out of her red bikinis, holding him, who was quivering and juicy, with her eyes.

Up on her hands and knees without one shred of covering, she let him fill her any way he wanted. She cried out with the sun in her face as it changed positions in the forenoon sky, the breeze blowing slick sweat from the cracks of her body and skin.

"Hey, baby," Curtis's voice was panting and husky, "what got into you?" He was still squeezing her engorged breasts, rubbing himself along the folds of her open physique and gradually cooling down.

"I feel liberated and really safe here outside." Inside, she had preferences and refused to make love in bathrooms.

"Man, you're full of surprises!"

"Are you complaining?"

"Hell, no. I must bring you to the woods more often."

She craned her neck to give him a nibble. He licked the salt off the end of her nose. "Yum-yum."

"I can see that you love my stuff."

Curtis responded, "I love you."

Had he really said that? She untangled herself and began putting on her jeans and sneakers while he did likewise.

"Curtis, remember our conversation? You're the guy who doesn't know what love is."

"That's not what I said. I said, what it means to me seems to be different from what it means for everyone else."

"So what does it mean for you?" She went further out on the limb. "What does loving me mean to you?"

"Loving you means I see who you are way deep inside. That's beautiful to me. I want to touch it and make it light up even brighter than it already is." He answered like he'd been pondering the question.

With his steady gaze on her, she felt her insides blazing and melting in the heat of his true regard. If she stayed with it, she would be liquid gold spilling all over, but she feared she would lose her grip. Could she take in his love? What did it mean and what would it call for?

"Curtis, I don't know what to do with that. I don't know if I can handle it."

"You seem to be doing just fine."

"But we hadn't spoken it. I hadn't felt it like all of what I'm feeling now. I'm not sure I can love you the same way. I've always given the best of myself to my work. I get inside it like you say you do me and want to make it shine."

He nodded with understanding. "I have to hold on to the way I love, too."

"What? How?" She was puzzled.

"You asked me how I loved you. I was surprised that you didn't ask a thing about Cynthia or Mavis." He was watching her closely.

"What about Cynthia and Mavis?" Then recognition struck her. "Do you love them, too? Is that it? Is that what you didn't say?"

"Yes."

"Fuck you, Curtis! What kind of lame shit is this?" How could he have touched her so deeply and made her feel so special, then turned around and snatched it away!

"Try not to curse me like that, Neicy. It makes me feel bad and I don't think I deserve it."

"But, Curtis... "

"I know," he said softly. "It's hard to take. It's hard to accept."

"You can say that again!" Inflamed, she sprang off the blanket. Curtis came up to the tree where she stopped.

"It's like this, Neicy. If I get into anybody I'm attracted to, I can see their goodness and their beauty and I love them. Loving just one person at a time has never worked for me. People pop up on my doorstep – Mavis literally did when she had an accident – and for one reason or another, it gets serious."

She recalled her own history with him. How his intensity at that court hearing had drawn her, how she had lingered after it was over to speak with him, how their first conversation over coffee had created a compelling chord between them. She scrutinized him in the dappled sunlight. She let the reality of her feelings for him seep through her consciousness. She felt the tenderness, the knowing, the desire to touch him. She felt love. But it had been easier for her when they didn't use the word.

"I can love you and somebody else, too," Curtis kept on explaining, "in the same way you can love me and love your work. And I want to keep letting it grow."

They began walking back to the cabins.

"Can you love me as much as you love your work?" Curtis pressed.

"I don't know. The work I can always count on."

"You can count on me, too. I'm here, Neicy. We're good together and we could be even more solid. But you have to come and meet me. You're still holding back..."

"I can't help it if my body..."

"I'm not talking about the way your body tries to close up before intercourse. Like I keep saying, I think that's some kind of an unconscious defense you need to work with somebody to figure out. I'm talking about you not holding back your heart and soul."

"I'm giving you all I have, Curtis."

"I don't think so. I'm here for you, always will be as long as you let me and stay with me. What are you afraid of?"

"I'm not afraid." He just looked at her. "But why do you have to have sex with all the women you love?"

"You want to be the one to give it up?"

"Curtis!" Now he was definitely messing with her.

"That's a big part of the loving, Neicy. Why cut that part off?"

"Pun intended?"

"Seriously, do you want to talk about it sometime?" he asked.

"Maybe."

"Hey, Neicy!"

She spun around when she heard Vivian's voice.

"Hey, girl!"

It was four o' clock on Friday and she was rummaging around in north Philly hoping to find an LP by Arthur Prysock. When the older couples at the "Pines" got tired of "Fever" and "Blueberry Hill" and "Sixty Minute Man," they had played Prysock over and over as she and Curtis sat in with them for a few hands of bridge. At one point, they all laid down their cards and slow-danced with their partners around the room, warming up the sweet, fading lodge. She wanted to surprise Curtis with more of that full-bodied crooning when she went to his place this evening.

"What are you doing up here?" Vivian called as she came down the aisle.

"I'm hunting an old album. Aren't you supposed to be at work?"

"The bosses sent me to see a block of buildings they're turning into a residential and business complex. I was walking back to my car and spotted you through the window." She glanced out the square of plate glass. "Actually, I meant to call you last night. How are you and Mr. Lockhart doing?"

"Things have never been better between us. Why do you ask?"

Vivian glanced around, then pulled the two of them toward an empty corner. "I don't mean to be spreading rumors, but I think you ought to know that the grapevine has it that Cynthia's pregnant."

Cynthia pregnant? Her knees almost buckled. All these years she'd acted out stage directions for characters with buckling knees, she'd never exactly known how it felt. The weakness, the wateryness, the abrupt loss of muscle starch made her look around for a chair. Vivian grasped her elbow.

"Oh, Neicy! Heavens, girl, I'm sorry. I see I shouldn't have sprung this on you."

"No, I guess maybe you shouldn't have."

She was still lost in ridiculous metaphors, thinking, this is what they mean by having the wind knocked out of your sails. She seemed to be able to fathom anything except the implications of Vivian's statement.

"Who said Cynthia's pregnant?"

"I heard it Tuesday from one of the secretaries whose sister is a nurse in Cynthia's doctor's office. And then Wednesday night, I ran into Margo at King of Prussia mall and she asked me about it. I don't know where she got it from."

"The grapevine." Had servants and slaves really hid behind grape arbors and whispered news to one another? The latter-day leaves were definitely carrying this story along. "Sounds like it's true."

"That's what I thought, too."

"Curtis is probably planning to tell me tonight. We haven't seen each other since we got back from the mountains on Monday."

"And it's not the kind of news you break on the phone," Vivian added. "Look, I'm sorry, but I really gotta run. Can I leave you here? Are you okay now?"

"I'm feeling better. I'll be alright."

After Vivian left, she stood in the corner a few minutes longer and then exited without a record.

On the drive across town, she thought, yes, Cynthia could very likely be pregnant. She could be pregnant. Any woman screwing a man on a regular basis could find herself with a child – even using menstrual calendars, diaphragms, pills, and juju charms. So, yes, Miss Chocolate Drop Brownie Fudge Cynthia was probably pregnant by Curtis.

Doing forty-five on side streets and running nearly every stop sign, she let up on the accelerator and volumned down the blaring brassy classical music. She didn't know what this new development meant, but she'd soon have a better idea.

Curtis had gone all out with dinner. Cornish hens stuffed with wild rice and mushrooms plus mushroom gravy, a gorgeous salad, and French bread. He seemed like his usual self, only with a slightly rushed edge around him. She'd resolved to let him be the one who raised the big subject, but heard herself saying, "I bumped into Vivian on my way over here."

"Don't tell me." He sprang from his chair on the other side of the table, came and knelt beside her. "Let me tell you. Cynthia's pregnant. I found out after we returned on Monday and decided to talk with you when I saw you tonight." He pushed her empty plate toward the center of the table, making space to lean closer.

"So, what are you all going to do?"

"Cynthia wants to have the baby. I told her that was okay with me as long as she doesn't expect me to change my life."

"I'm assuming that this was an accident, right? That Cynthia didn't get pregnant on purpose?"

"Absolutely."

"How do you know? Did the two of you ever talk about having

children? I didn't want to have any, but every woman you hook up with doesn't have to feel the same way."

"Well, yeah, we've talked about it. I knew Cynthia wanted to be a mother and she'd been joking lately about her biological clock getting ready to alarm. But, no, we hadn't decided to have a child."

"'We' didn't have to."

"Neicy!"

"Well, am I right? Cynthia could easily have made that decision and taken matters into her own hands."

"Cynthia wouldn't do that!"

Curtis may not have thought so, but she wasn't so positive.

"Why would Cynthia do that?" he persisted.

"For the same reason that women since time immemorial have made sure they had a baby for a man they wanted to rope in."

"That's really low-class thinking."

"Well, all of us ladies weren't fortunate enough to be born with silver-plated spoons in our mouths."

"Neicy, I guess you must be having a problem with this."

"To be truthful, I don't know if I'm having a problem or not."

Curtis got up off his knees and dragged his chair around to sit beside her.

"You know I'd welcome you having a child too, if that was what you wanted."

"No. That impromptu ritual at Vivian's released all that for me." Truly she didn't envy Cynthia having a baby. Whatever was bugging her definitely wasn't about that.

"Neicy, you and I can do whatever you need. Just tell me what that is."

"Well, maybe if I had a regular boyfriend, I could figure it out." As bizarre as his life was, why was he throwing the relationship ball into her court?

"Low blow, Neicy. What have you ever wanted that I didn't give you? When have I ever let you down?"

"The way you live is just too fucking complicated!" How could she ever trust that he truly loved her? Did he like her as much as he did his other two women, especially in bed? She couldn't bring herself to ask that question and, even if she did, he would answer in some kind of complex way that still wouldn't give her the satisfaction she was seeking of being in an exalted category all by herself.

"My life doesn't feel complicated to me. An easier way to exist might be to make everything and everybody expendable, but I don't feel that's how it has to be."

"Oh, Curtis..." This was all too much. In the final analysis, Cynthia couldn't tie him up or take him away unless that was what he wanted. Okay. Now Margo and Vivian would have a whole other set of questions to ask her, like what in the world was she doing and had she utterly lost her mind.

She started humming her slave woman's song. "I'm running on, to see where the spirit's leading me. Do believe I'll run, run on, to see where spirit's leading me." Selfhood. Stable loving. Someplace the soul can call home. Black women walking, running, stepping on whatever roads they hoped would lead them there. She tapped out the rhythm on the tablecloth. "I'm running on..." Curtis moved his hand alongside hers and joined in the beat.

"So, Curtis, you really think the baby won't make much of a difference and everything can go on, business as usual?"

"Well, maybe some adjustments here and there." He was trying as usual to honestly assess the circumstances. "But, no, I don't think anything basic will have to change."

She would keep hanging, just wait and see.

On his coffee-brown sheets after they'd cleaned up the kitchen, she let him love her up, his mouth soothing worry between her widespread thighs. After she came, they rolled over and she straddled him. He dropped into lush receptivity, lying open as a pasture, muscular and unmoving, with all the excitement she was building in him going straight to his erect penis. As she orgasmed again in that position, one part of her was repeating, over and over, "What can you do with a man like this except be crazy about him!" while another part of her raced frantically around the room.

Walking up the beach in St. Croix more than nine months later, she told Curtis how she had wanted this Easter vacation for Christmas.

"And I haven't forgotten that I have yet to lay eyes on your baby." Vibrantly happy to be sauntering on this stretch of uneven sand with him, still, not seeing the child was a definite sore point.

"You will, you will. Those two weeks around Christmas were really strenuous. A brand-new baby, the baby's mother yellow with septicemia, and her sister who was supposed to be helping coming down with the flu. And I don't know what happened to you. You just disappeared."

"I told you what happened to me. I didn't disappear." She refrained from saying "you did," took a long breath, and looked down at the ocean sucking through a fortress of cavernous rock. "After your baby came, I was hoping we would get here for New Year's. But given all the drama, I could see that was not about to happen. Tony and Esther rescued me. We worked on the script at her grandparents' cottage in Rehoboth and cooked up a storm. That was better than the days I spent waiting for you."

"Let's not go back there." Curtis started sprinting. She ran alongside him until they started panting and slowed down. The sea grapes had gotten bigger and the sand more hilly, enough to make muscles in her calves like a dancer if she did this every day.

"Have you ever thought about trying to connect with your family?" Curtis's breathing was returning to normal.

"What family?"

"Isn't your stepfather still living in Arkansas? And what about those cousins of your mother?"

It always amazed her that Curtis remembered the random stuff she told him. She had mentioned those distant cousins once.

"So, are you trying to help me drum up some family so you can get rid of me?"

"No, I..." She had caught him off guard. "I just thought it would be nice."

She filed away his unusual loss of cool to ponder at a later time.

"Sometimes I think about going down there, rather up there, at least up from down this side of the world." Easily turned around geographically, when she knew it, she liked to get her direction right. "Maybe I will. It's really odd the way things work out. The last time I sent my stepfather a letter, this woman named Erma Jean Sommers wrote back with him. She was an even poorer little girl in our neighborhood that we used to feed. Now she's helping to look out for Daddy Riley. Strange, huh?"

"Not really. I always think of black people doing things like that, especially in the south. Come on, race you to the condo."

Running hard, she matched his pace for about fifty yards and then lagged as he kept going the distance. The warm ocean breeze cooled down her skin. She studied the rocks and tough yellow-green algae under her feet and stared off at the far horizon. Every now and then, she stooped to pick up a lone seashell. Glancing over her shoulder for a last view of the water as she turned up toward the concrete walk, she changed her mind and bolted back down the soft sand to the damp packed receding water line. She ran in, letting the pale green force carry her into a platter of stillness as she floated motionless on her back, the ocean's underground plugging her ears with sound. Heavenly sky, heavenly water! Everything one. Since her first visit during a grad school dropout summer, she'd been drawn over and over again to this Caribbean sea. As mysteriously as it came, whatever hit her slowly let go and she leisurely paddled ashore.

When she walked into the apartment, Curtis was hanging up the phone. She wouldn't ask who he was talking to, went, instead, to the refrigerator and poured a glass of limeade as he got in the shower. She shed her silver bikini. Mama Chocolate Drop Cynthia wouldn't be putting her fudgy stretch-marked ass into anything like it for a while. It was probably her that Curtis was talking to.

As he finished in the shower, she went in behind him. "Being down here agrees with you," he slapped her buttocks, threw her a puckered kiss. "You look like a yellow rose."

They lazed on the airy bed, cuddling and smooching, dozing on and off into light, lacey naps. Curtis had slept prodigiously the first couple days. She loved it that the two of them were now in sync with their rhythms and rested, waking near dawn and enjoying each other all day.

Curtis asked if he could put some oil on her hair.

"Not too much," she warned as she dropped into a floppy pillow on the floor beside their bed.

"Who's skinning this cat?" he challenged.

"You are." She gave him the stock reply.

"Well, you just hold the tail, okay. I know with this humidity and you being in the ocean, it's not that dry."

"Actually, you're the one who likes to hold tail!"

"Neicy, that's obscene!" He pulled her to him in the authoritative way that made her feel like his woman.

Totally relaxed, she settled between his knees, letting her head loll any way it wanted. Curtis enjoyed dotting on the oil and really got into massaging her scalp.

"Did your father ever do this for you?"

"No." His question roused her. "But I tended to him. When I was ten, eleven, something like that, I used to haul out the kleenex, alcohol, and a bobby pin, and work on his bumps."

She was feeling Daddy Riley's presence or feeling the hole where his presence should be. "I hadn't thought of that in god-knows-when. Last time I talked to him, he and that Erma Jean were laughing about some catfish dinner she had barged in on and got our whole house upset. I don't know why it was so damn funny."

"Did you remember it?"

She wanted to say, "kind of, sort of," but answered truthfully, "I don't think so, no. I really don't remember anything that happened to me before I was six or seven years old."

"Were you close with your daddy?"

"Stepfather. We were closer when I was little than after mama died." Musty memories and broken sequences crowded the outskirts of her mind. When she left home, she put those arid and ashy badlands as far behind her as they would go.

"That's too bad..."

"No, it was alright."

"Yeah, I know it was alright because it had to be. But he was your only daddy. Whose else's little girl were you going to be?"

"I can be your baby girl!" She swirled around and caught his legs, hiding her head in his lap.

"Stop! You're making me spill this oil!"

By the time they got into their tropical white evening clothes, the sky was flaunting a spectacular sunset, changing moment by moment its wifty patterns of oranges and blue. Locking Ms Dorothy's condominium on their way out, Curtis said, "If some entrepreneur could buy up this scene, we'd be paying dearly for our ringside seats." They walked leisurely into town, wanting to check things out when one of the tour boats docked at the harbor and tourists swarmed all around.

Apparently, Fredericksted didn't bother to exert itself for the few visitors who chose this side of the country for their island stay. The two sparsely-patroned good restaurants, and the Kentucky Fried next to the vegetarian Rastas, and the dressmaker's and apothecary and all the regular hangouts and services were basically good enough. But when the big ships slowly swam in from San Juan or Miami, the town put on a different face. It was like somebody literally rolled out the sidewalks.

Fancy gem stores appeared, lining the harbor, where solid blocks of walled wood had stood. The painted wood had been the barred entrances of business establishments, now unbuckled and flung open for foreign exchange. The British pub became more inviting, its sandwich board broadly beckoning at one of the busiest corners. What had been quiet, nondescript alleys lit up with booths and shops, selling everything from three-for-ten-dollar tee shirts to pattees, blender rum drinks, leather bags, and custom toe rings, fitted by dark women kneeling attentively at their customers' pale feet. Music came from everywhere. The bass boom of the alley sound system was overlaid by melodies from a steel band in front of the wharf punctuated by jazz drifting sideways from the Night Moon café.

It was very clean, almost sterile, except for an occasional raw hit of sewage, and not a beggar in sight. The passengers discharged from the mammoth vessel wandered around the six block square area, forced either to eat, drink, or purchase something because there was nothing else to do. She felt like she had stumbled into a live movie set.

Eventually tired of looking, walking and munching, she and Curtis hailed a taxi van to their condominium. They went straight to bed, her head sinking on Curtis's shoulder as she said, "That was a trip." Her only life dream besides making it to Broadway was someday having an island home.

In her just before daylight semi-sleeping, Curtis brought her almost awake snuzzling her cheek and gently pressing against her body. She moved – a soft gesture of animal receptivity – and he began sliding back and forth alongside her thigh.

"Woman, woman, my woman," he was breathing into her ear. "Let me show you how much I love you."

She felt him lift up to continue his stroking and kissing. Her full breasts warmed, her belly began tingling toward him. Her thighs opened a fraction wider of their own accord. She was so wet she could smell herself. Was she already dreaming lovemaking? When Curtis put his hand directly on her, his searching finger tentative with her insides, she registered his excitement. He parted her and firmly circled her clitoris and her excitement jumped higher, too, heat spreading from her sexual center through her buttocks, hips, and spine. She swam in the pleasure of her nipples, of all her dancing parts, alert to each delectable sensation but still fuzzy in her head, knowing at her root, though, that this fuzzy with him was alright.

Curtis entered her with passionate fierceness, "Neicy, Neicy," his beautiful voice a substream of sensuous resonance, calling out for more response. Her female desire was right up there with the drive of his maleness. He went in and out, out and then into her body, pulling her hips off the mattress to meet him.

"I love you, baby. Love you, my darling sweet woman." His words and their frenzied movement was dizzying both of them straight to the top.

"You're my sister, you're my lover," he was saying, speaking from a kingdom united, way beyond ordinary sense. "Nobody means to me what you do, precious, precious."

She couldn't help it – not that she was trying. The walls of her vagina started their rhythmical spasms, undoing Curtis's last little bit of control. He thrust so far and so hard up inside her, it felt like he was unleashing the whole of himself.

"Neicy, baby, don't leave me." His muffled cry rang in her ear at the height of his coming as she tightened everything that she had around him.

"Curtis, oh sweetheart, sweet daddy, I won't."

She and Curtis kept doing well as the next several weeks rolled by. Maybe his idea of multiple loves and loving could work after all. Every now and again, they felt a little creakiness in their circumstances, but nothing seemed to present a real problem. But Vivian and Margo still refused to believe that things like Curtis strolling around town with Cynthia and the baby didn't bother her. They accused her of stuffing – Vivian's word – her feelings. "Do I look like an unhappy turkey?" she laughed, as they shook their heads.

She was absorbed in her first Penn Rep production, which had opened in April and now had its run extended through June. Inhabiting the role of a concentration camp trusty was stretching her to the max, maybe because it was pushing hidden places within her. She had heard other actors say that. With the play, with her jobs at Penn Two and the Center, with friends and then Curtis, she was busier than ever before.

When she was extra jammed, though, Curtis didn't hassle her. When she needed to see him, he was there. In a way, it was too easy. But why should loving somebody require an arm and a leg or bend you all out of shape? She ran out of the bathroom where she was applying a final layer of lip gloss as she heard Curtis in the hall outside. Without a doubt, what they were celebrating this fine night in May felt bigger than her thirty-sixth birthday.

Curtis's key was fumbling in the lock when she got to the door. She tapped and swung it open. "Hey, sugar!"

He stared blankly at the ring of keys in his hands, looked up, and finally said, "Wrong key."

She backed inside and he put his arms around her. "Happy birthday, lady." He was gorgeous in his after-six clothes.

She let her nose graze his warm, firm neck. "You smell like a baby."

"What else could I smell like? I just finished taking care of Timothy..."

The phone rang.

"Yes, he's here. It's for you, Curtis." She handed over the receiver. "Cynthia." She didn't even know Cynthia had her number.

"It went up that fast, just since I left?... No, don't bother to call her... Yes, yes, I get it... Okay." She couldn't piece together meaning from the fragments of conversation and she absently heard controlled panic in Curtis's voice. But that was muted by her own emotion rising in her ears.

Curtis hung up and stayed by the counter. "Timothy has a real high fever..."

She couldn't help but interrupt. "Why didn't you tell me you had given Cynthia this number? She was the last person I expected to hear on the telephone."

"I was trying to tell you when the phone rang. Timothy..."

"But that's not what I'm asking. Why didn't you tell me – no, ask me if it was okay – before you gave her my number?"

Curtis threw up his hands. "Damn, Neicy. If you'll just slow down a minute, I can explain."

"You don't have to raise your voice. I'm the one who should be upset."

"I'm not upset, just a little exasperated. You're getting all bent out of shape before I can even tell you what's going on." He took off his jacket and draped it around one of the dinette chairs.

She fiddled with the magazines on her coffee table, willing herself to keep still.

"Curtis, it would be a hell of a whole lot better if you just explained instead of trying to put me in the wrong."

Curtis spun on his heel back toward the kitchen. He opened the fridge and lifted out the carafe of water.

She flew up from where she was sitting and snatched the glass he was taking from the cupboard out of his hand. "Now. Not after you drink your water. Now."

"No, not now, later," Curtis snapped, walking pointedly past her. "I'm on my way to the hospital. Timothy has a fever of a hundred and six and you're being totally unreasonable."

"I don't see how you can even begin to say I'm unreasonable. I put up with you tipping off every minute to call home when we were down in St. Croix..."

"Twice a day, Neicy, just two times every twenty-four hours."

She kept on. "And I haven't pitched a fit about not seeing the baby. Or said a word about you always rushing here smelling like sour milk and baby powder..."

"So, now, you don't like how I smell?"

"If I liked baby powder, I'd be buying Johnson's instead of Bouchelle."

"This is stupid," Curtis burst out, resuming his thunderous march toward the door. "I'm sorry this had to happen on your birthday. I'll call you from the hospital as soon as I get a chance."

"'This' what are you sorry had to happen?" She was dogging his heels. "That you showed me no respect, that you're ruining my birthday..."

"All of it, Neicy, fucking all of it. I'm sorry for it all." Curtis swept up his jacket, yanked open the door, and strode out.

She had never heard him curse like that, she'd never seen him so upset. Fear constricted her chest. Curtis wasn't supposed to leave her, he wasn't supposed to treat her like this! And Timothy? Fever of 106? Dear God, please let your little one be okay. She felt her own blood racing, pulse pounding in her ears.

Now that she and Curtis had finished yelling at each other, what the hell was she supposed to do? Sit here in her slinky sequined dress and wait for him to call from the hospital? They were already missing their dinner, although dancing went on through the evening. But would Curtis be in the mood for that? Would she be in the mood?

Slow down, she said, slow down. She stopped pirouetting around the open space in her living room and sat straight in the middle of the couch, breathing, carefully, slowing herself down. Behind closed lids, she saw fractured images of herself going defiantly out unescorted, of Curtis bending over Timothy at the hospital, soothing Cynthia's hand. She had alternatives. She could sit here, and calm down, and choose them.

She sat, letting the shattered glass fit itself back together so she could see what the new picture looked like. It was not nearly as rosy as it seemed before. Yes, she was sick of the milk and baby powder and of Curtis making last-minute adjustments. Ultimately, she didn't have a lot of control. His other girlfriend, Mavis, could up and decide to get pregnant and there'd be nothing she could do! Curtis's inattentive air was occurring more often and he was beginning to look his age. Yes, he said, he'd certainly be happy when "the boy," as he put it, "crawled out of his infant stage." And she would, too. Now that she thought about it, she'd been spending more time than usual making love to herself.

But, if she had to be honest, all this didn't justify flying off the handle because Cynthia dialed her number. Curtis may have only given it to her when he left to keep their birthday date. Truly, she had been like a keg of explosives waiting for the right spark to go off! Anger and resentment had already been seething. What was it about?

In many ways, she and Curtis had a marvelous relationship. What had he called her that passionate morning in Fredericksted? Sister. Lover. Precious. Strong words, magical and musical, going into her someplace that needed to receive them, securing the bond between her and this sweet brotherman. But maybe she was bothered by his other women more than she realized. Maybe there was truth in what Margo and Vivian tried to tell her, that she had gotten herself into a dead-end rut. Bad girl Margo had even tramped into her business and asked was she staying with Curtis because of the sex. They wanted to know if where she was with him was where she'd like to be three, five, seven, ten years from now.

She wished she knew, but she didn't have a clue about how to answer that question. She couldn't even say coherently what she wanted now. Guess she needed to "unstuff" her feelings before she could find out. She wanted the good things, for sure, but she didn't want what bothered her. Did the two have to go together? And she'd never even thought to ask whether what she was getting from Curtis was what she needed. Was it true, what he kept telling her? – that she had to open, trust, risk, go deeper and extend further before she could figure that out and they could fulfill their relationship potential. The little she could hazily grasp about going deeper always felt dangerous and scary. Maybe gaining something richer meant getting bent and shook up and re-shaped! But did their non-monogamous arrangement make a more profound union impossible?

She shot up from the couch, on overload emotionally and mentally. The one thing she understood now for certain was that she needed to radically reconsider everything she was doing with Curtis and how she was living her life.

She stripped bangles from her arms, taking off her party glitter. She'd share these revelations with Curtis tomorrow – or the next time they saw each other. He would understand.

August, 1994
New York City / Philadelphia

CHAPTER 8

"Get out the way, willya!" A cabbie honked and yelled and almost sideswiped her. Gaining the curb, she wondered whether she would have been such an aggressive driver if she had brought her Celica from Philly to New York. The August heat was making everybody evil. She quickly walked the long block over and short block down to the Center, hoping to catch Richard before meditation so she could get him to send her some special prayer for her callback audition.

The Center for Enlightenment always looked like it was winking at her. The ivied stone of the handsome old structure made one statement, while the painted Center sign above the entrance – only a shade less bright than neon – made another. She was sure all that kept that sign from coming down was the fact that the Center itself owned the whole building. Founder Hugh had shrewdly purchased it after he began his "meditation ministry." In the 1950s, the property was affordable for a man with a few inherited millions and a driving vision of the world he wanted to help create.

Scion of a family of wealthy Chicago bankers, Hugh Masterson went to Europe toward the end of World War II as a newly-commissioned first lieutenant from Dartmouth. When his leg was shot off, he held death at bay by doing the mental exercises a British medic named Thomas guided him through. When he recovered, he traveled with Thomas to the ashram in southern India where Thomas had learned the techniques. He got hooked on the high-powered meditation and said that during one of his sitting sessions, he received the directive that adapting and teaching these trainings was to be his work for life. Thinking about founder Hugh and his mission, she entered the building and ran into his son and successor, Richard.

"Sister Nee," he greeted. The same salutation that the brethren and sistren in Jamaica had bestowed upon her. And something in his voicing of it had the same embracing ring.

"Whew, glad I made it before meditation. I'm looking for you."

"Did you turn on the lamppost light?"

He was cracking his favorite Nasrudin joke, the one where the Persian mulla has lost his door key and is groping around the lamppost in the street searching for it. When his neighbors ask him where he lost the key and he says inside the house, they ask then why are you looking for it out here. Because there's more light, he answers.

"Brother Richard, I'm serious."

"Well, you know what the old rabbis say? The only time seriousness sits next to godliness is when god falls asleep."

The first time he said that to her, she accused him of making it up. He knew more slave John trickster tales than she did and reached into a grab bag of teaching stories from all over the place, half of which she suspected he concocted on the spot.

" Richard..."

"Alright. We can be serious as you want soon as I'm done with this open house intro session."

"Oh, I'd forgotten this was an introduction Saturday." Richard was in one of what she called his onstage outfits, a green, gold, and purple top that looked like something between a tunic and a dashiki. Usually, he wore white shirts. Recycled from her original audition, her swirling aqua skirt and loose chiffon blouse was an oddly perfect complement.

"Come on, sit in." He stepped nearer, as if to fetch her away. She looked straight into his clear blue eyes. She and he were the identical height and physically matched, like different colored, different gendered twins. His medium brown hair and her dark bushy crinks bounced off one another. He crooked his arm through her elbow and led them to the meditation hall.

She slid around the perimeter chairs and took her favorite floor spot. One arm resting loosely on the skinny lectern, Richard welcomed the ten or so people and laughed that, with the infernal weather, the citizens visiting uptop from Hades were feeling right at home. Then he began his compact little rundown of the Center's mission, his father's founding of it, and illuminative meditation.

Her gaze wandered to the exotic plants and brocade wall hangings, the carved wood and skillfully recessed light. The day before she first walked into the room five years ago, she had slipped coming up out of the subway – with no visible fruit skins, oil spills, or slicks of spit in sight – and found herself face-to-face with a bright yellow flyer announcing a beginning class the very next night. It felt like a sign from her mother, who had made a rare dream appearance the previous night with some odd, angelic people grouped on sunrise hills. Sitting in the hall with a dozen other newcomers, she plunged into the meditation, following the instruction they had been given to zoom as high up in their heads as possible and hold on to light.

An amazing thing happened to her. Something she could only describe as Spirit rocked her upward circling body. Then an eye in her forehead strained open and burned the skin. Her heart started to whir in living colors and the "I" of her voice in her thoughts blended the sound of many ones. When a light in her head suddenly bloomed like an orchid, she – or somebody inside – said to herself, Look sharp, some magical soul work has begun. A luminous string of words were chanting through her – love wisdom service knowledge power sharing giving caring the group the one right path right human relations good will human and divine matter and spirit heart hand serenity and strength mineral vegetable animal human harmony through conflict the fifth kingdom of souls.

It was the first time since her ten-year-old conversion that she had been so palpably touched by Godspirit. She'd long since given up looking for religion among philandering and shaky patriarchs, whether in churches or at Rastafarian stomps. Attunement to her ancestral past and unnameable guidance had gotten her through. That just happened to include her crazy mother, whose dying promise never to leave her was about the only one she'd kept. She hadn't had another such off-the-charts experience as that initial Center orientation, although every time she sat, something good flowed through her and she knew that, at least for now, this was her right path.

Richard moved from the lectern to the slightly raised dais and invited all who were willing to sit for a short meditation with him. Those who wanted to leave could do so at this time and thank you so much, he added, for coming. Nobody left.

She closed her eyes, opened her mind, and zoned immediately into a high, clear frequency of energy. Richard. Sitting with him was like that. Him, plus the united force of even such a fledgling group. She loved, loved, loved that feeling of being one with and touching the consciousnesses of others. If only she could connect like this with people in everyday life! After Richard directed them to come gradually back into the reality of the room and slowly open their eyes, he continued to sit with his eyes lightly lidded. Waves of glowing power emanated from him. Even the threads of his shirt cast off a brilliant sheen. She felt the energy retract little by little back into his body, leaving the room and all of them in it both poorer yet richer and cleaner at the same time. Most of these people were coming back. She could tell. They couldn't linger to say so because Richard had asked them to take the silence of the meditation with them, but they were quietly catching his eye to convey their enthusiasm.

They didn't even know him and were already being comforted by him. Finding that dimension in Richard was definitely a boon for her. She had fled to New York after her breakup with Curtis, battered, confused, and defiant. The two of them hadn't been able to regroup from their birthday night fiasco, no matter how hard they tried. They began promisingly, talking everything over, but then, according to him, she started picking fights and making problems where none existed, raising theoretical objections and finding imaginary faults.

They argued about starting a community agency with her as head of the arts. "I don't want to be an arts administrator," she finally yelled. "I want to be a great actress." Curtis swore they wouldn't let the nonprofit effort take any more time than her job at United Neighborhoods already did. But she hadn't trusted that any more than she could wrap her head around becoming a part of his relationship with his young son. That piece felt almost like getting in bed with him and Cynthia.

Curtis got tired of hassling with her. He accused her of running scared. And she fell into exhaustion fighting him and herself. When she had to say what happened, she retreated to the noncommittal, "It just didn't work out." If Curtis wanted to insist she ran away, then let him.

She went back to dating whoever came along. Not every Tom, Dick, and Harry. But Trevor, Michael, Eugene, Larry, Omar, Keith and Crosby. She'd never been fully engaged by any one of them, not even Trevor, whom she stayed with for two years, or Omar, whose loving commitment to grassroots black activism stirred her heart. To a man, they were even-tempered and easygoing and busy with what interested them, whether it was getting their realtor's license, opening a new nightclub, becoming a dentist, or, like her, furthering their acting career. None of them was "lighter than a rusty skillet," as Virginia would have said, definitely with disapproval since her preference had run to light skin. They all knew how to treat her like a lady and knew what to do with a woman when they got her in bed. Her body didn't shut them out, so she nixed that as a problem she needed to investigate. But she could feel that she wasn't letting them in the way she had Curtis. And that was alright.

Something about Richard's energy filled the void in the same way he helped her not to miss her black friends so much. When he unfolded from the meditation dais and reached her waiting at the back of the hall, she gave his arm an affectionate squeeze.

"I'll catch you later, Richard."

"Hey, I thought you were looking for me."

"I was. But I found the light." It was fun playing his silliness back at him. "Truth is I came by to put you to work. I'm on my way to a very important callback audition and want you to send me some energy."

"Special energy coming right up for a special lady." His eyes and voice had that tone she still couldn't read, that sometimes made her wonder if he liked her in a man-woman way. But there was no reason for her to even wonder that. Richard was just being Richard. Pitiful that she was so insecure she needed to think that every man on the planet was attracted to her!

When she got to the theater twenty minutes early, only one imposing, older white actor was waiting his turn. She went to the bathroom, pulled her hair in a bun, stretched a bit in the hallway, then sat down and focused. No need to make herself hyper by dwelling on it now, but this was her chance to break into a starring off-Broadway role, and one with a high profile because the producer and director of this original play, "Obsessions," had decided they would cast disregarding race. Maybe their decision to experiment was partly a publicity ploy. If so, it was already working. There'd been articles in the trade news and more people had shown up for the original audition than anyone had anticipated. To be called back was a real coup, especially since she was audaciously aiming for the leading female role, a sexually-neurotic 1920s white woman from an incestuous German family.

This time, not only the casting director but the poobah director himself, Steve Elliot, was present, arrayed with three other people she didn't recognize in front orchestra seats.

"Ms. Jones, thank you for coming." The casting director, Tom Savage, was still in charge. She'd been introduced to him at a fundraising gala and didn't know if he remembered it or not. But she certainly wasn't going to mention it this time either.

"Thank you for having me." She made it sound like a dinner party, almost laughing as they smiled.

The assistant handed her some pages. A cold read. A synopsis of the play had been available, but not the play itself.

"We wondered if you wouldn't mind reading from the script," Tom continued. "It's a first act scene where Katherine, the wife, gets upset about her husband's apparent infidelity. Robert will fill in the husband's lines."

She plunged in. The woman was slightly over the top, but she wasn't stone nuts. Wrestling with ambiguity day in and day out could make you seem crazy.

"I hear what you're saying, husband. But I can't help it. Something doesn't feel quite right."

Katherine's jealousy was both raging and controlled.

"No. No. We don't have to do that. No, I said. But, if ever I find out you're being unfaithful..."

The edge in her unnaturally lowered voice carried the lines near hysteria.

At the end of the scene, it took her a split second to realize there were no more sides to turn. The orchestra seats applauded. They weren't just being polite. They had liked what they saw.

"Thank you." Apparently Tom was going to be the sole spokesperson. Then Steve joined in.

"Ms. Jones, very nicely executed. What in your experience do you think prepares you for this role?"

She highlighted her experimental work in the drama program at Wisconsin, mentioned that her off-off-Broadway lead in "Call Me Etta" required her to be both a black and a white singer, and added, chuckling, that involvement with shoestring community theater had thrown her into all kinds of roles.

"I've played many black parts, but it never bothered me to take on white characters and characteristics."

"A little odd, maybe, for someone who, as I see from your resume here, chaired the Black Students for Black Drama group and worked for years with Baltimore's Uhuru Theater." Sounded like he was pushing her, trying to determine something.

"Not really. As an African American woman in the United States, I've also been exposed to white images and learned the reality behind them almost as well as I learned myself. It's stood me in good stead in this line of work. I'm an actress and, to me, that means being able to create whatever character is placed before me."

It felt as if she had handled that well, not only negotiating a potential pitfall but turning it into a positive.

"Well, thank you again for coming." Tom was closing things out. "I'll be in touch. We're assuming you're free for rehearsals starting in September?"

"Absolutely." She gave them a nodding bow, exited the stage, and left. She didn't want to count unhatched chickens, but this part might just be hers.

Turning the corner away from the theater, she gave herself the luxury of a wild "hooray!" Finally, her too light for some, too dark for others complexion might truly pay off. Now that she'd gotten into the script, she was powerfully drawn to the play. She wanted the role so bad she could taste it.

She crossed Sixth and ducked into the produce market, then streamed with Saturday pedestrians to the subway, catching her train just as it pulled from the station. Chris was unpredictable when it came to meals. She could be oblivious to food and working or making an elaborate nicoise salad. The banana and smoothie were nutrition insurance. She settled in for the long ride to the Village, sipping the blackberry shake. If anyone had told her a year ago that she was about to begin a relationship with a woman, she would have said, "You're out of your mind."

The evening they met, she had left a bummer of an audition for a long-shot campy, noir part and was consoling herself with some dinner. Waiting for her dessert, she went to the bathroom and found Chris contorted in front of the mirror, trying to reach through the back of her blouse. Their eyes collided in the shiny glass and the room instantly heated up. Holding the contact, Chris laughed. "My bra strap slipped completely out of the hook and I can't retrieve it. Could you reach in and grab it for me?"

She had looked at Chris's laughing red mouth, at her lithe body and full, blonde hair, totally excited by the shameless come-on. She wanted, unexpectedly but unequivocally, to be sexual with this woman. Without hesitation, like an old trick somebody had taught her, she started unbuttoning the blouse. "Yes, I can get it for you." She took her time fishing around ivory skin and black lingerie, letting her fingers and hands touch whatever smoothness they encountered, as she stood behind Chris, their eyes still locked in the mirror. She almost, almost slid her palms under the armpits of this woman she did not know to reach into the loosened brassiere cups for her breasts. She was throbbing from head to toes. Collecting the runaway strap, she withdrew her tingling hands. "My name's Deneice."

Still gazing at their reflections, they both took in the mocha makeup, heavy eyeliner, and leopard print scarf she had worn for the campy tryout. Chris had about an inch and a half worth of height on her, but otherwise, they were evenly matched, the power playing back and forth between them. Chris held on to the dangling bra strap without putting herself back together.

They finally broke eye contact, got done in the bathroom, and returned to the restaurant where she met two women Chris used to work with at a textbook publishing house. Dinner over, she and Chris exchanged numbers.

Lust continued to rage between them. She liked rolling Chris over and making her moan, and liked it when the tables were turned. This whole development was a surprise from the blue that she was simply accepting. It was definitely something she was capable of doing, no doubt about that, although it wasn't her basic orientation. And that seemed like enough explanation.

The train slowed and then jerkily regained speed. A well-groomed Mexican guy swinging on the strap in front of her was having trouble staying out of her lap.

Chris loved plays, bright people and theatrical circles, and knew a ton of folks in the business. It balanced her occupation as a science book editor and provided creative space.

"If I could choose to be something other than what I am, acting would be it," she confessed right after they met. Lately, she had been cajoling her to play "dress up" in costumes some nights. "What costumes?" "Oh, you just let me know when you're ready and I'll take care of that. But don't worry. I think you'll like it!" With a glint in her eye, Chris winked and pulled down over the corner of one brow what could have been an imaginary monocle or a pirate's mask.

When she got off the local and walked up to Chris's apartment, Chris was not editing some geeky person's manuscript and she was definitely not into cooking. She was straightening up her desk and raring to go to a garden party.

"But aren't you curious about my audition?"

"Oh, sorry! How could I have forgotten about that? Tell me." She sat down in her office chair and listened.

"Wow, Deneice. They may have box office draw in mind with their non-traditional casting, but you'd still be able to be yourself as well as this disturbed character if you sink deeply enough into both parts, so to speak. That would be fascinating to watch."

Just like that, Chris had done it again – one, enlarged her outlook and, two, affirmed her as an actress. That was the kind of thing she liked about this new lover friend.

"So, now, " Chris stood up, "let's go share the good news. I bet somebody at this party will have heard something."

"Aw, can we just stay here, or maybe mosey over to Ashby's for an early dinner?"

"You don't like to spend time with me and my friends," Chris complained.

"Alright, alright." They'd been down this road before.

"Neicy." Chris retraced her steps. "I need to ask you something. And if you're starving, there's some potato salad in the fridge."

That earlier vibe about potatoes and salad was right on.

"Why are you with me?" Chris popped one of her famous questions, only this one didn't sound idle.

"For the same reasons you're with me." She gave her best short answer.

"'Cause I'm exotic and sexy, an amazing actress, and teach you things about the world that you don't already know," Chris shot back in sharp-aleck mode.

"Shit... Chris. You don't have to be such a smartass."

"Well, would you please answer my question?"

She took the chair in front of the computer and Chris dropped into the rocker-recliner.

"I'm with you because we both love theater. We're compatible in bed. Our minds click well together. And when we're not arguing about something, we really enjoy each other's company."

"All good and true. But what I want to know is why are you with a white woman? Maybe you haven't noticed, but the two things we clash about are race and hanging with my gay friends."

"First thing you mustn't forget, Chris, is that I didn't set out to be with any woman, of any color. And yes, I do wish you were a little more conscious about racism."

"I'm getting it every time some incident occurs and we discuss it. But I'm white, I grew up white. In Muncie, Indiana. My mother was a bookkeeper. My father was selling Ford cars when my mother took my brother and me and left him. You know all that. Background-wise, about the only things we have in common are our early-dying mothers and our absent fathers. I can't wake up and see with the eyes of a black person overnight."

That was true. But it still didn't keep race from being a problem between them. As quick as Chris was about everything else, it was hard for her to get it about race. Like having to question why an African American woman raised in Arkansas in the 1950s and 60s had an ingrained phobia about cops. She had dredged up her story of being followed every day by a squad car as she walked home from her summer job at the NAACP office and recounted being run off the road when students from the thespian society drove to a regional competition in Fayetteville. Then, Chris understood. But the process had taken too long. Yet white people at the Center could be just as blank about race, but she didn't let that perturb her. She looked past it and viewed them as co-travelers on the spiritual path. Why couldn't she do the same with Chris, who was much closer to her?

"I'll be right back." She headed to the kitchen. "Do you want some potato salad?"

She returned with the two small plates of salad, napkins, forks. Set hers on the desk. Got the tray table from against the wall, flipped it open, placed Chris's salad, napkin and fork on it, presented the food to her, sliding the table comfortably in front of her knees.

Serving. Here she was serving. Was she just being nice and natural? Was it in her genes? Did she help at too many white women's houses with her mother? Was she being ultra-sensitive? All of the above.

She reclaimed the office chair.

Suppose Chris had gone for the salad. Jumped up, saying, "You stay put, I'll get it," and served them. Chris's first thought might have been, "Am I simply being nice and natural, or am I trying to keep Deneice from waiting on me? Do I feel guilty about black people being servants to whites?" Then she could have thought, "There's guilt, and then there's responsibility and restitution. It's fitting for me to bring her this salad. But am I just making myself feel good? Not only am I not uncomfortable now because of Deneice serving me, but I can pat myself on the back." And Chris could have expanded her thinking further. But the problem was she wouldn't have had the first thought. About a whole slew of other things she would have. Not about this.

"Chris, I'm sitting here thinking about me serving you your salad."

"What about it? Oh, wait. Wait. Don't tell me. Historical context. Black people servants and slaves to whites. Right? I don't mean any harm when I say this, but, for crying out loud, do you have to see everything from the perspective of race all the time?"

"I can't help seeing the world from that perspective. That's how the world sees itself. What I was about to say on the salad serving, though, was ask how it feels to you when you think about how I might be feeling."

Chris pushed aside the salad. "Irritated. Impatient. Like I'm being called upon to do something hard and unpleasant. And that says a lot. I get it. But, heavens, Deneice, I can't imagine that every inter-racial couple is dealing like this. If there are good things going for the relationship, there must be ways to peacefully handle race."

"I don't see this as fighting."

"I wouldn't call it peaceful. And, then, with you and me, there's the gay issue."

"Well, yes, I'm comfortable liking to be with you, but I don't fit in with a gay crowd, black or white. Sorry. Can't count me in the ten percent."

"Ten percent! Hooey and horseshit! Ten percent of the population is naturally gay. Ten percent is left-handed. Why don't we keep going and say ten percent sleep on their right side ten percent of the night, then after that they turn over. Ten percent blow on a cup of hot coffee before they taste it, ten percent don't. Let's see. What else? Ten percent..."

"Chris, stop!"

"... of the people south of the equator live ten percent shorter lives than their counterparts north of the equator – which is counter-intuitive. Bu-ut, ten percent of all babies born with a full head of hair get married by the time they're twenty, and it's their offspring who ultimately make up the ten percent gay while..."

"Please, Chris, will you just stop?" In the middle of their important conversation, she was splitting her sides.

"These experts theorizing about people's sexuality don't know what in the universe they're yakking about."

"Now that you've provided comic relief, do you want to get back to the serious discussion?"

"What makes you think I wasn't being serious? If the experts spent more time educating us about things that mattered, there'd be fewer people running around screwed up about sex."

Chris looked at the clock beside her, one of those ultra-sleek designs where the numbers float in the air without any visible mechanism.

"Being gay is the other half of this conversation we need to have. But for now, I've done all I can manage, if that's alright with you."

They ended up having the early dinner, then coming back home, then wandering into the magic that sometimes happened when Chris made love to her with their toy. Chris said, "I want to be inside you," and her womb began to quiver as they sorted out straps and warmed the length of excitement with their hands and thighs. Something in Chris wanted to touch the something in her that wanted to reach that touching place in Chris. She called the reciprocal, matching yearning male and female and, when they came together like this, it played out that way. But they also went into another dimension where color clouded and gender bent back and forth as strange selves morphed and emerged.

She opened and they entered that magical world. This time, it was innocent and green, windy and hot. Ocher grit swirled around them, the grains settling in Chris's sweat instead of salt. Her own body kept its knowing experience, tightening and teasing, but her spirit was virgin earth. She felt like a young girl giving herself to her sweetheart for the very first time, both guiding and trusting what he did, and his every doing was right. So shy she could only say, "Fuck me," way way hidden underneath her breath.

But he heard the meaning if not the words and groaned further and further up in her, no longer a lean white woman with pinup breasts but a red-skinned warrior who used his masculinity like a clean, bright sword, in the same natural way he would draw bow and arrow or step around a pine tree to pee. She just drew him to her and held on, held on, lips burring on his shoulders, senses exploding in her clitoris exploding against the tip of him, red honey, deep inside of her. He was her Indian brave, and she some plum and wayward black girl he had found to give his fierce love to.

Later, as she grazed her woman blonde forehead with kisses, she sensed the blaze of his wild palamino take shape beneath her lips, the long diamond whiteness emerging, brushstrokes from an unseen hand. Who made this magic? Like ancestral memory in her blood. Where did this connection come from? He was brave and he was a woman, lying open, her pink parts glistening, the girl in the slit of his eyes running scared and looking for somewhere to hide. Like a woman, needing not to worry about soft belly flesh. Like the Indian other, wondering if he's been on his back too long and whether something more assertive ought really to be done to her. But everything was alright. Propped on her elbow, stroking the cheek nearest to hand, she kept her gaze on the fearful girl and called her, gently, home.

This ethereal dance of male and female spoke to some unknown longing, some other places and times. It needed to be talked about but never said, needed to be shared but intensely private, needed to be passed between them like an invisible goblet filled with stars. She couldn't bring herself to ask Chris if she went to the same dreamy dimension. At these times, she fervently wished she could remember every snippet of family story her mother had dropped before she died. When people invoked past life connections, maybe this transformation of Chris and herself into warrior and wayward black girl was the kind of phenomenon they were talking about. Vagueness about Indians, wilderness, and what she'd researched regarding her own Creek ancestry played at the edge of her mind. She could never make anything of it.

Content the next morning, she snuggled into Chris, their heads alternately safe in each other's cleavage, arms enfolding, thighs and legs resting together. That womanly comfort did as much for her as their other-worldly, riveting sex. She shifted.

"Are you awake?" Chris's unused voice was gruff.

"Yes, I surfaced a little while ago."

"Me, too. I've been lying here thinking about the conversation we didn't have yesterday about you not being gay. Us together in bed is special, but I need to tell you that I really want a lover who's also my gay girlfriend. It's like you're my lover, you're my buddy, but you're not my girlfriend. I need that."

"Have you found somebody else you're interested in?" Chris wanting to break off what they had just because it wasn't perfect was hard for her to fathom.

"That's the way it's usually worked, but, no, not this time."

"Well, I wasn't expecting this." She sat up. "I knew we had our differences and all, but our relationship has been fine with me."

"No, I mean, yes, it's been good in the ways that it's good. But all you seemed to want was company when you wanted it and sex when you needed some..."

"Geesh, Chris, that sounds horrible."

"But 'is it true' is the question."

"I never would have put it that way. That makes it sound like I'm body snatching, just using you."

"That's not what I meant to say. But I am wondering if you have some kind of automatic monitoring device installed that keeps your relationships at a certain level. We've been together ten months now and, except that we know more information about each other, the emotional involvement is still pretty much the same."

"I don't know how to respond to that. I do want your company, I do like the sex..."

"Yes, but is it just a novelty, just convenient filler for your life? Something happened to me a couple years ago that made me realize we human beings definitely need to figure out what we're up to when we're rolling around in bed. I picked up this cute girl at a party and was going through the seduction motions. I got us in bed and then realized I didn't really want to have sex with her. If I had been a guy, it would have been one of those 'can't get it up' cases, no hardness to go on. But I followed through. Without the energy, it wasn't spectacular. Afterwards, we cuddled with each other. That's when I realized it was species contact, physical closeness that I was craving and satisfying."

"You know, before you roused us this morning, I was thinking how much comfort I got from our female bodies lying together."

"That too."

"You're way ahead of me here, Chris. I've never considered any of this. Having sex is just what I do, just what's done. This is deep." And a little bit scary. "I'm still adjusting to your wanting us to end our relationship."

"But I still want us to remain friends. Can you handle that?"

"Yes, I want to keep on being friends, too. And I want us to keep talking about all this other stuff?"

"Of course. Why couldn't we? You just let me know when you want to. We'll be seeing each other."

Yes, that was a good thing. But, clearly, the amorous connection had just ended as speedily and painlessly as it began. Disappointing. Shocking. Still puzzling.

Chris rolled over and looked at the clock.

"You look at the clock a lot." She'd noticed that from the very beginning.

"How else am I supposed to know what time it is?"

Nothing she could do with that but laugh, and then get up to go to the bathroom as Chris said, "I'm supposed to meet Sandy Salazar for breakfast. I can drop you home since I'm using my car again. I think you ought to talk to her. If you ever decided to take another movement workshop, she would be fabulous. Everybody respects her."

"Thanks. Not today. I have to exercise, do the laundry, get some food in the house. Between my temp assignment and more of the rich girls than usual wanting their private lessons I got one hell of a week coming up."

Her phone started ringing the minute she got in the house. She was planning to meditate and let Chris's rejection settle in a bit further, or maybe throw on her togs and run.

"Hey, girl!" It was Margo.

"Madam Reverend, fancy hearing from you."

"I told you to stop blaspheming and call me by my name." These days, Margo was good-natured every time they talked.

"How's the Reverend Rev?"

"He's doing fine. Over in Elizabeth running a revival."

"How come you're not over there with him, sitting on the front pew dressed to the nines?"

"To tell you the truth, I was tired. I'm taking a break and kicking back for a while."

"You're not getting fed up with the ministerial track, are you?" Margo marrying this highly respected preacher who was twelve years her senior felt like either perfection or a colossal mistake.

"Nope, it's still a good deal. Definitely beats anything else I would probably have ended up doing."

Old paranoid antennae shot up. Was she taking a swipe at her life? Margo had been like a different person with her for a long time now, so much so that she was actually closer to her than with Vivian. After she moved to New York, it was Margo who periodically checked on her, who rang her up for some shopping or lunch when she came into town, who dropped her those corny "so we're not as young as we used to be" cards for her birthday, who kept her up on the gossip about Cynthia and Curtis. Marrying the Reverend gave her even more time since she quit her job teaching and let him, as she put it with emphasis, "Sit. Her. Down." No, she hadn't heard that Margo undercurrent of veiled nastiness since forever.

"Margo, you wouldn't be trying to hint that something's wrong with how I'm living my life, would you?"

"You mean how you hang out now with so many white people? You know I'm not in love with Caucasians, Neicy. I don't make any bones about that. But I don't think I've ever said anything judgmental. Or negative. Not about Richard or any of your people. Not about Chris."

Margo had met Chris during one of her jaunts to New York. The two of them had hit it off. They swapped hilarious and painful stories about growing up with hardworking and loveable, but hopelessly alcoholic fathers until their mothers finally ended the marriages.

"No, Margo, you haven't been negative. Sorry." She was deciding whether to tell Margo the news about Chris or save it when Margo said, "I called to see if you wanted to come visit next weekend."

"Does it have to be this particular weekend? I promised Mercedes I would brainstorm with her about how to pick up some new clients."

"Who's Mercedes?"

"You don't know her. She's a Puerto Rican sister who worked wardrobe my first play in New York. Now she has her own business. We were supposed to do this last week."

"Funny I've never heard you mention her. Well, you could bring her with you. The more the merrier. And you all would have time to talk on the train."

She wasn't sure she wanted to do that. Mercedes didn't seem to belong with the rest of her life and they could probably reschedule again.

Margo kept describing the two events – a poetry reading where her old Curtis co-girlfriend, Mavis, was performing and a teen girls conference at the church. "Go look at the websites. I emailed you yesterday."

CHAPTER 9

Sitting next to Margo at the poetry reading, she felt the energy exploding from the low platform at the front of the room. Mavis, the last of the four poets on program, was concluding her performance.

The memory of Mavis in her skin-hugging leather and shiny Corvette flashed behind her eyes. How many years ago? Ten, at least. Yes, the same woman. But bolder and even more angry. Listening to Mavis, she wanted to play back what she knew in bits and pieces about her, but she also wanted to keep her attention on the here and now. Only a few syllables of Mavis's bridging remarks had seeped in, something about the problems women face truly loving themselves. She was going, she said, to end with two poems related to that topic.

The first poem, apparently, didn't have a title --

> not outside you
> or above you
>
> only within yourself
>
> whether it is
> the tenderness you break for
> the dick arousing lust

the never hurt you, never leave you
palpitating heart of love

find it
stroke it

fake it
make it

yours —

She was surprised at the gentleness with which Mavis read this poem, the catch in her voice, evoking the same emotional response. Caught there, she missed Mavis's final poem, except for a sense of confusing sensuality and some "fuck's" and "beat's." Looking around, she saw that everyone was clapping, genuinely appreciative of Mavis and her work. An assortment of black women who appeared to be Mavis's posse was especially animated. Two of them stood and applauded. Then they all gathered up bags and programs and headed for the platform where Mavis was making her way to the floor.

"Come on," Margo nudged, "let's go up and speak." And before she knew how she got there, she heard Margo saying to Mavis, "You remember Deneice."

"Deneice. Yes." Each word was a sentence in itself.

Mavis came forward and shook her hand, then abruptly gave her a hug. She smelled like some heavy essential oil musked up with sweat. Why was Mavis hugging her? They'd never really met one another, although they slept with the same man for almost two years.

"I used to think about doing that, giving you a person-to-person instead of a secondhand hug." Mavis's laugh was indecipherable, interrupted by Margo.

"I brought Deneice to hear you read. She's in town for the weekend."

"So what did you think?" Mavis tilted backwards, waiting.

"I don't know what to think." Then, despite Mavis's brashness and her toe-to-toe presence, she began collecting herself. "I liked it. Your work is very powerful."

"Here in the middle of this room ain't no place to talk about Mavis's poetry." Margo glanced around. The audience was rapidly dispersing. A small knot of well-wishers still hung around two of the readers. The third one, alone, was slipping through the front fire exit. "Mavis, you got time for a drink next door?" Margo asked.

"Next door" turned out to be a café that felt oddly familiar, like the site of an encounter she no longer remembered or a prop from some weird dream. She followed Margo and Mavis through a tight maze of tables to a spot in the far right corner and ordered wine and a sandwich with them, still ruminating about Mavis's poetry.

The chit-chat of the other two women barely grazed her consciousness. At what felt like an opportune moment, she leaned forward.

"Mavis, I'm still thinking about your poetry. All of it was powerful, but the last couple of poems really hit hard."

"You mean the two 'love yourself' poems?"

"Those – and that 'Forgiving White Women' poem you read before them."

"Oh, that poem." Mavis chuckled, scooting back in her seat. "Laying that old business on the line is easy. But that's the last time I'm going to read it. I don't want to give the topic any more of my energy. But there's so much sexual rivalry between us and white women. I've had one good white woman friend, who died a couple years ago from breast cancer. Getting to know her made me see how women are as polarized racially as everything else in this messed-up society."

Mavis's words triggered a memory she hadn't thought of in years. She and a local guy she had been staying with in Ocho Rios during one of her trips to Jamaica were playing in the ocean when noise, voices from a small oncoming boat broke into their fun. As they stood in the water watching, the boat passed some yards in front of them. A young blonde woman was topless at the prow, sunning her breasts, with two very dark Jamaican brothers behind her, grinning and enjoying all the attention their scene was creating. Her own guy had stood there, transfixed, his penis rising into a full-on hard that he made no attempt to conceal as he openly stared at the girl. She had felt like the fifth wheel at a party, the superfluous guest at the feast, uncertain about how she should feel, and what, if anything, she should say or do.

She told Margo and Mavis the story as they nodded, yes, yes.

Margo leaned forward. "This lecturer I heard at a public sorority meeting – the Delta's, AKA's, and Zeta's organized it together – kept saying African American women have to scrape the white woman off our eyeballs before we can see and affirm ourselves."

"And what we never really see is our beauty." She surprised herself with her outburst. "If we're petite and not bad looking, we can be cute. If we put concentrated energy into 'fixing' and 'keeping' ourselves up – the makeup, fashion, diet, exercise and etcetera – we can manufacture pretty. If there's something compelling about us that people can't help acknowledging, they will dub us attractive. But beautiful, BEAUTIFUL, we can hang that up! When I was a girl, nobody would ever say I was beautiful. I thought, I'm ugly, I'm ugly, and could never be beautiful, no matter what anyone might say."

"That's too sad," Margo admitted, sounding sad, "and too true."

"Both of you are stunning right now," Mavis declared.

"You're really beautiful, too." She couldn't help telling her sister.

"Thank you. This is what I've decided to start writing poems about. It takes a whole lot of courage to reach inside and talk about self-love."

"Like that 'only within yourself' poem?" She was glad she remembered the phrase if not the actual title.

"Yes. Like that." Mavis answered.

"I felt you really feeling it as you read it."

"I've had a hell of a holy lot to feel these past twelve years."

When her brow quizzed upward, that expression set Mavis off.

"And why are you of all people giving me one of those clueless looks? You should know how much I've suffered."

"Me? Tonight is the first time we've ever spoken to one another."

"Are you trying to tell me that you didn't know anything about me? Didn't know about my life?" Mavis's tone completely changed the atmosphere around their table.

"What I knew..."

Mavis interrupted.

"That whole period when I was falling apart because of Curtis, what were you thinking about me?" Mavis's voice slapped the air between them. "Or was the only thing on your mind the next time he was going to see you?"

Stunned, trying to calm her buzzing insides and stammer out a defense to Mavis, she looked at Margo for help, who returned her gaze with level comprehension but didn't open her mouth.

"I know you heard the gossip," Mavis continued. "I know you and that prissy Cynthia DuPree knew I was drowning. Wrecking my cars. Almost losing my job. Serious ongoing depression."

"I didn't know all that!"

"You knew some of it. And you could have found out the rest. If you cared about anything other than your own satisfaction."

"Hold on a minute now. All of us were having a difficult time. That one-man, three-women thing we had going was nobody's easy ride. You can't blame me for your problems."

"I can't blame you for my problems. But I can blame you for not caring that I had them."

"I had mine, too."

"So, is that an excuse for not giving a shit about me?" Mavis was ramrod straight, eyes blazing.

She wanted to jump up and push her over or get up and leave.

She was powering her legs to stand when Mavis raised her opened hand in truce, her anger seeming to drain as quickly as it had swollen.

"What the hell? That pain is long over and done. I don't know why I'm sitting here yelling at you about it. But during all that time, nobody asked me what I needed or reached out a hand. What kind of something did you think I was? Don't answer. 'Cause whatever you thought – or didn't think – I wasn't that." Mavis slid her wine glass back and forth in a tense track on the table.

"I'm sorry." Now that Mavis had calmed down and she had also, that much she knew was true.

"I'm sorry, too," Mavis answered. "I really didn't mean to go off on you like that. After recovering from our Curtis thing, I had two other relationships. Neither one turned out to be any good. That's when I started writing poetry and beginning to know myself. Now, I'm still writing poems. And I finally love myself." Mavis's face dropped into sagging lines that aged her.

Remembering the agony of that co-girlfriends time, she reached over and covered Mavis's hand. Mavis let hers rest there, hand under palm, for a few seconds, then pulled it away. "It's alright. I'm alright." She ghosted another one of her indecipherable smiles and pushed up out of her chair.

"I gotta run. You kept women can stay out all night. I've got to hit the government ridge in the morning."

"No, my treat," Margo stopped Mavis from dragging bills out of her purse.

Mavis leaned down and cheeked Margo's cheek, said "Take it easy, Deneice, here're the poems that you liked," handed them to her, and strode through the room out the door.

"Ohmygod, Margo!" Too exhausted to say anything else, she slumped in her chair. She'd only taken three or four bites of her sandwich, a few sips of her wine. Now, she just drank the shiraz. "You could have told me what to expect, and you were no help at all."

"There was no way I could have predicted what happened tonight," Margo countered. Everything she said was true. I couldn't save you from that."

"So, you thought I was being selfish, not worrying about Mavis?"

"Look, Neicy, you and Cynthia were battling your own issues, but Mavis had the roughest time. The only one who was trying to think was Curtis. And his hands were full with way more than he could handle."

"I'm seeing him tomorrow," she dropped.

"For real?" Margo sounded about sixty percent surprised.

"Dorothy ran into him and mentioned I was coming to town. He asked her to ask me to give him a call. So I did."

"That should be interesting."

Margo looked at her watch. "C'mon, let me pay this bill and run you back to your nook. It's nice that Dorothy lets you use her guest efficiency whenever you come to town. If you're going to see your old flame tomorrow, you need to get your beauty rest!"

Curtis promised to pick her up at twelve, and he arrived right on time. He pulled up outside the apartment in his customized Accord and jumped out at the curb to greet her.

Going on fifty and looking damn good. Slightly heavier, with a little bulge of prosperity under his casually elegant Havana shirt, touches of silver in his becoming bush, a pair of expensive brown shoes. The only times she had thought that he didn't look great was when he wore his country boy blue jeans rolled up at the ankles. Clearly, Cynthia and the two kids, and his other woman or women, plus his demanding job as executive director of a showcase non-profit hadn't worn him down. His energy brimmed even brighter than she remembered. He came toward her, sparkling with his special brand of Curtis appreciation.

"Madam Neicy," he actually kissed the back of her hand, "how long has it been since I've seen you?" He led her to the car, opening the passenger side and securing her in as he leaned on top of the door to close it. Once in himself, he turned and faced her. "Gracious, woman, it's nice to lay eyes on you!"

He was breathing her in and she suddenly saw herself as he was seeing her. Oval face subtly matured, hair cut short, still full of itself and oiled glossy, impeccable day makeup, zingy lemon and ginger colors. How glad she was that she had taken the time to put herself together like a woman who wanted some old boyfriend to wish he'd married her instead of his wife.

"You're a sight for sore eyes, too," she smiled. "I think the last time we glimpsed each other was at that hoity-toity jazz auction four years ago."

"Five." He glanced at the side view mirror and eased into the street. "I had just come from Michelle's four-year-old birthday party. Remember, she was born two years before you took off for New York."

"I can't keep up." She heard her own dryness. "So, they're how old now?"

"Twelve and nine. Are you hungry?" Curtis quickly changed the subject. "We could walk for a little and have lunch someplace nearby. This whole area around the university is getting pretty upscale, not like it was at all when you lived here."

Walking sounded like a fine idea. They strolled the streets, pausing at a shop window, or monument, or historic house. He asked about her father – "stepfather," she corrected – down south and she told him that Daddy Riley had moved from Arkansas to Houston with Erma Jean.

"Have you gotten down there to see him?"

"No, not yet." It seemed like something always came up to stop her.

"Well, I haven't married Cynthia either." But he had caved in to her persistence about having another child, although he wouldn't let them all live together. He found a four-bedroom house for her and the children and a smaller home for himself nearly back-to-back on parallel streets.

"Is Cynthia okay with you all's arrangement?" It was hard to believe that she was still as content as he was.

"Yes, I believe she really, truly is. I overheard her talking to her sister on the phone, who must have been asking the same question. Cynthia told her that full-time children, a part-time husband, and no outside job was what she had always wanted. She said she didn't need the father of her children to be breathing down her neck all the time."

It was working out well, he declared. He had his space and his freedom – she knew what that meant – although the arrangement might stand in the way of him running for public office. "But I'm not keen about that. Too much wasted time in dubious limelight." The agency he headed for children and their families had an eighteen million dollar budget and did a million times that worth of good for the people it served. He was content.

"Come on, let's duck in this Italian restaurant and see what they have to offer."

They did takeout and shanghaied a park bench. The meatball gyros and antipasto salad were messy, but with the styrofoam balanced on her lap and a supply of napkins, she was relaxing into familiar comfort.

"So, Neicy, tell me, how are you really doing?" Curtis's voice was mellow with invitation.

"I'm doing fine." Her old sensual response bumped against irritation at his pointed question.

He kept waiting as she picked up an olive.

"Neicy, are you happy?"

"Happy, smappy..."

"No, Neicy. This is not a joke. Lately, I've been thinking. I was hoping you and I could talk. Did you forget about everything you said before you left? How you couldn't get settled with what we had and decided to take your chances finding something, actually someone, else?"

"Look, Curtis, I'm busy with my work. I hang with alright people. There's no need to scrutinize my life."

"But I've been wondering if you're making it possible to get a relationship you want. With me, it was definitely something unorthodox that didn't have much social support. We were brave to try to pull off our non-monogamous arrangements."

"You were the only one who was being non-monogamous."

"That's not the point. You know what I mean. Where in this culture is there precedent for honoring the love we feel for all of the people who touch us that way? Imagine if anybody, just one person, hadn't thought you, me, and Cynthia were crazy, and had accepted what we were doing, plus the baby when he came! Things would have been a whole lot different for everybody."

She wasn't sure about that or anything else related except that she wasn't interested in having this conversation. But she found herself asking, "Do you think support from people would have meant that we – you and I – could have gotten more solid, even with everybody else still in the picture?"

"I don't know. You said you wanted more, but you never gave us a chance to have it."

"I never gave us a chance? If you hadn't had Cynthia and the baby, I might have been able to."

"I think that's an excuse. There was nothing you ever wanted that I didn't give you – except for a couple of jammed times. And that would happen in any form of close relationship. I loved you, Neicy. I still feel you were running away – from us and from yourself."

"That's easy for you to say. You having those other commitments didn't make it any easier for me to stay and take the risk."

"Loving is always risky business – under any circumstances. You just wouldn't give it a chance."

"And this sounds like one of the arguments both of us got tired of having before we broke up." This was worse than the scene with Mavis.

"But, Curtis, suppose I had said I wanted to marry you, would you have done it?"

"Absolutely. I told you that. You were my match in so many ways. I didn't understand how you couldn't see that."

"And what if everything had turned out to be more than you could handle? What then?"

Her question didn't faze him. "We all would have gotten so deep we couldn't stand it." He laughed, long and hard.

"What's so fucking funny?"

"That's the first time today I've heard you curse. I was beginning to think you'd given up the habit."

She decided not to reply.

"Nothing's really funny, exactly. The only way I learned who I was and learned how to grow further was to keep hanging in there with Cynthia. I've always known I was a good man, but I didn't know how good or how bad, if you want to use that language. It just made me laugh to think that I might have grown three times as much if I'd had Cynthia and you and maybe also Mavis pushing my ass."

"Curtis, part of your problem was that you thought you could do everything, superman."

"The new baby did put extra stress on me. And, yeah, some things frayed. And, yeah, maybe I do over-stretch myself. But most of the time I make it."

"Don't be so fucking cavalier." He winced. "Yeah, I'm cursing again. People aren't bubble gum or rubber. Those were our lives you were playing with."

"And you were in the game, too. I always gave it everything I had and would have kept doing that no matter what. You wouldn't even go talk to anybody – about what may have been underneath the way your body acted, about your fear and lack of trust, nothing."

"And it really doesn't matter at this late date." Somewhere inside herself, she knew that wasn't true as she began consolidating the garbage. "Rehashing this shit is a waste of time." She was ready to get back to Dorothy's apartment.

"Neicy, I'm really sorry. I didn't mean to upset you. I hoped you were finding fulfillment."

She didn't look at him.

He reached for her shoulders, tried to swing her around to face him.

"I wanted you to talk to me. About relationships, about purpose and passion, about commitment, those things we touched upon at the end. About being in a union with somebody that wasn't necessarily easy but that the two of you had decided was worth working for. I've figured out some things and I thought maybe you had, too." Urgency was back in his voice.

She couldn't meet his beseeching, his desire for this plumbing with her. She sat heavy as Arkansas mud, with nothing to scrape it.

She wished she'd never seen Curtis. Instead of calling him and agreeing to lunch, she could have thought about his motives, her expectations, how their meeting might be – said "no," not "yes" and saved herself from upset and confusion. Even after pumping through a vigorous exercise routine – every push-up, she reminded herself, a prostration, every jump a bid for transcendence – and even after meditating for forty minutes, she still felt terrible.

But Margo bubbled on the drive over to the mini-conference. Thirty-eight girls, fourteen to seventeen, had signed up for the big event. As they drove the last few blocks, Margo begged her to save one of the workshops. The sister who was scheduled to run it had caught a bad cold.

"But you can do this, Neicy, without hardly trying. Please."

"So, what's the workshop? What would I have to do?"

Margo started sounding hopeful. "Basically, just be you. The workshop's called 'Self-Presentation: Putting Your Best Foot Forward.' You can do anything – voice stuff, how to walk, impromptu social situations, anything. Just get them going with something entertaining. This is their fun session."

"I'm not feeling like fun. I came here because you invited me to see you in your element."

"Aw, Neicy, please. Help me out. It'll cheer you up." Margo threw her a quick look. "You don't seem too bright this morning."

Now was the moment for the question about her time yesterday with Curtis, but Margo was too preoccupied with the conference to raise what would ordinarily have been a very compelling subject. They turned into the church parking lot.

"Neicy, if you don't pitch in, I don't know what I'm going to do!" Margo slid to a stop in one of the "Reserved for Pastor" spots at the rear door, practically wringing her hands.

"Okay, okay. I'll do it."

In her seat during the opening, she read the program. The event was mainly for the young women, but almost as many grown sisters were present for a component that Margo had added when teachers, counselors, mothers, and others concerned about the girls they loved and worked with wanted to attend and caucus together. It looked like this whole thing was a little big-shit of a deal. What was she going to do in her workshop? – no, workshops? Well, actually just one. The second would be a repeat.

What she did was wing it. As the participants entered, she met them at the door and got them to take off their shoes. They were nothing like the rich girls she coached in New York. And they were loud. Half of them were dressed like Sunday church, the other half like Saturday night. At their age, she had read outdated editions of young ladies etiquette manuals from the branch library and walked around her three-room house with a book balanced on her head.

She interrupted their chatter and told them to, one, choose something of theirs to place on the communal table, and, two, think about what positive qualities they brought to the workshop and what they wanted to take from it. And, as new girls came in, to convey these assignments to them. There. That would get them self-reflecting plus talking to and taking care of each other. Kneeling or stooping, they deposited earrings, bracelets, key chains, wallet pictures, silly buttons, crosses, a tube of lipstick, an ornate book of foreign matches on the makeshift altar.

"Okay now," she quieted them again. "Let's introduce ourselves. Watch me. I'm going to walk into the center of this room like I own it and say 'My name is...' as if that's the hottest news on the planet." A few of them giggled. Semi-circled in two irregular rows at the rear of the room, they were excited and nervous. "Ready?"

Her back to them, she strolled to the far front corner, paused, turned around like Hedy Lamar crossed with Cicely Tyson, her wrists held in loose grace almost in front of her, and walked with head-high precision to the middle of the room. "My name is Ms. Deneice Jones." She threw in the "Ms" on a whim to be more impressive. Then she stood there, letting the name, authoritatively vocalized, and her total being extend around her. After three or so seconds, she shifted slightly, relaxing from one leg into the other, breaking the spell.

"Dang," a big girl with a lot of bosom in the second row burst out, "I don't know if I can do that."

Good. "Why not?" Her question set them going about what she had just done. She made them break it down analytically – movement, pauses, style, stride, attitude, pitch of voice, demeanor, concentration, sense of self, the whole nine yards. They talked until they got it.

All nineteen of them completed their introductions – some with finesse, some lively with personality, others falling to the extremes of either Coretta Scott King or bad bitch with a chip on her shoulder. But, without exception, every single one of them tossed their head, swinging a mane of imaginary hair.

"So, what's that about?" she asked them.

"Aw, Ms. Deneice, there you go sounding like Ms. Allen." Ms. Allen was one of their teachers, they told her, who still wore her hair in a natural and tried to talk to them about black female consciousness and racial pride. "We just do that," a tall skinny girl insisted. "It don't mean nothing. We know we're black."

They were giggling, but getting uncomfortable. She didn't want to bruise any feelings or turn them off. Maybe they were discussing race and beauty in some other workshop. She decided to let go of the hair flinging. Partially.

"Okay, promise me something."

"What?" some chorused.

"That when you get home, you'll try to do the introduction we just did without tossing your head. See if you can, see what it feels like, try to imagine how you're looking as if you're your own mirror. And think of yourself, really, really, consciously think of yourself as black. See your self, your own self, your own peach, brown, and black skin and body. And notice what that feels like. Promise?"

"Okay." "Yes." "Promise."

Fine. But she would bet dollars to doughnuts that what was in their heads and their mirrors wouldn't be a perfect match. It hadn't been for her at their age.

"See if that makes any difference in how much power you feel within yourself as you do it."

"What do you mean by 'power'?" Shanelle was dead serious. She was the only girl who had floundered three times before completing her introduction.

She decided to stay personal with Shanelle, but infused her voice with both gentleness and fact. "It's what would have gotten you across the floor like a champ the very first time you tried it. How many of you know what I'm talking about?" About half of them raised their hands.

"What's power?" She pointed at the young woman directly in front of her, who playfully cowered and said, "I didn't raise my hand," as everyone laughed.

"Give it a whirl," she partly directed, partly coaxed.

"I think..." the girl hesitated. "I think power is the confidence you have to do whatever you need to do."

"Great! And where does it come from?" With her body language, she opened up the space, inviting any and every one to respond. "What gives you this sense of confidence and power that..." – she waited, head cocked, for the young woman to supply her name – "... that Autumn is talking about?"

They went straight to the heart of the question. "God." "My mother and father." "Something deep inside." "My grandma who always made me know, 'I am somebody.'" "The belief I have in myself." "My experience. All the things I've ever done right."

"I have some of that," Shanelle protested, "but I still got shaky trying to la-dee-da across the room." She exaggerated, undulating her upper body and blinking her eyes.

The girls laughed at Shanelle's antics.

"You probably needed us to be doing something comic. Everybody can't be equally talented at everything. But what we all need to be able to do for each and every task and occasion is reach down into the place of confidence and power inside ourselves and operate from there." She let her words sink in. "I bet many of you did that. But I bet not many of you were conscious that you did."

That was true. So they spent the last few minutes of the workshop discussing how to be conscious and how to remember to go to their place of confidence when the going got rough. She closed the session on that note, having them make their object on the altar a charm they would use to call themselves into their power. They loved it and filed jubilantly out the door with wonderful hugs and sweet, funny handshakes.

In the afternoon session, the girls got right into their

introductions, likewise slinging long hair. When she asked them why they did it, they told her they didn't want to hear anything else about how they should stop trying to be white women. They had talked about that during the morning. They had white friends and knew white girls were okay.

"Why do you all sound like you hate white women?" A prim girl dressed for church asked.

"Yeah," one young woman smoothing her brow with a red fingernail added loudly, "my grandmother told me that anybody who goes around making a job out of disliking white people doesn't love their own self."

"What?" Had she heard that right?

The girl repeated herself, in the same exact words.

"But we're not talking about disliking – or hating – white people," she argued. "We're talking about affirming our own brand of beauty. About not buying into the media images of how a woman is supposed to look in order to be attractive, which usually means a white female pattern."

"Not all the time." The girls named a few singers and supermodels.

"Those fall into another category that shows something else – black women being made into super-sexual or exotic creatures. All the hair lets everybody know they're hot."

"Well, I don't care." The pert girl speaking tossed her head. "Hair or no hair, my boyfriend thinks I'm sexy – and I still wanna be Tina Turner when I grow up."

They all laughed, and she had to laugh with them. She hadn't had the joy of being with young sisters like these since she left Philadelphia.

She gave up debating with them. The issues were too complex to handle in a one-hour workshop that was supposed to be fun. The girls weren't buying what she said anyway. They didn't have to be on guard against white women, they told her. "And we don't have to fight anybody to be our black self."

She stood in the room where the girls left her. "Anybody who goes around making a job out of disliking white people doesn't love their own self." Anybody black. The black was understood. She hadn't made a job of disliking whites, but it hit her that beating up on them did make her feel hip and morally superior. And, yes, the only reason she would need that was not feeling good enough about herself in the first place.

The thought was so revolutionary she dropped into one of the nursery school chairs, her legs flowing over the floor. While putting adversarial energy into white people, what in her own self was she neglecting? Not looking at? Escaping from? And would using race in this way, as she'd certainly done with Chris, keep her distanced and unconnected? She didn't like what this said about her. This was not who she wanted to be. She most definitely needed to get her head straight on the subject.

The last half of the grown women's caucus was uplifting, as were the closing remarks by Margo and her Rev. Otis Dunne. His tone conveyed none of the "head rooster bestowing his imprimatur of approval" that most speeches by men at a women's gathering carried. A large, dark man, well-dressed with a lot of presence, he was just as genuine and pleasant on the conference platform as when she spoke with him on the phone or their paths crossed when she and Margo hooked up with each other. He and Margo looked terrific together.

Margo rushed her when it was over. "Thank you, dear Neicy, I really truly thank you. Otis is taking me and a couple other people out for a debriefing dinner. Shanelle and her mother will drop you off. You had a good time, didn't you? I'll pick you up at ten tomorrow for your train."

Margo insisted on coming inside 30th Street station to wave her goodbye. But a freight derailment north of Wilmington, Delaware had delayed the train to New York. They settled for their wait on one of the worn wooden benches.

"I'm glad you came, Neicy."

"I'm glad I came, too. It was good to get away before I start rehearsals." Landing the "Obsessions" part had sunk in. "This play is going to take everything I've got."

"You enjoyed your workshops, right?" Margo's mind seemed to be stuck on the conference.

"Very much. You know, the one thing both sets of girls did was swing heads of long, imaginary hair."

"Sounds to me like you're doing pretty much the same thing in this role of yours, playing a white woman."

"Margo, there's no comparison." What an appalling idea! "What I'm doing is... "

"Okay, okay. You don't have to give me a lecture. I want to ask you something. Are you happy with your life?"

"Why is everybody asking me that question? Do I look miserable or something?"

"No. You don't. But why do you get upset just because I ask? If you're happy, you can say yes. If you're not, the answer is no. If you don't want to talk about why you're not, that's your business."

"I'm just tired of being asked."

"Pardon my repetition, but you still haven't answered the question. Are you happy?"

"I don't think about whether I'm happy or not." A toddler jerkily walking along the bench at their backs dropped his rubber duck between their shoulders. She retrieved it and handed it to his dad.

"You really are sounding defensive. I don't mean to pry, but I'm getting worried about you."

"Don't worry about me, Margo. I'm fine."

"I don't think so. It looks to me like you keep choosing the wrong kind of people, ones you can't have lasting relationships with. When you were with Curtis, you couldn't commit to him because of his other women, right?"

She kept silent. Maybe it was more complicated than that. The little boy and his father drew her attention again. They got off the bench, the father following the child around as he careened and squatted over the train station floor. She brought her eyes back to Margo.

"And the string of men you dated since Curtis you yourself said weren't ones you'd make a life with. Furthering your career has been the main thing on your agenda. And then up pops Chris. I never saw the two of you getting serious. I'm pleased you're staying friends, but I still don't think I know what that lover thing was about."

"I don't understand every piece of it, either. Obviously, someplace in me has the ability to be attracted to women and I don't have any problem with that." Vivian's astrologer once told her that being a Gemini predisposed her to sexual relationships with both men and women. "But you're right about commitment. I knew Chris and I were going nowhere near that."

"That's the point. You keep running that same pattern."

"Okay, Margo." She could admit the possibility. "If it's true that I'm ducking and dodging real relationships every way I can, what am I supposed to do about it?"

"Recognizing it is the first step, I guess." Margo stopped to listen to a station announcement and checked her watch. A good thing she was paying attention. "There're things we can't know even about ourselves until we get to the place where we know them. Take me, for example." Margo looked up, making sure that the couple slowing next to their bench kept walking past and didn't sit there. "I used to be out for the biggest, juiciest dicks I could find. And if I told you now that Otis is impotent, you'd probably have trouble believing it and wonder what in the world has come over me. But I've learned there're all kinds of wonderful ways to put together sex and love. Not to mention kindness and caring and depths of satisfaction..." Margo ran out of words.

"I never would have... I can't... I... Damn, Margo... " She trailed off, her mind a staccato mess. Was everything deeper than she'd ever imagined? And was she missing out?

"Otis and I have a union with each other. We do our outreach work for the church. We have common goals and compatible ways of living. I think being happy in a way I'd never dreamed possible made me force this conversation on you." Margo lowered her head and nudged a loose tile with the toe of her shoe. "I've only talked like this, Neicy, because I care about you."

Margo's softness helped her to say that she also wanted a compatible, committed union.

"But, Neicy, if that's what you're wanting, then it really looks to me like you're sabotaging yourself."

"That's how it looks to you, how it looks to Curtis, how it's beginning to look to me."

"You're the only one who..." Margo cut herself off, focusing again on the station announcements. "They've been calling your train! Hurry!"

She grabbed her luggage and pushed through the gate to the hot August tracks. Margo yelled, "Let's keep talking. I love you" and — two months before she needed the luck — "break a leg!"

October, 1994
New York City

CHAPTER 10

Nudging up the underarm zipper of her Act I outfit, she couldn't believe it. The damn zipper popped!

Jackie eased the pale yellow fabric back over her head. "I thought this was too small," she fussed as she hurried out to fix it.

There was no mystery about where to lay the blame. The potato chips day before yesterday that she didn't stop eating. The scrumptious raspberry and chocolate dessert after last night's dress rehearsal. Just a taste. Then a third of it. Then, before she knew it, the whole thing was gone. Rarely could she not control her eating. Obviously, she was more jittery about this "Obsessions" play and her strange role in it than she realized. Turning all four sides of herself to the mirror, she didn't see the flesh that had ripped her dress.

Where was Margo? Out there in the audience was what she needed. She threw on her backstage robe to peep the house and bumped into Charles at her door.

"Hey, leading man."

"Fifteen minutes to opening night fame, and you're not in costume."

"I will be in a minute. We had a minor accident."

He was beautiful, holding a bouquet of roses, togged out in gray slacks and gold watch chain. If all the white men making capitalist empires were truly like this, it would have been a romantic era.

"Cheers, Deneice!" He lifted a make-believe glass. "I wanted to dart in before we went on. Here, these roses are for you. The box office was bringing them as I got to your door."

"Oh, thanks. And thank you for everything." Charles stopping by was just one more way he showed his support.

"Are you ready? Still okay with the knee scene and everything?"

Director Steve had decided during the final week of rehearsals that Charles should pull her into his lap and keep her sitting there as he tried to soothe and pet her after one of their tumultuous fights. They jokingly called it the knee scene and, sure, she professionally handled it well. But that smack-on contact between her bottom and his front carried a lot of energy and both she and Charles knew that she was having trouble staying peacefully confined in his lap. Just one more thing about this edgy, sexual play to keep her pumped up and off-balance.

"I'm as okay with it as I'm ever going to be," she answered Charles.

"I heard that." He chuckled and walked away.

The roses were from Curtis, with his handwritten card. "A shining night to the most magnificent woman who's ever entered my world!"

She set the roses on the floor by her table and threw the card in the wastebasket. Then fished it out. Then picked up the roses to stand them in front of the mirror, then halfway there, dropped them back down on the floor. Hell!

With no one around at the moment, she'd better perform her little ritual that was something between a meditation and prayer.

But Jackie rushed back as "two minutes" sounded over the dressing room speaker. "Stand up! Quick!" Jackie slid the dress down over her head, ran up the zipper, and right at her rib cage, in the same exact spot, the zipper seam popped again. Unbelievable! Was this a bad omen or what? Rummaging in her big apron pockets, Jackie found safety pins to control the damage and flew with her to the stage just as Ian called "places." She needed to be there – sitting on the divan, yellow voile spread around her, when the curtain rose and Charles, playing her husband, Victor, strode through the door. The last glimpse she got of her face – dashing from the room – her made up light skin looked ghastly next to the hue of the dress.

Scene one had gone well. She could feel it. The stage crackled with the sexual excitement of Freud-crazy New York in the bohemian 1920s. The audience was flowing easily with the quick cuts between real and imagined occurrences, signaled only by the dimming and brightening of lights. Charles in the lead was perfect as quintessential middle-aged male, sexually obsessed but repressed. And best of all, her performance was proving to skeptics in the audience that she as a black woman actress could pull off her white woman part. She ended up being the only cross-racially cast actor in a major role, so was left carrying the burden of that publicity hype.

Scene two was ending as it should now, taut, tense, and controlled. She stood outside the closed door of Victor's study, speaking Gretchen's fearful fantasies of him having sex with someone else. Inside the room, the lights dimmed and Victor began the fantasy seduction of his secretary, Miss Morgan, exactly as Gretchen was imagining. They were her imaginary fears, but perfectly congruent with his suppressed desires. This fantasy sequence lasted a hot minute, then came back to lighted reality just before she knocked, opened the door, and summoned Victor – while dismissing Miss Morgan – to afternoon tea.

Quietly seething, she bumped Victor's cup as she poured cubes of sugar in the fussy china bowl.

"Husband, are you being true to me?" She stood dangerously still as she asked him.

"Now, sweetheart, please. . . please, Kath. . . Gretchen." He almost called her Katherine, Gretchen's old, original name before Steve changed it. Her sizzling energy augmented the nervousness he was supposed to feel. "Don't take yourself through all that agony again. Don't needlessly carry me through it. How can I convince you that no other woman is getting my amorous attention?"

"You say that. I hear you tell me that over and over, but I know, I know it's not true. I know something's not right!" She screamed the last sentence and violently shook her hands. She was playing Gretchen's distress to the hilt, the intensity ratcheting up even further when Victor reached to pull her on his knee.

By the end of the play, everything was rolling like a gorgeous tsunami. At the big office visit, Dr. Bonn told them both they were suffering from childhood sexual trauma, that buried hurts and twisted longing were sickening them. As if hearing it for the first time, she listened with her Neicy mouth open, her Neicy brain clattering, "Could this be true, could this really be true?" He instructed them to act out their fears and fantasies together, which meant they had to communicate what was hidden and then give it elaborate form. She listened as Victor squeezed out how his mother had sat him on her bed as she slowly slipped on sheer lingerie and then playfully petted him. She stammered through the little she had begun to remember about clandestine trips with her father and his brother to Berlin brothels. It was all so fascinating. Could she be Victor's mother as a brothel girl? Should he fondle her like her uncle?

In their separated rooms that are both visible to the audience, they bumble through garters and black lace, thin whips, moustaches and toys preparing for their therapeutic tryst. Victor doesn't know what to do with his cock piece, and she covertly closes up the plunge of her negligee. As the play concludes, he yells, "Ready?" and she calls back, "Ready... yes, ready." The scene touches light comedy, but no one can predict whether what ensues will be cause for laughter or tears.

A loud moment of silence. Did the audience stay with them?

Did they buy what the play presented? Ultimately accept her in her role? Her heart was thumping, mind racing in a thousand directions, trepidation blocking her ears. Finally, she could discern clapping. The audience released the tension of skirting too closely their own untapped stuff. Now, with the daring and tricky drama over, they could acknowledge the novel experience that had taken them to outlawed brinks and then brought them back to safety smiling. What she thought she heard in their applause was exactly what she needed to hear.

She took her curtain call just before Charles. When she backed aside to make star space for him however, he hesitated for just a moment, then grasped her hand and pulled her front and center with him. They smiled and bowed to the audience and each other as sound from beyond the footlights washed over them.

Joy. Yes. And gratification. The attention and validation made her feel real, never mind the white woman guise. This was love she could always count on. As good as sex, and, like she'd told Curtis during one of their seismic arguments, better than any relationship she'd ever had.

As she entered her dressing room, there was Margo, with a cascade of yellow roses.

"Oh, Margo, I was trusting you were out there! Did I kick butt, huh? Did I do it?

"You sure as hell did something! But, girlfriend, I had no idea..."

"I told you my character was extreme."

And that was all she got said before undressing, dressing, hustle and bustle took over the crowded space.

By the time she changed into her gold sheath dress with the shimmy fringes and her metallic gold tee-strap shoes, the room had quieted down. Margo, who had stood observing it all from the corner, came and sat next to her in front of the bright mirror as she finished fixing her face.

"How was I, Margo? Now, really."

"You were brilliant, I think. That scene where you go from accusing and threatening to cajoling and crying to on your knees begging then seducing was something else. But, Neicy, is that what you want to be brilliant at?"

"As long as it doesn't hurt me or go against my values. It's my beloved profession, Margo."

"Okay, but what does it say about you that you could do that part so well?"

"It says that I could go there. Don't ask me why 'cause I don't have the answer to that. This play compelled me and Gretchen's problems shake me up." She started laughing. "Look at it this way. There's probably a neurotic white woman somewhere in all of us."

"Not in me. Being a neurotic black woman..."

"Deneice." Charles knocked and stuck his head in the door. "Are you ready?"

"Yes, ready." She couldn't resist the line and Charles picked up the echo, chuckling with her.

"We're leaving for the restaurant in a minute. The car's waiting outside."

"Charles, this is my friend, Margo." She rose to give a proper introduction. "Up from my old town of Philly lending me moral support."

"Are you coming to the party?" Charles walked in closer as Margo stood up, too, green eyes flashing in her pretty skin, the drape of her expensive silk dress accentuating plump, pleasing curves as she lifted her bosom and chin.

"Neicy, I have to catch the train back tonight. Otis is meeting me at the station so we can get to Detroit."

"Oh, right." She'd forgotten that Margo and Otis jimmied their schedule so Margo could make it tonight.

"Nope, Charles. I guess she won't be joining us." He was reversing himself out the door.

Stooping a little, she gave her buddy a squeeze. "I can't tell you how happy I am that you came. Call me when you get back."

"Neicy," Margo sounded suddenly serious, "you take care of yourself." Margo looked her in the face and reached out to tuck tenderly into place a straying strand of hair that was swelling black and crinkly now, freed from Gretchen's tight bun.

Her post-performance daze didn't dim at the after party. People filling up the large private room hugged her and kissed her, plied her with food and champagne. She could almost see the glow on her own odd, pretty face, the sheen bouncing from her eyes and peachy skin. Daddy Riley's hunting buddies used to say she resembled a fox because of her eyes. They were perfectly round in the center, but dropped curlicue down at the inner corner and lifted way up at the end. Her lips were nicely balanced, an inviting dent at their upper center. As she aged, that babyish bow had widened. She liked to think the change made her look like a gospel singer with a powerful mouthful of gleaming white teeth.

Standing by herself for half a minute, she glanced around and thought, "These people are my family." Just like every cast she'd ever played with. The realization felt new as the folks around her came more sharply into focus. Myrna. Danish with a touch of Sioux Indian from South Dakota. Big soul, off-brand sense of humor. Odessa, the designer's assistant. She always got tight with them. She liked Bud, who played Hiram, and even aloof Carmella, who was Miss Morgan and her conscientious understudy. For the time they made magic together, they were bound together like family – only to scatter back into separateness after the play was done.

Margo would think it was off as hell that she called these people a family, however temporary. But Margo still couldn't fathom what it was to be as alone as she had been almost all of her life. Rebelling against her stepfather after her mama died and hanging out with other kids who were struggling to raise themselves. No relatives to love and correct her, teachers who mistook her stubborn drive for real strength. And even as an adult, always feeling like an outsider. Not tonight! She tossed down the champagne left in her glass as if it were a neat whiskey. Like the previous two servings, it went straight to her head.

On her way to the bathroom, she bumped into Charles, who grabbed her and spun her around, into the arms of the dot-come backer from upstate she'd been flirting with, who waltzed her in a narrow circle, then swung her back toward Charles, whereupon her high heel twisted and, totally losing her balance, she went slamming to the floor before either one of them could catch her. She went down like a rag doll, her splayed leg taking too much weight. When she got to the doctor, the injury he identified as a twisted hip-femur connection was giving her a fit and she was howling in disbelief about having to take time off from the play.

But the good news, she kept telling herself over the next few days, was that her leg would mend fairly soon. Some initial rest, then taking it easy for another short while, then back to work. Carmella stepped into her part. But Carmella's Gretchen was tame.

"No, Neicy," Charles agreed, "she doesn't have your power."

Ironically, this power of hers was what had gotten them their worst review. Old fart critic Arnold Baxter vehemently objected to it and "the taint of Freud's jungle." He wished for more ladylike charm and sophistication. In the end, he dismissed the whole production as a dubious experiment, notwithstanding what he admitted was its unusual interest, overall topnotch cast, and superb directorial talent. Yet, despite Baxter's review and Carmella's tepid rendition of Gretchen, the audience turnout held steady, not dwindling into failure yet not rising to hit proportions.

"Just wait 'til I get my part back," she kept saying to Charles whenever he called to check on her.

Steve counseled her to concentrate on getting well. "By then," he added, "we'll know where we are."

She couldn't remember when in her life she'd ever felt so vulnerable and helpless, so at the mercy of forces beyond her control.

CHAPTER 11

Breathe in-2-3-4-5-6. Hold it for four slow counts. Breathe out, all the way down to eight, and stay for four more beats. Breathe in-2-3-4-5-6. Hold.

She sat, trying to meditate. After three and a half weeks of rest, her hip joint and thigh were healing and she was no longer on drugs or crutches to blunt the pain. But meditation wasn't the refuge that it had been before she was sidelined from the play.

Upright this morning on her burgundy cushion, with legs stretched out straight in front, she was breathing in-2-3-4-5-6. Holding. Breathing out-2-3-4... On and on in cycles of repetition for what was supposed to be about thirty minutes. In and out, up and down. The upward stroke, then the gathering. The outbreath pulsing with heat – warm nostrils fanning her neck and shoulders, fat tendrils flaming along her spine. Breathe-2-3... out-7-8. Suddenly, without any warning, her sphincters tightened and her panties went damp. She ignored the spasm that almost happened and kept her attention fixed high on her internal point of light.

Richard had explained that something physical like this could occur. Third eye and crown, feminine and masculine, the altar of union at the spiritual meeting place in the center of the head. A mating more true than any earthly copulation, sometimes causing even palpable bodily reactions.

Another almost spasm, which she again ignored.

Richard had said, "When that happens, to the familiar Father-Mother-God, add Lover, and ask, 'What serviceable thing am I going to use this loving to co-create?'"

"What serviceable thing am I going to use this loving...What serviceable thing am I going to use this loving... What serviceable thing am I going to use this loving, use this loving, this loving... " But, to no avail. Sphincters tight and swollen clitoris tangy, she came, the pent-up spasm jerking out of her as she bobbed helplessly on her meditation cushion. A no-hands, no-touch orgasm! Though the heated beating was dying down, her open vagina was still pulsing – pulsing – gradually relaxing. Why was naked sensuality intruding this blatantly as she visualized the light? The lowdown part of her wanted to say she just needed to get laid. She hadn't been with anybody – other than herself – since she and Chris stopped sleeping together, and that was two months ago.

Sexual matters had definitely been on her mind. With time to reflect, it hadn't taken much to see that Gretchen's jealousy and anger tapped into old emotions that she hadn't allowed herself to feel with Curtis. Who knows, it might have blown open their situation in a positive way if she had cursed, screamed, yelled, threatened, and stalked him and called the other women on the phone to leave fucked-up messages when she thought he was at their house. Wonder what he would have done? Wonder why none of his women did it? Mavis came closest, but she ultimately turned her violence inward on herself.

But what had really gotten to her about "Obsessions" was the atmosphere of sexual saturation and personal helplessness. That people could be so driven by their urges and yet so haplessly blind was amazing.

Carefully, she maneuvered off the floor. She should go to the Center and talk to Richard. Having an orgasm during meditation definitely qualified as a spiritual subject!

At Richard's office an hour later, she got comfortable in a leather armchair while he dropped down on a cushion beside her and turned up his lean, squarish face.

"I'm having trouble with my meditation," she plunged in. "I can't concentrate and my sexuality is getting triggered."

Richard nodded. "Well, you know how spiritual energies sometimes manifest on the physical level."

"Yeah, but this was a full-blown eruption! I know what you all teach about meditation being true union with God or Spirit and that that's original sex. Physical. Spiritual. – Spiritual. Physical. All one, right? But it still seems like some boundaries are being crossed when my body interprets the spiritual as physical and takes it to the max."

"Not when the centers are in the process of opening up. Things like that can also occur when we're too much in our head and essentially out of our body. That sounds contradictory, but…"

"Given what just occurred, I would say that I'm too much in my body and not enough in my head!"

"Have it your way," Richard backed off. "But sometimes deep disconnects between mind, emotions, and body can cause that type of reaction. In the final analysis, though, you're the one who has to sense into what feels right."

"Look, Brother Richard, do you experience sexuality in the midst of your meditation?" All this theory was fine. Let him talk from his own experience.

"I'm not sure that dragging my stuff into the picture would be helpful."

Something in his voice stopped her cold and made her peer at him. Could Richard have "stuff" around sex? And sound dreary about it? He certainly seemed wistful now as he softly added, "The only thing I can say is that it's good for us to live out our physicality, which includes sex, and our spirituality."

"And so I've just got to keep running with that?"

"If you can. It's a huge subject, Neicy. Many wise ones believe sex is the problem we have to master before this planet can evolve. Our sister, Venus, is beaming energy our way, trying to aid us. Maybe you should come sit in the atrium some propitious evening after meditation and soak up the rays."

Well, that could be pleasant, hanging with him in the penthouse he occupied at the top of the Center building. Whenever she was there for a function, he walked her around, showing off the special plant breeds he air layered and tended himself. Once, he'd taken her into his private suite so she could see for herself an unusual piece of African mudcloth, the characteristic pattern rendered in black and orchid. They'd spent the time standing in front of a large aquarium watching an emperor angelfish flash its brilliant blue and yellow body through tall algae and waterlogged castles before Richard reluctantly decided he'd better get back to the reception. Everything was beautiful, even a bit dramatic, but in a natural way, not at all like the stagey elegance of some men's homes she'd visited with Chris.

"But I am thinking one more thing," Richard rushed. "Sexual fruition and finding life partnership often go hand in hand. How well are you doing with your intimate relationships?"

This was further than he'd ever ventured into her personal business, but he plowed on.

"You know those intimate relationships are why we're here. That's really how we're tested and grow. Usually, you can chart your progress on the path by looking deeply at whom you've chosen – or not chosen – to be with and how you were in the relationship. Would you say that your intimate unions have been successful?"

"I wouldn't say that I was batting a thousand." Flustered, she resorted to flippancy.

"Three-hundred would get you in the majors." He was still pressing her.

"I'm probably playing in the minor leagues."

"Why do you say that?" He pulled up a chair.

She found herself telling him about Curtis – how they met, what it was like when they were together, why they broke up.

"So, what you're saying is you were looking for something that he couldn't give you?"

"No... No... I didn't think we were getting anywhere. But I may have been running away."

"Even if you were, I could understand that. It's hard to be intact enough to give yourself up to another person in a healthy way." There was a lot of emotion in Richard's voice and she felt her own self shaking. "We just keep working the question, what serviceable thing can I use this loving to co-create, whether we're talking about meditation, our life work, our life partner, or a conscious person's one-night stand. I believe the greatest relationship achievement would be to unite male and female, sexual and spiritual with a partner and within one's own self. That would take a lot of courage and commitment, as well as love."

His touch on her arm was gentle and light as he smiled. "Who knows, dear Neicy, you're worried now, but maybe all heaven is about to break loose for you!"

She couldn't respond. This surprising conversation was turning her inside out.

"We can talk more anytime you want. Don't forget my Venus invitation." Looking drained himself, Richard leaned back and closed his eyes.

Finally, she stood up. Unhurriedly, he did the same. She retrieved her bag from where she had dropped it on the floor beside her chair. She usually forgot not to "set her money low," as one of Margo's Philadelphia big mamas put it. Well, there wasn't much money in her purse, anyway. She slung it over her shoulder and walked in front of Richard through the door.

Turning around, she gave him a hug. He lingered for a moment in it.

"So long, Sister Nee."

"Bye, Brother Richard."

Later. She could think about everything Richard said later.

Idling in front of the Center, she watched traffic whiz up the tree-shaded avenue.

Losing her part in the play, she'd lost a huge part of her life. Calls and visits from the cast had dwindled to naught and she wasn't strong enough yet to throw herself into her regular routine.

She wished she had someone to run home to. A mother who was peeling potatoes and carrots and seasoning pot roast wouldn't be half-bad.

Out of the blue, she thought of plantains and beans. Escovitch fish. Spicy jicama salad. The eclectic Afro-Cuban take-out down the street from Mercedes's shop. And then she thought of Mercedes, whom she hadn't seen since "Obsessions" opened. She could drop in on her, even if Mercedes was not her mother. The two of them had been hanging out since her early days in New York, drawn together by their love of clothes and Caribbean cuisine. Frustrated at the barriers that kept her stuck in wardrobe instead of making designer, Mercedes quit working theater and opened her own tailoring shop. It would be good to see her friend, to cozy down in her cluttered back room. Mercedes closed the business at twelve on Saturday, but she stayed there the whole afternoon.

At the take-out, she picked up food and walked the two short blocks to Mercedes's door. Setting the food down in front of her, she banged on the thick plate glass. No answer. Banged again. Still no answer. She cupped her hands around the glare, nervously peering inside, then balled up her fist and, with escalating insistence, pounded the door once more. The policeman on the corner who looked her way made her realize she needed to cool it. Mercedes suddenly appeared through the curtained partition and came around the front counter.

"Hold your horses, baby girl, hold your horses." She was laughing as she made her way to the door. "I was taking care of business in the bathroom."

When did taking care of business in the bathroom become something to laugh about! She almost asked, who did you have back there with you? Didn't you hear me calling you? She felt like a troubled child.

"What kept you so long?" Stooping for her bags covered the strangeness of her question and helped snap her into composure. "I brought us some grub."

Mercedes's looks never failed to amaze her. She was a big, brown-skinned woman, the only female she knew who made her feel little. The sparkling whites of her eyes, long sloping nose, and wide, wide luscious lips were so arresting that all one's attention went there. Even with her automatic Neicy eye for clothes, she could never remember what Mercedes had on. The blur of soft cloth that enfolded her now when Mercedes hugged her was another such enigmatic outfit. You'd have to look hard to figure one piece or two, long skirt or pants, where sleeves stopped and capable arms started, whether the color was brown, dark gray, or dark blue. Mercedes wasn't trying to hide her large, shapely body. Her clothes just seemed to be camouflage, a deliberate cloaking that gave her maximum options for being – or not being – seen in the world.

The closest she had come to broaching the subject of Mercedes's appearance was to ask who in her sprawling Puerto Rican family she resembled. Mercedes went to the purse she always carried, pulled out a large hand-tooled wallet, and showed her an old-fashioned picture of four women. She pointed to the one standing slightly rear and to the right. "Her," she said, "my great-grandmother." The stout, comely woman was several shades lighter than Mercedes. "The old folks forever said if I wasn't so dark, I could pass for her reincarnation."

Released from Mercedes's hug, she felt a bit steadier. Took one of the two stools at a corner of the gargantuan worktable and began sharing out food from her takeout containers.

"How's the tailoring business?"

"I got plenty work, but the people don't want to pay me or can't afford to pay me what it's worth. I make their taggled asses look like queens and they dicker me about my prices. If it wasn't for the weddings, I'd be in big big trouble."

True. Almost everything hanging on two of the three clothes racks were white marriage gowns and sets of bridesmaids outfits. She wiped her hands, got up, and fingered a few of the dresses, being careful not to touch any pins or accidentally smudge the chalk. "Why they so ugly?"

Mercedes laughed. "I can't stand the colors either. That's what they want, though. It's the style."

The drab golds, stained plums, and casket ivories weren't doing a thing for her soul. Okay if you were thinking about dressing for winter, but they looked like a funeral to her.

She sat back down and dished up another helping of fish and plantain, waiting, actually, for Mercedes to ask how she was doing. Mercedes averted her eyes, looking ill at ease.

"Have you heard what happened with me and my play, 'Obsessions'?"

Mercedes shifted on her stool and moved to a big, mauled office chair further down the room. "Yes, I heard." She sounded as distant as the space she'd just put between them.

"What's wrong?"

"Mathurlie and I saw your play the night it opened."

"So, what did you think?" She was holding her breath.

"We didn't like it." Mercedes looked defiant. "I never expected to see you demean yourself like that."

"Demean myself?"

"But I don't want to talk about it. Mathurlie said that even a good sister like you could finally get tired of not making it to the big time. I just never expected it from you. Coochie-ing up with a white man, getting debased..." She broke off, like speaking about it was too odious.

"Mercedes, the character is white!"

"But you black. And that's what matters. You think those people looking at you were not seeing your color?! You and those skinny brown girls in their skimpy cabaret costumes. It's all the same to them. Except you were crazy on top of it and groveling. No wonder you hurt yourself and lost the part. Good riddance!"

All these years she'd known Mercedes, she would never have imagined such narrow-minded garbage spewing out of her. Heat seared up from the hinge of her jaws to her ears and flaming eyes.

"Mercedes, it's a role. I'm playing the role of a troubled white woman with psychological problems."

"As far as I can see, you were up there on stage trying to pass for white. Why would a supposedly black and conscious sister even look at the part?"

"It was a great part, Mercedes," she was pleading. "I knew it would be a little odd. I knew the audience would have to get used to it. But the part is a gem – subtle, sophisticated, complex..."

"And demeaning for any black woman with sense enough to see it." Mercedes cut her off, pitch in her eyes. "Did you have any problems playing a fine white lady?"

Why she hesitated for a fraction of a second before she answered – to catch her breath, consider the question, soul search her response, whatever – she didn't know. But the tiny break gave Mercedes the chance to nail her.

"See. Like me and Mathurlie said. You were just dying for the chance to be white."

Jumping off the stool forgetting her hip, she winced at the sudden, sharp pain. Mercedes and Mathurlie judging her and her performance like that.

"I thought you were my friend. But nobody who was really my friend would think like you're doing about me."

"So, then, how do you think I'm supposed to think? That I'm supposed to just all the while praise you? Well, my job is not to sit here waiting for you to show up in your own sweet time so I can tell you how wonderful you are."

She was speechless, her shock and anger careening into another dimension as Mercedes continued her assault.

"All you ever wanted was for me to make over you, to help you feel good when you got tired of phoneying up with the white people." Mercedes farted with her mouth.

This was unbelievable. Inside herself, she was shrunken and wailing. She felt as if her own mother had told her she wasn't worth her attention and didn't love her anymore. Emotionally, she cowered in some low, filthy place scratching not to feel like shit.

"And another thing," Mercedes narrowed her hateful eyes, "just because I'm big and black, I ain't your mama. What you think? You can climb in my bosom and get everything? – just 'cause you supposed to be pretty!"

Snatching up her wrap from the top of the battered file cabinet, she walked with as much stride as she could manage past Mercedes and her heavy, old chair. And kept on walking from the canvas curtain to the horizontal door handle, the floor like crushed glass beneath her feet. Green shawl in hand, she made it out of the shop, into the November wind.

She couldn't hear, couldn't think, could barely see where she was going. She turned to drop underground and then veered back to the sidewalk, nearly bumping into a tall, hurried man, his bushy hair covered with a ratty knit cap, his arms loaded with magazines and newspapers. She couldn't sit bottled up on the train. She walked – plant your heel, roll forward to the ball of your foot, lift the other leaden leg, plant the heel, flex your ankle, roll forward – concentrating on this one basic thing her sore body and spirit could do. She kept it up until the devastation inside began to form into sequential thought.

How, how could Mercedes say such nasty things about her?! How could she even think them?! That the play was no good and she was prostituting herself for white people. That she had been using

Mercedes. That she wanted to be taken care of. She was so hurt she started to cry.

Suddenly, slowing, she recalled other women she'd had similar relationships with. Jamilah in Baltimore, with her precocious mixed daughter, Roshan, where she would stop almost every day on her way from work, Jamilah always at home in the messy house, the rumpled couch and bed, unwashed pasta pot on the stove, dirty clothes in the laundromat cart at the door. A place where she could come and not have to be anybody. And, before that, Elizabeth, her off-the-grid haven in Wisconsin, smelling of meat pies and buttery cinnamon-baked apples. Yes, another way to try to hit home. "I ain't your mama." Hateful, hurtful words. No, Mercedes wasn't her mother, but sadly, maybe somewhere inside herself, she had wanted Mercedes to be. Attention to her one and only daughter had never been Virginia's long suit. That had left a maternal deficit aching to be filled.

Mercedes was always there whenever she wanted to visit and never required her to do anything. And she had taken that homey retreat and acceptance for granted, like a narcissistic child. It must have been that air of entitlement that gradually pissed Mercedes off.

But why such a vicious attack? Even if she caused Mercedes's resentment, no way could she blame herself for what Mercedes just did.

She might never in a hundred thousand years understand what this cruel horror was about.

She was still hurting when she walked into the conference room at the theater and greeted Steve and Charles. Steve had summoned her to this Monday morning meeting. What other reason than to restore her part? The prospect lifted her battered ego.

Charles gave her a one-sided hug. "How're you doing, Deneice?"

Steve made a feint at a hug, ended up squeezing her on the

shoulder. "Sit down, Deneice." He held out a chair on the side of the table and took the one at the head for himself. Charles settled across in the seat facing her.

"I've made some decisions about 'Obsessions.'" Steve got right down to business. "And I wanted to tell you about them before proceeding any further."

"You mean you didn't call me to restore my part?"

Steve lowered his eyes. She threw panic in Charles's direction, looking at him.

"I told Steve you wanted your part back worse than anything, Deneice. I can imagine how much of a disappointment this has to be for you."

"You're not giving me back my part!"

"Deneice, I'm sorry." Steve's hands started toward her but stopped midway on the stained oak wood. "Things aren't working out like we expected. I think I made a mistake with my casting."

"So I was a mistake."

"No. No, Deneice, you're not a mistake." Charles was speaking to her distress. "You're an extraordinarily talented actress."

Steve piggybacked. "No question about it, Deneice. You're a wonderful actress. But I don't think putting you in this role was the right thing to do, at least not at this point in time, not off Broadway. Maybe for an avant-garde theatrical experiment, but not for a commercial venture. I'm really sorry."

"So, I was just an experiment, like everyone said. A little something different in the petri dish to get attention." Breath pushed through her chest in windy gusts. Steve's face momentarily blurred.

"Deneice..." This time his hand made it over to where she sat.

She snatched her hands away. "So I was just an experiment." Her voice was louder. "An experiment, not a commitment. Now you're trying to cut me loose without giving me another try."

"We've offered the part to Genevieve Taggert and she's accepted."

"You've what?" This couldn't be happening. "Genevieve Taggert!" Not just white, but porcelain. Thin. And blond. Famous for starring roles as a softly sexy, patrician beauty. She couldn't – and she could – believe it.

"And we've worked out a severance for you that Equity thinks will be fine."

"I'm outta here." It was impossible to sit in her seat for another minute. They had used her. And there was nothing – zilch, nada – she could do about it. Fuck them, fuck all of them. She slammed out of the room.

At home, her only recourse was to call Margo. Either that, or who knew what! As she vented, she could see her friend running to mute the television, turn off the stove, perch on a kitchen barstool, still leisurely home at eleven a.m. in tight pajamas.

"No, Neicy, they didn't do that! That's too cold, even for them. But I have to tell you, I had misgivings from the start about you playing that part. And what I saw on opening night didn't make me feel much better."

"Why didn't you say anything?"

"You weren't listening. Every time I tried to bring it up, I could tell nothing was getting through. I even asked why would a conscious sister..."

"Oh, hell no, not you too! That's what Mercedes spit at me."

"Who's Mercedes?"

"You never met her – the Puerto Rican sister, the designer I was thinking about bringing with me when I visited in August."

"Well, Neicy, if two of us..."

"If two, four, six of you, I don't give a shit. Acting the part of a neurotic white woman doesn't make me a racial sellout!"

"Okay, okay. But did you always know exactly where you were underneath the lines and the white girl makeup?"

"Yes. Where I always was. Where I always am. The same place as when I had to make my skin darker to be black enough. True, something about this Gretchen role got to me. It really shook me up. And I can't explain that. But it's for damn sure not because Neicy Johnson wants to be white!"

"I'm sorry. We probably shouldn't be talking about this right now. When your life gets back to normal, you might want to think about it. And, Neicy, dig deep. After I began therapy, I was blown out the chair at the crud that came up for me. And while you're digging, throw sex in the pile, too. An orgasm while meditating? And everything you told me about your reaction to that lap scene sounds like fallout from childhood. Are you positive you weren't messed with in some way when you were young?"

"Naw, Margo, I know all that theory." She felt confident about her answer. Onstage, the specter of buried nightmares had prickled. Offstage, she was sure that nothing traumatic had ever happened to her. She didn't remember the first five or six years of her life – so what – but knew from the stories her mother told over and over that she'd been doted on and gushingly cared for by a wide network of generous black people.

"What about that talk we started at the train station where you were wondering why you chose the people you did to go to bed with?"

"I don't want to figure out why I go to bed with who I go to bed with." This exchange was way past getting on her last nerve. "I don't want to worry about wanting to play a white woman." She was practically screaming. "I don't want to scrutinize sex scenes and orgasms. I just want my life back. Everything is falling apart!"

"It may be rough, I see that. But, Neicy, you're still blessed." This was the new Margo talking. "You're not broke or sick, not homeless or friendless, not dodging bullets..."

"Shut up, Margo. Just, please, shut up." Her anger and adrenaline were ebbing. Despair was kicking in. "Forty-year-old black female actresses don't get second chances. What am I going to do with my life?"

"Neicy, you're more than an off-Broadway part."

"Yeah, put it in the funeral program. At this point, Margo, I don't know what I am. And I'm not particularly interested in trying to find out. I don't want to deal with any of this. I don't know that I can."

"So, what are you going to do?"

"Go find the blue hole and jump in it." Her mother's old threat when things were going wrong. She was mumbling.

"What? What did you say?"

She didn't answer.

"Neicy, I'm sorry. Today it's tough, but I've seen you pull through tough times before. Go undress. Take a warm bath..."

"Margo, you aren't listening. I don't think I can deal with any of this! And I won't feel better tomorrow."

CHAPTER 12

"Neicy, where you been?"

"Out."

"Doing what?"

"Hanging. Hold on a minute, Margo." She quickly dead-bolted the door. "Okay, here I am."

"Neicy, what are you doing? What are you up to?"

"I was on my way to lock the door..."

"What was your door doing unlocked?"

"Guy went out of it. I was still in bed. Oh, my head is killing me. I truly can not drink anymore."

"Oh, Neicy..."

This phone call from Margo had been a daily ritual for the past three weeks. She wasn't suicidal like Margo sometimes feared and she didn't need to go stay with her and Otis. The only person she might kill if she met him in a dark alley with no witnesses was Steve.

"Margo, I'm okay. You keep calling me unstable, but I'm fine."

"No after-effects from your realizations day before yesterday?"

"Not a one." Finally seeing that inhabiting Gretchen's fine white lady body gave the little not-good-enough girl inside her a healing thrill of power was liberating. She could shake off that dust and put those ancient dolls away. She'd even apologized to Chris for beating up on her in order to make her own self feel better.

"Well, just like you got that..."

"Margo, can I check you later?" Her friend was worming around to yet another conversation about men, relationships, possible childhood abuse and what was she doing about them. She could feel it coming. "I've got to run to an audition."

That was a lie. What she had was an 11:30 date with Crosby. It was too much synchronicity that he called after months of no contact on the very same day she'd spotted his lost silver cufflink glinting among a stack of clutter in her top dresser drawer. This overnight guy in her bed who'd just left was a fluke. The information specialist at her temp assignment, he was sitting in the bar minding his own business until she started flirting and one thing led to another. She hadn't done that in eons!

Hey, what was this? He'd left something on the bedside table, neatly placed. No! Yes. Money. Her head reeled. Four one hundred dollar bills underneath his business card. He thought... No. He couldn't have thought that. It was a mistake. Had to be. They'd enjoyed each other. Money! She'd call him and they could have a good laugh about it. Was it a joke she couldn't remember? Was she supposed to buy something for him? She'd definitely better go back to her one glass of wine. How funny. Could he really have thought she moonlighted as some kind of expensive pick-up girl?

But now she needed to pretty up herself and get moving. No way she could not have said "yes" when Crosby invited her to lunch.

Maxwell's was packed, buzzing a little too loudly for her taste with a Friday crowd jumpstarting the weekend. They followed the maitre de around a large ficus to their small, corner table. If all someone saw were the handsome, olive-skinned waiters, they'd think this was a Middle Eastern restaurant. As this young man backed away with a hip, elegant dip, they settled in their round-bottomed chairs.

"That waiter couldn't keep his eyes off you."

"What?"

"But I can't blame him. Devastating, delectable, divine. I'm sitting here wondering how I survived without seeing you these past twelve months."

"You seem to have done alright. And you're still as smooth talking as ever. The glibbest tax advisor I've ever run across."

"It's your fault. Pretty and fine as you are, you bring out the poet in me."

She didn't comment about men's attributes to their faces, but this last year hadn't hurt him either. He wouldn't stand out in a crowd, but the longer your eyes stayed on him, the better he looked. The part that was so precisely etched it felt like an African scarification was still deep in his scalp-short hair. His eyelashes still curled, his beautiful skin shone, his whole aura bristled with health. And, yes, the oversize nugget ring was still on his right index finger. Besides the ritualistic part, that was his only ostentation. In his late forties, he had never been married, called himself "the fish that got away."

"Where have you been keeping yourself, lady? How have you been?"

"Let me see if they have what I like on this menu. Then I'll tell you."

The creamed salmon and asparagus crepes. Balsamic tomatoes and goat cheese salad. A glass of merlot. Food ordered, she let the meal unfold, the waiter come and go, and focused on their conversation.

"I'm basically okay. However, if you had caught me a couple weeks ago, it would have been a different story." She gave him the unabridged rendition of her "Obsessions" saga.

"Whew! I'm sorry. And I'm glad you recovered. It doesn't sound like anything I could have helped, but I would like to have known about it. I guess by then we'd really gone in different directions."

"True. Why did you stop calling me?"

"Do you want the poetic or the raw, honest answer?"

"Raw and honest."

"I met another woman who acted like she appreciated me more

than you did. You were always so absorbed in your plays and whatever. You didn't make me feel special like this woman did."

The fawning female image that popped in her head definitely wasn't her.

"So, what did she do that I didn't?"

"If you don't get it, I can't explain. She just made me feel like she needed me and I was real important."

It seemed like Crosby didn't know it, but she had liked him, too. He was a nice lover and an impeccable escort. No matter the occasion, with little or no prepping, she could count on him to show up perfectly dressed and to behave just as appropriately when they got to wherever they were going. Once she joked that he should hire himself out and he had gotten so offended she sent him an "I'm sorry" card and cooked him greens and cornbread and lamb chops with string beans and new potatoes, all in one meal.

"Are you with anybody now?" If the expectancy in his eyes wasn't feigned, he truly wanted to know.

"No."

"Really? That doesn't sound like you."

"What do you mean?" What was she picking up in his tone?

"Oh, nothing. I just thought you always kept a lover." Waving back the waiter and the dessert tray, he signed in the air for the check and leaned forward.

"What are you doing for the rest of the day? Is there anyplace you have to go? Come home with me and have some dessert. My mother sent one of her rum raisin cakes for Thanksgiving and I found that vanilla ice cream you're so crazy about."

"No." She didn't even say "thank you."

"No? Why not? You used to like hanging out with me when you weren't busy."

"What are you inviting me for?" Why did she feel like punching him?

"Ice cream. Rum raisin cake. A relaxing time." He leaned closer.

"Now, if you decided you wanted to take it further, I wouldn't fight you off. Being intimate with me was one thing you did seem to appreciate."

"'No' is what I said the first time. Can you handle it?"

"Sorry. I'm not trying to press or upset you. I've just never known you..."

"Never known me what? Not to want to jump into bed?" Seeing a line of men stretching back to her teen years whacked new truth between her eyes. Maybe she wanted to be offered something more than a nice body and good time. Take the cheap whore out to dinner! Come for some cake topped with vanilla ice cream and dark chocolate sex!

"Look, I just thought..."

"That I always wanted sex. That I always kept a lover. Isn't that how you just put it? Like I'm some bitch in perennial heat!"

"Deneice, I don't know what's wrong with you. Why are you making it sound so ugly? We always did things like this."

Whoa, yes, dial it back. He was right. She was the one putting that ugly spin on it. He was only offering her what she'd accepted before. How nuts could she be? Bringing home a man she barely knew last night and now raging at a nice ex-lover because he was still attracted to her. But it seemed like she was changing – had changed – and wanted something else. This was totally new territory – and how was he to know?

"I'm sorry, Crosby. I guess I'm being more impacted by stuff than I realized."

"You really leaped on me! No problem. Let me get you a cab..."

"No, please, everything's fine. I'd love some of your mom's cake."

His apartment was as comfortable as ever – traditional done up homey and bachelor hip. She wandered over to his entertainment center and started looking through a stack of CD's as he headed for the kitchen.

"Cake and ice cream coming up!"

"Actually, I'm still feeling full from all that lunch I put down."

"Oh, okay. I guess we can wait 'til a little later." He came, stood behind her, began gently massaging her shoulder blades.

"You're as tense as I thought you were."

"What you're doing feels really good. I think you missed your calling."

She'd forgotten how much she used to relish his impromptu body rubs. He stayed in place and continued, taking his time with her shoulders all the way from her neck to upper arms down through her mid-back, coming in closer as he smoothed deeper and she melted into relaxation. The CD she was holding slid from her hands with a clatter.

"Oops, sorry."

"Here," he said. "Come over to the couch."

He sat, pulled her backwards on his lap, and what she felt beyond everything else was the sexual hardness beneath her, propelling her up. Something almost as old as she was tightly coiled in her arm seemed to power the slap she aimed at him. Men playing nice. Preying on little girls and women. He deflected the blow. She swung again as he managed to wrest her down and pin her arms.

"What the hell is going on with you?"

"Your dick was hard. You pulled me in your lap with a hard-on. We were supposed to be having cake and ice cream."

"You are out of your mind. I can't help it if my dick gets hard when I'm rubbing on you. Whatever the hell is wrong with you, I didn't do it."

She stopped struggling and came to her senses. Put her arms around him, her head on his shoulder. "I'm cracking up."

"Do you want me to call somebody?"

"No. No. I'm sorry. I'm really sorry. Just give me a few minutes. I'm not really going crazy. A lot's happening, but I'm not totally out of my mind. Can I lie here a minute?"

He helped her stretch out on the couch, then sat at the other end and, cautiously, began massaging her feet.

Old pain, wounding, scars, and a heap of confusion. She could see it now, Crosby the culmination of a very long list, highlights playing behind her lids.

Being called a whore by her classmates when she came back into their sixth-grade classroom with the tree twig sticking out of her hair. Being shunned by the good girls because she was fast, which was as much a reason for not being chosen a debutante as her poverty and lower class. Macarthur still getting her to play with him, but walking another girl in white dress and lace home from mass. Bingeing on alcohol and sex when she was in high school until she went to college and straightened up. Still, there was the football star she had to fight off, who kept asking, "Why not me, what's wrong with me, how come you won't give me some?" He'd assumed she would screw him too because she'd had sex with other guys.

Virginia supposedly talking to old Beulah, but actually speaking loud to tell her, Neicy, not to be "no fish sandwich woman," which she didn't understand until she was grown meant don't give it up cheap. Four one-hundred dollar bills now laid in her face. That would buy a lot of fish sandwiches. She had never been calculating about money, so never applied the "don't be cheap" rule to herself. Too bad she didn't know to think of value in other, self-worth currency.

"Crosby, all my sexual chickens are coming home to roost. I'm sorry you got caught up in it. None of this is really your fault."

"I hope you can deal with what's happening. You know me. I like to keep it simple."

"That's what I thought I was doing, too – being ultra-hip sexually. Deep down I really needed more than that. Did you respect me? Did you honor me?"

"I never disrespect women and I gave you what you acted like you wanted. You were into being sexually attractive and having that validated."

"In fact, I would have felt rejected and worthless if you hadn't."

"No problem there. That was easy. Sex is good, sex feels good."

"I got a lot out of it, too. But it was my very limited default mode of dealing. I didn't trust you to really, truly care about me deeper than that. I think I expected you to leave and so I kept us at a certain level and held myself back."

"Yeah, you were, like, you could take me or leave me. At a certain point, that's the same as telling a man to leave you, especially if another woman comes along who acts as if she wants more. Not that this fish here is into getting hooked."

"Don't worry. I'm not about to propose." She was also not about to get in bed with him. Finally, for her, those days were over – even though his hands, which had eased up to include her calves as well as her feet, felt awfully good. All she would have to do is stop talking and keep lying here, receptive, letting her energy, his energy flow. Apparently, without consciously knowing it, she'd picked some splendid lovers who could fall into an exquisite zone of sensuality with her as easily and naturally as they breathed.

She bent her knees, fixing her skirt behind them, putting her feet in his hands instead of her legs. Either her thoughts shifted the energy or he got the physical message. Or both.

"Are you ready for that ice cream and cake?" he asked. "Come on, let's have our dessert."

CHAPTER 13

A sluice of wind cutting across the rooftop chilled her as she sat. Cold outside, cold inside. Her excitement over new realizations was now ebbing into despair. She was really messed up. Number one: No more sex for well-being. She hadn't been choosing it. The addictive habit had been running her. Number two: No more theater to feel good. That had to break down so she would stop using career success as an escape from her real issues. What was left? An unemployed actress whose future was bleak, and nobody to run to for comfort. Sexual connection that kept her from feeling like an alien was not viable relationship. It took a whole intact self and not just some genitals to truly make love.

She had screwed men without letting them in, except for Curtis. His sweetness, decency and love induced her to be emotionally open despite his multiple women. But he was still a man and that triggered apprehension and anger. The only thing her confused body knew to do was close up when it was time for him to enter and have him work extra hard to get inside.

Seeing everything wrong didn't show her how to fix it. What was going to help her "make somebody out of herself"? That phrase rang in her ears as she was growing up. According to the standards handed her, that was what she had done. Ha! Ms. Somebody was not even a passable human being. How could she think about a healthy and functional relationship with another person when she wasn't even healthy and functional herself?

One sane thing she could do right this minute was stop pretending that her beach chaise on the graveled top of her building in November was summertime at the French Riviera. The whole scene was New York neutral, a nondescript blend of tan, khaki, light brown, gray, drab, colorless that the city dissolved into on cloudy fall days. With the briskness and short daylight, the pigeons were already roosting and none of the other residents would be climbing up after work. What she actually wanted was to cry. She was more miserable than she'd ever been in her entire life.

Inside, she wasn't hungry enough for supper, wasn't ready to go to bed. She plucked Mavis's poems from the bottom shelf of her bedside table, sat down in her armchair, and read the one Mavis had laughingly called a "manual."

> I have fucked myself
> prodigiously
> with the energy of
> my own dick

Not "the" or "a" dick, but the energy, "dick" here seeming to mean powerful sexual desire.

> One me on the bottom
> tip out pushing
> wet womb sucking in
>
> The other one, me
> heavy breathing at the top
> hard grist thrusting
> pinkness wild wide open

Female wet womb lying flat, but clitoris, penis tip, pushing. Male heavy thrusting from above, but girl pink in the open center. Active and passive, giving and receiving on both the top and the bottom. Finally, at the end of the poem, the four metaphoric hearts crushing together, in love, with love. What really tender and complex images for sexually taking care of yourself!

She nudged up the thermostat on her way to the bedroom. Stripped off her clothes and got into bed. Soft sheets caressed her as she closed her eyes and lay still, sensation building with her breathing from the inside out. When she felt the aliveness in her fingers, she ran love through them and gingerly, reverently touched her clitoris. It answered with a surge and a happy extension. Reciprocity and slow exploration. She'd never made love to herself with this much affection before.

She took time to pleasure the plumpness alongside her breast and armpit, finally teasing her nipple into relaying the elation all the way down, to where stickiness pulled in her fingers. Oh, how marvelous. She was curling. Slithering and scrubbing. Back. Front. Back. Powering in. Receiving. Lifting up boldly, buttocks on fire.

She reveled in the acceleration toward orgasm. Then all of a sudden, she lost the track her mind was grooving and her rotating ass went cold. In love, with love. Nothing. Her own dick thrusting, nice fat clit front receiving. No response. She reached for every image she could think of, every tried-and-true erotic picture that had ever gotten her off. Everything just went flatter and flatter, her wrist started cramping, and her pussy rubbed dry. Drooling saliva onto her hand and concentrating directly on her clitoris didn't help. Nothing did. She rolled to her side and started crying. Hot, heavy tears. She didn't even have this any more. Nothing was going to save her or make her feel better.

But next morning, she sat in meditation profoundly more receptive than she'd been in a while. Began breathing in, expanding. Then hanging on persistently to the outbreath's dwindling tail. Time slowing and falling away. Mental chatter muted, brightness the surrounding sound. As-a-man-thinketh-in-his-heart-so-is-he. Each word plopped down, a discrete packaged lump, and lined up exactly like the burnt wood plaque in Richard's office. Then her whole consciousness abruptly dropped, too, into her waiting heart. The impact was like dry ice in a pool of water, sharp sizzles and bubbling smoke. In swift succession – subway cars she couldn't catch – came a crunch of pain, a waterfall's roar, and a mighty drench of tears. Sorrow washed away the foggy smoke so she could glimpse the things behind them – a broken skate, two worn little girl sandals, spilled milk on an oil-clothed table, one fat calf on a bed.

Her legs began to violently tremble and there was nothing she could do to stop them. From inside herself, she observed them jiggle and shake. She felt the nerves running from her feet that propelled them, how they connected with her thighs. She watched, fascinated, and for the very first time, knew herself, all at once, in her body of feeling and skin. She was one damp big eye looking, one same self being seen.

Then another wave of sadness toppled her to the floor. Cotton blanket pulled up over her shoulder, she focused on the misery. Breath. Consciousness. Thought. Centered in her raw and awakened heart. And the first thing she realized was that the pain didn't kill her. This was what she suffered when her mama died. She'd been enduring the abandonment, bewilderment, grief, anger these many years, along with all the loneliness, longing, isolation and fear. If her mama would leave her, then any and everybody would. If that bond couldn't be counted on, then there was nothing left to trust. She'd shut tight and there'd been no love wise enough or strong and determined enough to help open her up.

Now she hit bottom with nothing to hold on to except the pain. The pain and her breath. "The breath is life," said the teachings as she trained in the right use of both. She knew how to breathe, and she knew how to not breathe. It was a miracle she didn't just stop her breath and let the hurting go.

But she didn't. Not this day, or the next, or the next one. When she called Richard on Sunday morning, he begged, please, take it easy. He would come see her on Monday.

She was taking it. Easy? Not so sure about that.

She stood in the living room waiting for Richard, looking around with critical eyes. She saw the bent corner blind, slats faded and dusty. The nice philodendron, losing its run of luxuriant leaves. Where did she get that ivy? Ah, yes. She'd been descending the wide, concrete steps of the textile museum when a skinny brown boy with big eyes in a large pair of girls' canvas sneakers looked at her, spied something that allowed him to swiftly approach and offer the plant. "Three dollars, miss." He ran away with the five-dollar bill she handed him before she could say "keep the change."

The beige walls of the apartment were plain, except for two cherished batiks. Nothing wrong with the furniture, but nothing particularly right with it, either. She must have owned the funky old square brown hassock for the past hundred years. She frowned and turned the slats of the blinds so light fell in at a different angle. The room looked the same.

She went back to her bed and swooped up two of her raw silk throw pillows – one, a stunning peacock, and the other butternut gold. Once arranged on each end of the tan leather couch, they started a conversation with the gorgeous batiks. Better, a little bit better. Then the shrill bell, summoning.

Richard bounced through the door in his ubiquitous white shirt, a British bomber jacket, and well-washed pair of jeans.

"Hi," he twinkled, "this is Barney," introducing the largish dog strutting in beside him, who promptly jumped up to her chest.

"Sorry," Richard apologized, "black labs tend to be friendly."

She patted Barney and took Richard's jacket. She didn't even know that he owned a dog.

Unleashed, this one sniffed his way into her living room. Richard trailed behind. He stopped in front of the most abstract batik and tilted his head as if appraising a fine piece of art. If he made a frame with his hands and looked through them, she wasn't going to like it. Squinting, he made the frame. Barney ran from across the room and Richard stooped over, nuzzling. She got even more irritated.

"Can I get Barney a drink of water?" Richard asked. Barney barked.

She took them to the kitchen, found a bowl for Barney's water, and set it firmly on the linoleum floor.

"Richard, I'm going under. My whole life is falling apart."

"Yes," Richard murmured, his blue eyes kind. "I know. From what you said on the phone, I could tell you were in a crisis. Some people call this big expansion the dark night of the soul."

"Reading about it is a lot different from feeling like you want to die. Everything's messed up, nothing's going right. And then, there's all this pain, here." She caught herself patting her heart, as if tapping would ease it.

"Some of it's old, Neicy, from hurts you can't even remember. Some of it's new. Some of it's yours, the rest belongs to the world. You're in touch with it all and that can be devastating."

"Nothing I was taught prepared me for this." That was putting it mildly. "You all just say, meditate in your head, connecting mind and meditation. Nothing about this lightning that struck my body and blasted my heart."

Richard followed suit as she sat at the counter while Barney went and posed by the fourth floor window looking out at who knew what.

"I hear you, Neicy, and you're right. Our practice tends to attract people who start off from a head place. But sooner or later, as the work does its work and they're ready, they get to where you are. A whole self softening. A place of poise and integration, of receptivity and love. You're being called upon to take your life to the next level."

"I know I need to change my life and I'm gaining insight about how it's messed up. But I don't know how to fix it. I'm not happy. I'm sabotaging myself. I don't even have a self to hold on to. Forget figuring out how to create something serviceable with passionate purpose. If I could fabricate a halfway decent me to bring on board right now, that would feel like progress."

"Neicy, you're in touch with a lot of your stuff." Richard sounded thrilled. "Listen to you. You're holding on to your self even as you feel like you don't have one. The part of you that knows you're here on earth to manifest the glory of spirit is firmly in control. I could tell the minute I saw you that you're going to be okay, that you are okay."

"I wish I could believe that."

"Believe it, Neicy, it's true." Richard was lit up. "Just relax with it all – the emotion, the memories, your body unwinding, massive shifts and changes. Stay gentle, stay compassionate. Everything's going to be alright."

His happy faith spread through her as he pulled her in for a tight, quick hug. Holding on to the enveloping closeness, she leaned out and squeezed him in return, almost tipping over her stool before she could balance herself.

"Whoa!" Richard scrambled to the floor and braced her against his chest. "No more falls for you."

Barney trotted over to see what the laughter was about. Richard scratched him behind the ears. "Isn't he the best dog ever?"

Kneeling to also give Barney a rub got her a lick to the face. Ugh, yuk.

"He likes you," Richard volunteered.

Gathering the melon she had sliced, she led the way to the living room, trying not to trip over Barney who impeded their march with his obvious interest in the plate.

"Richard," she stopped, halted by the thought that hit her, "did your father let you stumble through your crises?"

Barney whined, and Richard unexpectedly moving past her jostled the fruit in her hands. She caught up with him as he seated his lanky body on the couch.

"Did your dad help you, you know, give you some special instructions or something, since he was the founder of this practice and all? Or did you have to pretty much fly blind, too?"

"We all basically are flying blind even if there's someone around who could ostensibly help us."

Opening her mouth to repeat her question, she realized Richard was being evasive. How absolutely unlike him. Looking closer, she thought she saw a cheek muscle twitch.

"I'm not fishing for any dark secrets. Now that I'm on this journey, I'm just really curious about how yours went for you."

Richard quit trailing his hand over Barney's tight coat and turned around to face her.

"If you really want to know the truth, my father has never been very much help to me."

Oh, my. "You sound like you didn't like him."

"I loved him. Then I hated him. Then, after he died, we made peace. He was a pretty unusual man."

"I'd like to hear, if you want to tell me about it."

Richard sighed, adjusting one of the pillows to the small of his back. "Nobody knows what I'm about to tell you. Are you sure you want to hear it?"

A pact was getting set up between them. She looked at his sincere face, both pale and ruddy, looked deeply into his transparent eyes. "Yes, I do."

"I found out when I was fifteen years old that my mother was not my mother, that my father had me with an African woman who also bore him four other children."

"What?!" Richard half black and half white. No wonder...

"Just keep listening, okay."

"I'm trying to." She corralled her exclaiming mind.

"During one of his stays in India, my father traveled around Africa and, under some rather bizarre circumstances, got involved with a Ugandan woman. He installed her, the two children she already had, her brother and his wife with their children plus the wife's brother – all of them – in a small village in southern India. My mother – I mean, his wife – knew about it. She couldn't have children and didn't care for sex. Of the five of us, I'm the only one who turned out white. So my dad and mummy decided to pass me off as theirs."

"What a story! Did you know your real mother? Did you meet your brothers and sisters?"

"Yes to both questions. My father and I used to visit. Some of my earliest memories are being tended to by Bembi. That's what I called her. But nobody ever let it out that she was my mother. That stayed sewed up tight as a drum. I can see now that my father terrified me about sex all of my life. He used to put the stump of his leg next to my penis, as if something like that could happen to me. I must have been around six. And when I got older, he made me look at graphic medical book pictures of male organs with venereal disease, cauliflower clumps and open, red sores."

"Adults suck." How could anybody do that to their child? It made her sick to her stomach.

"The only reason my father eventually told me the truth about Bembi being my mother was he could see I was getting sexually curious. And the last thing in the world he wanted was for me to father a brown or black child. Can you imagine?"

She could.

"I felt betrayed and castrated. Pushed out of my self, my body, my sexuality – all because my old man was a flaming hypocrite who couldn't control his, like many of those upper-crust men laboring under Victorian conventions."

She thought about Victor in "Obsessions."

"I vowed never to misuse my sexual energy or wield my power as a man to oppress women. I was in another bind, though, since the only women I could safely marry would have to be black. At least if I wanted to keep his secret sealed for the sake of our spiritual mission."

He said it before she had gotten there, she was so caught up in grasping just the bare facts of his story.

"And, the last piece of this damnation you need to know is that he'd been grooming me since I was four to step into his shoes and carry on the ministry he'd started. I believed so much in the work that I couldn't turn away, no matter how I hated him."

Her head was bursting. "Stop. Wait. For a minute."

She got up and walked down the hall to the bathroom, thinking in some detached part of her mind that Richard and Barney, being males, would probably go through their whole visit without having to pee. But she actually didn't need to, either. She turned into her bedroom, flopped on the bed, and gazed up at the ceiling. All she needed was a few minutes by herself, a break from the stimulation. She let her mind wander, wondering how often that was what she was really taking time for when she left social situations for the restroom. Rest room. Rest. When she noticed a spider web beside the overhead light that she rarely turned on, she rolled up from the bed, energized, and stood for a grounded moment. Nina Simone singing "Ne me quitte pas" softly hit her as she came out the bedroom door.

Richard sat on the living room floor stroking a sleeping Barney and eating a slice of melon.

"I hope you don't mind that I got into your music. We have some of the same artists in our collections. That Nina Simone is one of my favorites."

He was still running excitement, but a calmer kind. She lowered herself to the floor, close to him and Barney in a spot that he made for her.

"Music is one positive legacy from my dad that I expanded upon. I saw her perform that song in Paris when I lived in London."

"How long ago was that?"

"During what I call my breakaway period. When I turned twenty-five, I ran away from home. Damned my father, dropped the practice, said goodbye to my mummy and friends and went to live in England on money that came to me in a trust from my grandfather. I slummed all over Europe, soaking up everything from Riviera sun to a Spanish diva who was as operatic offstage as she was on. It more than made up for my slow start in life."

"That's the same time I was junketing around the Caribbean whenever I got the chance. Every summer, I spent one month in a rural Jamaican village helping a sister teach her freedom school. I lived in a one-room structure away from Olive's house with the lizards, red ginger plants, and cold water outdoor shower and loved every minute. But what made you give up your exciting life overseas?"

"I guess you could say I outgrew my rebellion and accepted that this meditation ministry was what I was meant to do. I left London right after my twenty-ninth birthday, came home to New York, and dutifully took my rightful place as heir to the throne."

"You make it sound like a heavy kingdom."

"I've done everything I could to keep it light, can't you tell? Have you heard the story about the African king who went out periodically and, one by one, conquered all of the neighboring monarchs. Each time he subdued a territory, he'd banish the king and confiscate his throne. All of the thrones he stowed in the attic of his own grass hut. This went on for years. One day, the victorious king was sitting at home when his ceiling caved in and the thrones fell on top of him and killed him. So, the moral of this tale is that people who live in grass houses shouldn't..."

"... stow thrones! That's corny beyond belief!"

"I know. But the point is that I don't need or want to maintain a kingdom even though I have to constantly resist followers' attempts to turn me into their version of a guru. Some like 'em saintly, some like 'em hot. I fight off both definitions."

"What I still want to know, though, is how did you get past hating your father?"

"I didn't – not fully until after he died. It took the grace of one of those dreams that is more than a dream. If you haven't had an experience like that, you probably will. It's a special blessing that changes you in ways you don't even know."

"What happened?" She lay down with her head on Barney's side. Not a bad pillow.

"In this dream, for lack of a better word, I was sitting on the ground with a group of people, waiting for the teachers to ready themselves and come. A beautiful, dark man with liquid velvet eyes sat next to me with his folded legs somehow, strangely, resting in my lap. He squirmed and fidgeted until he finally moved completely over, merging the back of his head and torso to my head and chest as I recognized the shift, saw the moment coming exactly when it happened. Oh! I cried. He sank molten in my breast with a love piercing sweeter than any orgasm. I knew then what was meant by the master in the heart. The biggest and best part of myself fused with all of me. When I woke out of that, I didn't hate my father any more."

She stayed quiet.

"I could now love and serve. I could now risk my heart, even when it might be broken." He maneuvered around Barney's legs to stretch above her as she lay on the floor. "I never thought I'd be able to tell you my story. At one point, I almost decided to just keep it simple and let you know how I liked you without saying anything about being half-black. Oh, Deneice, I can't tell you how good it feels to finally confide in somebody and to have that somebody be you."

In his voice, there was so much relief and yearning. Yes, the implications were enormous. But this part was moving too fast. She needed to sit up, forcing him back. "Oh, Richard..." Still, the tenderness inside her spilled out to him. Her heart and belly wanted to pull him in.

"Richard, I'm feeling you. You've always seemed like a brother to me mixed in with the teacher and it would be so easy to take that into lover. But I know I shouldn't go there. There's too much work I still need to do getting my head together about sex and men and piecing together a new me, period." She probably needed to stay out of bed with anybody for at least a year!

"But you don't have to push me away while you work on yourself, do you?"

"I don't believe I would ever have to push you away. But I think there's something I ought to tell you. I've always seen myself with a black man. You're not exactly that."

Richard looked as if she'd stabbed him with a butcher knife.

"Richard, I'm sorry." She got the pain.

"It's alright. No, it's not alright. I've found you, and I'm not going to let you get away. Race is about externals. You and I, we connect on levels deeper than that, almost like twin souls. Tell me you don't feel it."

"I think I feel it. And I'm open. But I've wanted my partner to be my racial twin also so that, as we move through this world, I'm carrying my roots and support with me."

"With all we would have going for us, we could figure that piece out. Funny, this morning as I got out of bed, I imagined you in my place with me. You were strolling among the flowers in your silk bathrobe, teacup in hand, sunbeams dancing on your naked neck and uncombed hair."

"The hair you've got right. But the way I look in public has you fooled about the rest. Try an old oversized tee shirt and a gaudy thrift store mug."

"Externals, all externals. We could buy you silk robes or old tee shirts. What really matters is that we're both complete enough within our selves to take on true union with another person."

"Richard, I'm not there yet." She saw herself on Crosby's couch and curled up in misery under her meditation blanket. "I've been alienated from myself and other people. And I'm being real careful because I've used sex to create false closeness. I want what you want, what everybody wants — love and happiness. And I definitely see how our shared spirituality could help us make something magnificent, you know, what you've always taught about uniting male and female, sexual and spiritual and being of service. I guess all I'm trying to say is that I need time."

"I think you're already more together than you realize, Neicy, but, yes, I can give you the time you need."

"It might be a lot – and I can't make you any promises." But she let him hold her, tight and tangled, sitting there on her living room floor.

Barney twitched, started waking up noisily, opening his eyes, moving his rousing body. They looked at him and laughed. He stood up, legs wobbly, gave himself a violent shake and barked.

"Ne me quitte pas, Neicy." Nina Simone was still singing in the background. "Please don't leave me. And, oh, the other thing I did while your back was turned was give that little ivy some energy."

Her eyes followed his to the accent table beside the stereo where her freshly-groomed plant perked up attractive and sunny. He had a nice touch.

As she went about her business the rest of the day – picking up grocery treats, checking Caesar's for casting calls, stopping by the cleaners – she mused about fathers. About Richard and his, about her own two daddies – the one she didn't know and Daddy Riley. Before he and Barney left, Richard asked her, "Did you love your father? Did he love you?" She told him what she knew about the biological sire who had planted her in Virginia's belly before striking out from Arkansas to Chicago. And Richard was very curious about Daddy Riley, the good man who had helped raise her, even after her mother died and she turned bad and unmanageable, a drunk-as-a-skunk teenager cursing him out. Her recent details were sparse since Daddy Riley had moved last year to Houston with Erma Jean.

What she didn't tell Richard, though, was that, as she communicated the bits available to her, a spellbinding image rose up from some locked recess of her mind: Daddy Riley's long middle finger slicing down the crack of Virginia's buttocks in her faded print housedress as he stood with Virginia leaning on him against the refrigerator. The image was mesmerizing. It was like a pointer into sexual territory she desperately needed to unlock.

She couldn't reconcile this rank, sensual moment that they were enjoying to the fullest with Virginia's unsexy housedress and Daddy Riley calling her "mother" most of the time? Or the fact that she who had lived in their three-room shotgun house had never seen them so much as hold hands or kiss. What else had they kept hidden under the unpaid bills and Virginia's loud arguing? And how were kids supposed to learn what grownups knew about quality probing and opening amidst grunty everyday life? The incongruity of it all. The innocence and the devilishness.

She couldn't figure out what Virginia was thinking or feeling. That was troubling. She herself had been on the receiving end of many men's fingers. What was on her own mind during those times, and why did it seem as if Virginia was experiencing something much richer? Was this married love? Spiritual union? Raunchy as a juke joint jelly-roll blues yet sacred as carvings of Shiva in coitus on southern India temple walls.

The unanswerable questions, the dark secrecy of it all was what bothered her the most. If she didn't understand this, what else didn't she get about this thing that she'd been doing and letting boys and men do to her since she was twelve? That slicing finger was a hint, a warning, a lure, an invitation into everything she didn't know – but should – about her own sexual self and psyche.

That night, she carried a host of fathers, sons, husbands, brothers, and boyfriends to bed with her. She woke early the next morning, straight out of an upsetting but unremembered dream, her heart pumping, head half blanketed, a string of thoughts racing through her mind. She was fascinated by men and their masculinity, but afraid of them, too. And that fear had sucked power from every aspect of her life. She put dicks in the place of a daddy. Had lots of dicks — but no daddy. Instead of a mother and father, she succored herself with what she found, with what came to her — tits and dicks, so-called "lovers." No parents, just body parts. In her own self, she was turning around a lot of the stuff, especially the female stuff. And maybe if she found daddy, she could come clean with the dicks.

She'd had moments before of knowing what she needed to do — like the dim realizations after her birthday night fight with Curtis, like what she understood at the 30th Street train station with Margo. But she hadn't made good on those flashes of illumination. That wasn't going to happen this time.

Flinging off the cover, wide awake, she shot up out of the bed. Booking a flight to Houston. She had to see Daddy Riley. If he could stand there against their old fridge, a man, as solid and calm in the midst of emotion as he'd been all of her life, he should be able to help her. With luck, she could arrive in time for his birthday. She was storming her past and her future — ready or not.

December, 1994
Houston, Texas

CHAPTER 14

The guy who asked her was she coming home as they waited for the carousel to spin out their luggage was one of the ones she had caught ogling her body the hardest when she reached up for her carry-on bag, her short jacket having risen high enough to give a full rounded view of her figure in stretch knit pants.

"Not exactly. I'm paying my stepfather a visit."

"You look familiar."

She couldn't decide if he was being fresh or southern friendly, but would have bet money that he'd never seen her before.

"People tell me that all the time." She almost gave him her name, "Deneice."

"Well, I grew up here. Just moved back to take a new job." He reached in his suit jacket pocket and handed her a card. Bright yellow seashell logo. Oil company manager. "Call me if you have time. I can show you the city."

He wheeled away without retrieving any more luggage. All he wanted was to say something to her. It wasn't even a decent pass.

The taxi driver was another story. He loaded her and her two bags into his gold and black cab, verified the address she gave him, and then put his attention on getting to their destination. Okay with her. Before she left home, Daddy Riley got her on the phone, talking back and forth with Erma Jean about picking her up. Erma Jean really brought back their old Kirby Street neighborhood. Who would have predicted that the stray child Daddy Riley had helped feed was now, years later, helping him? Eventually, they figured out the transport details. Told her to take a taxi and come over to the restaurant.

Out of the window, loops and multiple lanes of freeway, wide open expanses of well-cut commercial grass, undistinguished strip malls, tall steel and brick buildings. Closer to what seemed to be town, hardly a person in sight, except in their American-made cars and trucks. She sneezed violently, then sneezed again and swiped her eyes with the back of her hand before remembering not to do that. It was the best way to get germs in the body. She really didn't intend to be sick while she was in Houston. Whatever was down here for her, she wanted to be present for it.

On December 9th, Daddy Riley would be seventy-nine years old. "79 on 9," he said with satisfaction. Why not have your big bash when you're eighty? she had asked him. Seventy-nine's fine as wine, he rhymed, and eighty ain't promised to me. She told them she was on break and wanted to come for Daddy Riley's celebration. But she worried that, with so much going on, she wouldn't have space to be one-on-one with him. Erma Jean's "it's only gonna be us" still rang like a lot of folks – all of whom would undoubtedly be making each other feel like boon skin blood kin. She'd never felt that sense of inalienable belonging anywhere, with any group of people.

The two of them had been too polite to ask why after all these years she was making the visit she'd never gotten around to before. Once, right after leaving State, she had returned, and never set foot in Arkansas again. Three or four times, in a flurry, she had talked up plans to do so. But something more important came up each time. She always knew Daddy Riley was there and that the years were passing. But the connection felt anchored in some other arrested life, like those people in the airplane magazine article about cryogenics who remained frozen in suspended animation.

So, now, she was having this father-daughter revival to establish

– finally – who she was, what she wanted, and how to be happy, to heal her issues around men and sex. If Daddy Riley and Virginia on the refrigerator was the powerful union of body and spirit that she knew deep inside she yearned for, could she learn what she needed to co-create it?

Richard used to have a sign in his Center for Enlightenment study, "Transform or Die." He had taken it down, saying it was too harsh for most people. But now she got its truth. There were points at which, if you didn't change, then you could just give it up – whatever the "it" was – until the next time around – whenever the hell that might be. She hadn't made it this far for nothing. No stopping, no dying now.

The scenery outside the cab had drastically changed. Gas stations and bars were popping up, and black, brown, and white people appeared, not just in cars, but on the sidewalks. Kids riding their bikes. Repairmen getting in and out of generic minivans. Voices and radios and angry horns honking. Late afternoon noise. Welcome sounds of life pulling her forward to see more clearly out of the tinted front windshield.

She spied the sign as the driver slowed and pulled in. "Swanky Jean's" in bold lettered lights, and slightly smaller under that, "Soul Food Restaurant." It looked like a big, friendly house, glass windowed across the front. Just eyeing it made her smell catfish, string beans and potatoes, fried okra, and coconut cake.

Getting her stiff legs out of the car, she saw the two men waving at her as one of them got up from their booth by the door and came slowly down the steps. A regal old guy, with only the hint of a stoop in his shoulders. Full pleasant face, tan lines and creases, a neat moustache. Not Daddy Riley! This elderly gentleman was more vigorous and twinkling, but also thinner and darker than she thought Daddy Riley to be. She tensed. What if she couldn't recognize him after so many absent years?

At the bottom of the steps, he met her eyes and said "Neicy." It was his voice, the quiet, measured one she remembered, and the sound made her heart catch in her throat. He stood self-possessed, even if a bit awkward. She felt awkward, too. Still, her arms reached out hesitantly toward him and he gathered her into a welcoming hug. The two of them had probably never embraced before. Dizzy, she gave him a smile.

"Daddy Riley."

"Neicy."

"It's me. I finally got here."

He was checking out the features of her upturned face – down-turning almond eyes, even brows, nice nose, and smooth, dented lips. "You still just as pretty as ever. I thought you'd maybe make it one of these ole days."

Her momentary guilt didn't stop the happiness. She saw acceptance in his stare as he threw back his head and regarded her. The port of stomach that used to jut out from him wasn't there anymore, disappeared like some of his hair. She was so glad to be here.

In the dense, muggy air and muted gold sunshine, she sensed the taxi driver waiting on his side of the car.

"How much do I owe you?" Daddy Riley asked, reaching into his pocket.

"Thirty-eight dollars."

Daddy Riley gave him a five and two twenties, and they shook hands.

"Thanks. Take it easy."

"Thank you."

Faced with the gentle rectitude that had always been Daddy Riley, with this homey restaurant whose steps she was climbing now, carry-on bag in hand, she could no more have discussed her earlier thoughts about tits, dicks, and sexual power with Daddy Riley than she could have talked with him when she was in ninth grade about her period or the boys she messed around with! Never mind her galvanizing image of his finger hugging Virginia's rear in their Little Rock kitchen and her do-or-die determination.

Before they could fully make it inside the door, the elderly gent who had been waiting at the window with Daddy Riley began beaming at her.

"This is my friend, Horace Dinkins," Daddy Riley introduced.

Mr. Dinkins made an effort to stand, pressing his hands on the tabletop and gearing up to get on his feet.

"Nice to meet you, Mr. Dinkins. Please, keep your seat." She waved him back down, marveling at the instant emergence of that old, engrained courtesy. Please, keep your seat.

"Neicy, you hungry? Are you thirsty? What can I get you to drink?" Daddy Riley was situating her on the side of the booth opposite Mr. Dinkins. He stood at the open end, in an aisle between the row of booths along the window and some small tables in the center of the clean, black and white tiled floor.

"Some hot tea, with lots of lemon. And honey if you have it." After being flushed outside, now she was feeling a chill.

"We got that. Rest here a minute while I go find Erma Jean." The way he settled her in her seat, the hesitation as he moved away, his purposeful gait – all felt familiar. He walked down the row and around the counter into double swinging doors. Two tables on that end and the farthest booth had people eating. She turned and saw that the side of the restaurant behind her was empty.

"Things'll be filling up soon." Mr. Dinkins made a play for her attention.

"So, the restaurant is busy, huh?"

"As a run full of chickens at feeding time. Folks here was just too happy when Miss Jean opened the place."

Daddy Riley had said they were doing well with it. She kept looking around.

"Riley says you the only child him and your mama raised."

What? He'd finally captured her interest, so she gave it completely to him.

"I had six boys and one girl. Me and my wife put 'em all through school, three of them went to college. I was working down in Port Arthur when they called me to come home, my wife had taken sick. I told the boss man to give me what was coming to me and got on back up here. She died the next day."

Had she been ill? How long ago did this happen? Were the children still around? Mr. Dinkins didn't look happy or sad.

Returned and standing by her side, Daddy Riley asked, "Is Dink here keeping you company? Erma Jean's busy in the kitchen. Let me take you on back."

Busy was an understatement. The kitchen was a fury of food-laden surfaces and pots boiling on the institutional stove. One dark man in a very stained, white butcher's apron was seasoning a large pan of chicken. A girlish young woman worked at one of the sinks, washing iceberg lettuce. A stout, older woman was dangerously cutting up raw sweet potatoes. In the middle of it all was Erma Jean, brushing a stray piece of sweaty orange hair out of her face. Broad-faced and freckled, big-boned and bold, she looked like she had a long lifetime ago hellishly glaring at her from beside Daddy Riley and his truck when she passed them on her way home from school. That must have been around sixth grade, right before Erma Jean's mama moved her motley flock out of the neighborhood.

"Neicy!" Erma Jean started to walk around the large steel central rectangle to greet her, but a bubbling lid pulled her back. She lifted it off and turned one of the knobs on the stove. "We're glad you got here. How was your trip?" Erma Jean gave her an all-over scrutiny and then glanced back at the pot.

"It was fine." Her curiosity piqued by what all was on the crowded table, she moved nearer to the center. Saw the long casseroles of elbow macaroni, onion, mushrooms and cheese in front of Erma Jean, then walked closer to Erma Jean's side.

"I've got to do this butter and white wine secret to pour on the mac and cheese. These colored folks love it, even though it's real different, but it's one thing I make myself." Erma Jean stirred the thickening, hot sauce.

"Ouch!" A big pop of it splatted out of the boiler – "Watch out, Neicy!" – and landed on her hand. She rubbed the burned place as Daddy Riley and Erma Jean added, "Be careful." The other three quit what they were doing and stared. Then she sneezed, and they all recoiled, automatically protecting the food.

"Dar," Erma Jean was speaking to Daddy Riley, "you'd better take Neicy back out. Neicy, we'll get a chance to visit later." Erma Jean raised her voice to the cooks and helper, "Miss Bea, Walter, Whitney, this is Neicy, Mr. Riley's daughter and my play sister from New York."

"Hi." "Pleased to meet you." "Nice to meet you."

"Nice to meet you all, too." Daddy Riley's hand on her elbow steered her through the swinging doors.

"Her tea is on the order-up shelf," Whitney spoke softly as she shook a colander of lettuce. "I put it in a styrofoam cup."

They said goodbye to Mr. Dinkins on the way out. Tea in hand, she realized she was being hustled. But she was ready for some rest. Daddy Riley promised they'd come back to the restaurant for dinner. One nice thing about this visit was she wouldn't have to add food to her list of worries!

"Why does Erma Jean call you 'Dar'"? she asked as they pulled off.

"I used to question her about that, but I finally stopped. She says she can't remember. Says she don't know." He made another slow, left turn.

This block was more residential, with lovely oak trees. "Swank was Erma Jean's husband's name, right?" She thought she recalled that accurately.

"Yep." Daddy Riley paused. "One of the nicest men you'd ever wanna meet."

"What happened to him?" That part was a blank.

"He fell off the roof, not that high up. But he landed head first on the concrete patio and severed his spinal cord." Another one of his pauses. "Not long after that is when Erma Jean persuaded me to move into their house with her, so what if people would gossip. We knew we weren't doing nothing such as that. She's like a daughter to me. My place was getting bought up by the government for a piece of the interstate highway. It was her idea to name this new restaurant after him."

She wanted to ask why Erma Jean decided to go from Arkansas to Houston, and how come he came with her, but her head started hurting. Actually, her eyes were hurting and her head was throbbing. She would feel better after a nap.

She did. So much so that when Daddy Riley came down the steps of the split-level to the guest quarters on the lower third and tentatively called her name, she had already opened her eyes and was taking stock of her physical condition.

"I'm up, Daddy Riley," she yelled back.

"How you feel?" He'd moved closer, but still stood somewhere beyond the door.

"Much better, thank you."

"That's good. We can leave whenever you're ready. I'll be upstairs."

Driving over, she really noticed the car, a beautiful old black and silver Lincoln in auto show condition.

"I would've been just as happy keeping my truck, but Erma Jean said a little luxury wouldn't kill me before it was my time to die." He chuckled.

"It's a really nice car. The closest thing you'd see to this in New York are some real limousines. A lot of them pass where I live on their way to the U.N."

Walking through the restaurant door, she saw that Mr. Dinkins was right. The place was practically full.

"It'll slack off in about an hour or so," Daddy Riley explained. "Not like on the weekends where it's packed until closing time."

He seated her at a table on the other side, away from the kitchen. There was a back room over here that she hadn't noticed and a couple of people entering it from the dining room. Before she could ask anything, Erma Jean came from behind the counter.

"Not still sneezing, are you, Neicy?" She seemed jovial but still busy, like she was keeping her mind on a few too many items. And she'd changed her clothes. The blue, red, and yellow dress patterned with hibiscus flowers made her stand out even more. Her own pale blue slacks and matching striped sweater were schoolgirl demure in comparison. "I've still got my eye on the kitchen. Carrie didn't show."

"Do you want me to handle the seating?" Daddy Riley asked.

"No, it's alright. You take care of Neicy. Oh, but you could do one something that would help me out. Jonai and 'em are expecting a bunch of new people for the Raffers meeting tonight. If you see any folks looking confused, point them to the back room. Okay?" Erma Jean was already pivoting to go.

"Okay," Daddy Riley said to her loud-printed back.

She was trying to process what kind of meeting. Rappers? But Daddy Riley had lowered himself into his chair and was beaming like someone about to spring a surprise.

"Neicy, do you still love rabbit?"

Rabbit? Who was Rabbit? No. Rabbit. An Easter bunny ran 'cross her mind. Then a squirrel. Then, a rabbit. Do I love rabbit?

Daddy Riley sat expectant and beaming. Obviously, this was supposed to be something real good. Nothing she could do 'til she got her bearings but improvise.

"Rabbit!... Boy!"

"I bet you haven't had any rabbit since you left from down here." He was so pleased with himself.

"Naw... naw. Wow..."

"You remember how you used to like it? Crisp fried almost done

215

and then lightly smothered in its own juices with onions and bell pepper."

It still wasn't coming back to her. She couldn't believe she ever loved to eat rabbit.

"You want me to fix you some? Frank and his sons had luck hunting. I got one dressed and saved up for you."

"Wow... yeah... that would be great." There was no other answer to give him.

"Hold on a minute." Four people were hesitating in the middle of the entrance, looking around. Daddy Riley headed toward them. "Must be the Raffers."

What were they saying? Rappers? Raffers?

He directed the group to the back and returned to her, still happy. "It's gonna take me a little while to get that rabbit cooked up for you." His voice trailed off as he tried to figure out what to do with her, giving her a chance to ask her question.

"What are you and Erma Jean calling the people going to that back room?"

"Raffers. R-A-F-F-E-R-S. R-F-S'ers. Raffers. The real name is 'Recovering From Slavery.' That's what it stands for."

"I've never heard of anything like that."

"They meet here every night God sends at seven o'clock. Says as hard as it is to make it through each day being a black person in America, you have to have somewhere to come whenever you need it."

"What do they do?"

"Anybody can go to the meeting, anytime, long as they black. You want to see for yourself, let me take you and introduce you to Jonai. When your rabbit is ready, I'll come back and get you."

There were about twenty people in a room that would hold maybe five times that many sitting in a raggedy circle. A few were talking, a few others eating, some were as quiet and still as meditation. When Daddy Riley stopped, hand on her arm, just past the door, a man at the rear came toward them looking for all the world like Huey Newton on the steps of the Oakland, California court house, only with a seasoned set of dreadlocks on his head.

"Jonai, how you doing?" Daddy Riley greeted.

"Keeping the peace, one minute at a time. How's life treating you?"

"Can't complain, especially right now. I want you to meet my daughter, Deneice."

"Deneice, welcome, sister. Where're you from?"

"New York City."

"How long are you going to be here?"

"Only a few days. I arrived this afternoon."

"She was asking me about the Raffers," Daddy Riley thrust his hands in his pockets, "so I brought her on back."

"We're about to begin. Stay and sit in with us." Jonai's invitation was firm, but without any pressure.

"Thank you. Is it alright for me to get up and leave anytime? Daddy Riley's making me something to eat. When it's ready, I'll have to go."

"No problem. Just ease out whenever."

"I'll stick my head in the door when your rabbit's ready." Daddy Riley started beaming again. The kick he was getting out of cooking her that rabbit made her want to hug him.

Jonai bowed slightly, arm and hand extended sidewise like an usher in church guiding her down the aisle into an available pew. "Sit wherever feels comfortable."

A nearby chair with the door in full view felt right. Changing his place, Jonai took a seat in the center, looked at his watch, crossed his legs and leaned forward.

"Welcome, Sisters and Brothers. My name is Jonai. I'm the anchor for tonight." He uncrossed his legs, then re-crossed them, sitting up straighter in his chair.

"For those who are here for the first time, this is Recovering

From Slavery. A core of us black people in Houston started the group a year and a half ago so that any black person who needed someplace at the end of the day where they could vent, or be supported, or just rest in the company of other folks who 'looked like them,' as we say, and who understood their experiences – well, they would have some place to come. Our meetings usually last one to two hours, but we have this room for as long as we like and folks who have gotten to talking, or crying, or whatever sometimes stay longer."

Crying? She felt a tingle of apprehension.

Jonai slowly looked at everyone in the circle. "Let's introduce ourselves and, if you'd like to, share what brought you out tonight." He cleared his throat and planted his feet. "Like I said, my name is Jonai. I've been with Recovering From Slavery since the beginning. I'm a survivor of the war against black men in this country, a Vietnam vet, trying to more fully love myself and all of my people. For the next three evenings, I'm going to be chairing the meeting."

The insurance salesman to Jonai's left was also a regular. So were the two women next in the circle, who didn't say what they did except they belonged to the same Methodist church. The sister beside them – skipping a seat – looked like she'd drifted in off the streets. She only said who she was, "Irene."

"My name is Neicy Jones." She was next, at this curve of the circle. "I'm sitting in as a first-time visitor tonight. I got into town this afternoon from New York to see my father and I'm happy to be here."

The people after her were the group of four Daddy Riley had guided in – a man and woman who seemed to be in their fifties, dressed in business suits, and a younger pair in their twenties, in student attire.

The older woman started talking, gesturing with her eyes to include all four of their contingent. "We're from the university." She sounded very authoritative, very professional, but then stumbled as she said her name, agony suddenly sweeping her face. "We just returned from Rwanda." She looked like she was about to lose it.

The older man took up where she left off. "We're shell-shocked." He glanced at Jonai. "Suffering from post-traumatic stress, you might say." His attempt at a wry laugh didn't make it to first base.

The young man waded in. "We went as part of an international delegation to find out whether or not genocidal atrocities had actually been committed in the war between the Hutu's and Tutsi's." His eyes glazed over, and he looked off blankly at the wall as the young woman placed her arm around his shoulder.

"They had." The older woman partially recaptured her poise. "We couldn't believe what we found out."

And then, compulsively, all four of them talked, recounting their trip and what they'd witnessed. How they'd embarked skeptical that things could really be as horrible as some of the confidential sources reported, what they went through to get themselves connected with Tutsis at the village level, the one mass grave they had seen.

Everything she had read during the spring months as the situation unfolded was coming back to her, revivified. She recalled the gray, bloated bodies, and the rivers red with blood. Images haunting her sleep for days after she'd seen them in news magazines. Descriptions of corpses frozen into grotesque postures, fending off machete blows. She was remembering it all, sitting with the others in the circle as if they were at a wake, contemplating the dead and wordlessly comforting one another, their collective emotion a palpable ring.

"Why?" The stoosh brother next to Jonai's original seat finally spoke out. "Why?" he said again. It wasn't a question requiring response or analysis, just a note someone sounded to encapsulate their pain and bewilderment, but, blessedly, not any shame, since eyes other than their own were not looking at them. She had asked herself that same question trying to find understanding. Some ancient stain in the blood of being human? Definitely not peculiar to black people. Post-colonial sickness? Brother-against-brother madness? Like the U.S. civil war. What?

Their sorrow hung around them. Would that there was some comparable way the whole country could sit in a bonding like this and grieve the ravages of slavery! What white people did to black people in Africa, what black people did to each other, what white people did to black people in the United States. All of it, the whole soiled tapestry.

Jonai drew in his chair, tightening up the circle, stretching out his arms to embrace both sides and pulling in everyone else to do the same. Standing up to scoot forward, she spotted Daddy Riley at the door, quietly looking. She walked over and the two of them stepped outside.

"You can stay longer if you want to." He was searching her face.

"It's alright." She gripped his hand holding hers a little tighter. "I can leave now, it's alright."

"You sure?" His grasp was firm and soothing. They'd never held hands like this before.

"I think I'm sure." Did she want to stay? Did she want to go? A part of her was still in the room laden with grief. "It's hard being black."

Daddy Riley snapped to with a little jerk of surprise, but came back quick. "Harder even than you think." There was a world of comprehension in his five words that acknowledged and absorbed her sadness. "But a good thing, too. Right?"

You're a good thing, she was feeling. Squeeze his hand. Just say, "Right."

"A lot happens in that room." He stayed with her mood as he led her away to the main restaurant area.

"Do you ever go to the meetings?" she wanted to know.

"I go for a spell, then I rest awhile. I'm resting now." He smiled.

She stopped a few steps from the dining room entrance, making an effort to rise to his smile. "Didn't you know there's no rest for the weary?"

"Rest standing up. Rest when you're working and hurting. It's always there, underneath. If we hadn't found that out, all of us would be dead by now."

She'd read something like that about the rest underneath. But the essay had been talking about jazz music. Same pain, same point.

"Come on and sit down. I hope you're not too tired to eat this rabbit." No, she wasn't, as she sat there and let her kin from Rwanda, the meeting in the back room, Daddy Riley's subtle comfort level in her bones.

Him bringing out the rabbit created a scene. It wasn't exactly sizzling like those tandoori dishes in an Indian restaurant, but the way he was carrying it, the steam and the specialness had the same effect. A mean-faced, very black guy at the next table sniffed and asked, "Is that rabbit?"

Daddy Riley grinned. "You bet."

"Man, I'd like a taste of that. I didn't see no rabbit on the menu."

"Ain't no menu item, sorry. This a treat for my visiting daughter."

"Pleased to meet you, miss." He reached over and extended his hand, not looking as mean anymore. "L.P. Barnett."

"My name's Neicy."

The heat from the rabbit was warming her face. It was in a pan, cut up into nice pretty pieces. "Daddy Riley, this looks great."

"I'll be right back with the rice and vegetables."

"Little lady, you gon eat all of that?" L.P. Barnett was only half teasing. He had a serious eye on her rabbit.

"Maybe, maybe not." She fell into the groove. "Depends on how the drop falls."

He cracked up. "You ain't no snotty-nosed cook and I damn sure ain't no greasy Sunday preacher, hanging over the dough tray." He laughed again.

"Okay, maybe I'll share."

Daddy Riley returned. Fluffy white rice. Candied sweet potatoes. Butter beans.

"This a feast, Daddy Riley."

"All I made was the rabbit. Dig in."

"I'm just about to. Please eat with me. And I promised I'd give Mr. Barnett a taste."

L.P. Barnett nudged his pork chops to the side of his plate and passed it. She dished him a healthy piece. "Daddy Riley?" She poised with the serving fork in her hand.

"You go on and get started. I'll chime in in a minute, when I cool down from the cooking."

She made her own plate, took a nice-sized bite of the rabbit, chewed, and swallowed. Her cells lit up like a Christmas tree, flooded with memory. The kitchen on Kirby Street. Her sitting on one side of the table, around nine or ten years old, Daddy Riley at the head end, smiling. The texture of rabbit flesh a little squeamish in her mouth but the flavor wonderful. And the taste of Daddy Riley's approval, his animated appreciation of her eating the wild game, even more wonderful than that. In the flood, she remembered that her mother Virginia wouldn't touch it, and heard Ray Charles in the background. Felt the naked light bulb hanging overhead.

"Good, huh?" Daddy Riley asked.

She was in both of the two places at once, nodding her girl head "yes," taking another bite of the juicy rabbit. The only important person missing from her split tableaux was Virginia, when Erma Jean, right on cue as emotional double although she wasn't Daddy Riley's wife, sailed in from the kitchen, railing, "Y'all still eating that nasty ole squirrel?"

"It's not a nasty ole squirrel" – she almost yelled, almost added "Mama" – "it's a real good rabbit!"

"Same thing. Dar, I'm not gon let you keep cooking that wild meat in my kitchen."

The red and yellow flowers on Erma Jean's loud blue dress were popping, thankfully helping to bring her Deneice self back into one here-and-now reality.

"Well," she said, in her most sophisticated voice, "I'm glad you let Daddy Riley make it for me this time."

As Daddy Riley and Erma Jean went on playfully bickering about Erma Jean's immaculate kitchen and his incorrigible love of possum, rabbit, and squirrel, she ate her food, daintily licking the points of her fingers. Daddy Riley took some, and she gave L.P. Barnett another thigh of the rabbit.

"I'm going home with you all," Erma Jean announced. "Miss Bea and Walter can lock up the place tonight."

Besides themselves, there were only two people left in the restaurant.

In the back seat of the car, full of a long exciting day, she almost laid down on the inviting black leather like a tired child. But sat up straight 'til they got her home, then fell out in her bed, their voices upstairs in the kitchen and their muffled footsteps sounding squishy in her sleepy head.

CHAPTER 15

"Nooo, Daddy Riley, I was not running from a rabbit." She felt way better this morning, laughing and protesting his teasing, sitting on her side of the breakfast table downing more orange juice with her vitamin C's.

"Well, maybe it was that devil coming at you out of the waterline cut-off box 'cause you didn't want to go to Sunday School. That's how Beulah used to scare you."

Another piece of lost childhood trivia that he was having fun with. "No, Daddy Riley. In the dream, I was running from a kinda short man with a felt hat on his head, like out in the middle of nowhere. But I jumped into the weeds in the vacant lot next to our house and he drove off in his car. There was some more afterward that I can't remember." Not being able to was frustrating.

"You're frowning just like your mama when she was vexed." Daddy Riley searched her face. "Neicy, do you remember your father? That dream of yours put me in mind of him. That's how he was built and your mother said he always wore stetson hats."

"I know his picture, but I never saw him in real life."

"Yes, you did. But seems like you don't remember it. Virginia didn't think I knew this, but he used to come 'round the house on the q.t., kind of sneaky, and try to get a glimpse of you whenever he was down visiting his ma and pa. A time or two he caught you playing in the street with the other children and tried to woo you over to him."

"I don't remember that." She couldn't stop frowning. "How old was I?"

"Around five to ten, something like that. Yeah, you were about five when your mother and me got together."

"So, what happened after that?"

"After me and Virginia got together?"

"No! After I was ten."

"He stopped coming 'round. I don't know why. Like I said, we didn't talk about him. But, yeah, you've seen your daddy live a few times in your life."

"He wasn't my daddy."

"Well... your mother said he was."

She pushed her chair back from the table, hard. "If he was my daddy, why didn't he make me know him? Answer me that."

"I don't know as how I'm the one who's got the answers, baby..."

The doorbell rang. Then, whoever rang the bell also lifted up the horseshoe knocker and clapped it five or six times. So did they think nobody would hear the bell?

"Excuse me." Daddy Riley swallowed the last of his coffee from the old china teacup as he got up from the table. "That's Jason next door. I told him I'd sit with his grandmother 'til the care lady came so he wouldn't be late for class. It's not gonna be long, less than half an hour. I'll be right back."

"Just a minute," he called, after the next two knocks of the horseshoe and stopped them.

Jason was a clean, good-looking white boy. He and Daddy Riley gave each other a soul shake, knuckling clenched fists, at the stained glass doors before they went out.

Her daddy. Her real father, David Walker. She knew next to nothing about him. She looked at herself in the vestibule mirror. Every part of her that was not her mother, Virginia, had to have come from her father. Virginia's frown and her luxuriant hair. High, slightly flat cheekbones. The roundness part of her eyes. But so much width between them. That had to be her daddy. The perfect curves of her mouth. Cute little ears. David Walker. She stepped back to insert more of herself into the picture. These sturdy shoulders belonged to Virginia and the long, graceful arms. But not this softness on her same frame. More behind than her mama had any day of her life, less bosom but fleshy thighs. Without a doubt, her daddy had left her his body, but he still took his body away. Before she knew it. Before she even knew herself.

Opening the door, Daddy Riley was surprised to see her, a bluster in the entrance hallway. "The care lady got there early. Neicy, are you alright?"

She scowled at her face in the mirror. "I'm trying to figure things out about my father."

Daddy Riley's "Oh" sounded like understanding. "I can tell you the little I know." He led them to the couch. "It's not much. Virginia got pregnant with you right before David Walker moved to Chicago. She didn't tell him you were on the way. If I got it pieced together right, he learned about you from Mamie Brown. You remember Mamie?"

She shook her head, "No."

"Mamie lived down the street in Miss Jackson's rent house. Sgt. Brown was at the air base. Anyhow, some kind of way she got news back and forth about him. From what I understand, Virginia didn't want you to have too much to do with him and she pretty much kept him away from you."

"Why did she do that? Why did he go off in the first place?"

"Well, he was a sporting man. Into gambling and fast money. Hustling here and there, whatever means he could. That's why he left, I think. A whole lot more fish to fry in the big city."

"Mama could still have let me see him."

"I'm not arguing with you about that. Like I said, I don't know all the in's and out's between them. When I met her, she was trying to settle down. She was tired of..."

His pause was so long it made her lift her head and look at him. He was rubbing bristles above one jaw and grappling for words.

"... shifting around. She wanted you to have a good life."

She still didn't see why she couldn't have a good life and her father.

"That's about all I know." He sounded tired.

She was feeling tired too, all of her morning freshness gone, and her throat was hurting again.

"Daddy Riley, I'm going and lie down, okay? If I drop asleep, will you please wake me up? I don't want to sleep too long."

What finally woke her was the sound of voices – Erma Jean's and Daddy Riley's. The clock radio red-blared 2:30. Why didn't Daddy Riley wake her up like she asked him? Flushed from dashing into her sweats and rushing upstairs, she confronted him with her question.

"I came down and called your name a couple of times."

"You don't know Dar," Erma Jean cut in. "He thinks sleep is sacred. If he sees you're out for the count, he's not going to throw a bucket of water. Here. I brought you all some lunch. Vegetable beef soup. Very good."

"Let me get you some, Neicy." Daddy Riley reached for a bowl from the cabinet. "Erma Jean, you want a taste, too?"

"No, indeed. I come home at lunch to get away from food. You know that. But since Neicy's not feeling too good, y'all can go on and eat in front of me."

"Look at this, Neicy." Daddy Riley set her soup down in front of her and drew an old photograph album toward them. He pointed to a picture of her perched in the crook of his elbow, a box of groceries under his other arm.

"I look so little."

Erma Jean pulled around closer so she could see, too.

"You're older than you look," Daddy Riley studied, "about seven right there. You didn't start growing good fashion until after then."

"That's about when I start to remember."

"There's that snapshot of me!" Erma Jean interrupted, grabbing at a photo on the opposite page and laughing.

There Erma Jean was, a bit older than seven, standing in front of Daddy Riley's saintly black pickup truck – harum-scarum clothes, wild hair, and blazing red eyes.

"I took that picture," Daddy Riley said, "and when Virginia got the roll developed and saw it, she pitched a sukey. She always accused me of being Erma Jean's daddy. Nothing I could say to make her drop that outta her mind."

"Well, you could've been. How do you know you wasn't?" Erma Jean was giving Daddy Riley a piercing scowl.

"Look, Miss Lady, I know. Men can know, too."

"Most men don't know nothing but what they're doing when they're doing it."

This sounded like an argument they had had before. Many times, as a matter of fact.

"Did your mother ever say to you that I was your father?"

"She didn't say."

"See..."

"But you could have been."

"Well, I know for a fact that Daddy Riley was my stepfather."

They both looked at her like she'd said something crazy. But it set Erma Jean off.

"Who the hell cares about stepfathers?! Anybody can be anybody's stepfather, that's no big deal."

"Hey now, it's alright. Our chillun belong to us all." He repositioned the photograph album and turned to a page at the back. "Look at this."

Erma Jean crowding her shoulder, they both looked. He pointed to a picture of a very attractive young woman, eighteen or nineteen years old. Dark, wavy hair upswept in a fashionable roll, flawless milk and honey complexion, direct, friendly eyes, a vulnerable mouth.

Something about the way the girl held herself, plus the print of her dress and her painted fingernails made her think of Frida Kahlo.

"That's my daughter, Pearl."

Erma Jean turned the album for a better view. "You never showed me this picture." Her voice was accusatory.

"Well, I'm showing it to you now." He paused. "Virginia thought you" – he was addressing Erma Jean, ignoring her – "looked as much like me as Pearl does in that picture."

Yeah, standing off to the side, away from Daddy Riley, Erma Jean, and the picture, she could see the resemblance. And she herself didn't favor any one of them. "Why did you want us to see this picture, Daddy Riley?"

"No reason." He sounded sad.

All those questions about fathers probably made him think about this daughter.

"What happened to her?" Erma Jean pressed.

"I lost track. It's a long story."

"Tell us, please, Dar."

"Yeah, Daddy Riley."

"It's not a nice story." He cleared his throat. "But I guess I can tell it to you." He cleared his throat again. "White men tried to get their hands on Pearl from the time she was ten. I did everything I could to keep them away, but back in those days – it was still the depression, and a Ku Klux Klan county – you had to be careful. They could've killed me and my whole family." He'd been staring out toward the door, now he looked straight at them. "I thought everything was fine until I found out that, unbeknownst to me, after Pearl got bigger, my wife was letting white men in the house to see her while I was at work and keeping the money."

She couldn't believe it. What kind of black mother woman would do a thing like that?!

"I did everything I could think of to stop her, but I couldn't sit at home everyday. I couldn't stop her. Couldn't stop the white sapsuckers. Couldn't do nothing. I knew if I kept staying around it, I was gonna end up killing somebody sooner or later, so I left. Joined the war and went overseas. Men killing men over there, for sure. Lucky for me, I just dug trenches and worked in the mess. When I got back and contacted my wife, Pearl was long gone. A few years after she ran off, she sent back this picture. Nobody ever heard hide nor hair of her since."

"Oh, Daddy Riley!" She was devastated. Erma Jean had tears in her eyes. No longer feuding like rival daughters, both of them were trying to comfort him. He lowered his head, then raised it.

"I been thinking lately that the only thing I didn't do was talk to Pearl myself. Try to sense her into helping herself and helping me fight her mama. But men didn't talk to their daughters about nothing like that. Leastwise, I didn't."

"Dar, there's no need for you to beat up on yourself..."

"Don't worry. I've already kicked myself 'til I wore my old ass out."

"Daddy Riley, please, don't do that any more!"

"I don't, sweethearts." He looked at the both of them as they straightened up from hugging him. "Something sorta made me tell you girls that story. I hardly ever even think about it anymore. I had to just let it go."

Now that would be a real letting go. When the sorrow is so big it pops you and it all runs out.

The three of them sat silent. Erma Jean finally roused herself.

"Time for me to get my butt on over to the Swank. Dar, come ride back with me. Oh, Neicy, I almost forgot. You have two messages on the answering machine. A girlfriend of yours calling from Pennsylvania to see if you arrived safe, and some sophisticated-sounding man."

The sophisticated man had to be Richard. He and Margo were the only people she'd given this number to besides building manager Birhan, and Birhan wouldn't phone unless her place was burning down. On his message, Richard was encouraging and asked in brief, sweet code whether the red amber bracelet he'd given her as a going-away present was fitting well on her wrist. When he clasped it shut at the airport, it had seemed a trifle big. Margo was out of Philly with Otis and dying to talk about Vivian staying in Italy to start a business with a man she had met over there. Well, she'd try to catch them both tomorrow. Right now, she wanted to enjoy the warm weather.

Out on the deck, she set her chair so the sun fell on her from behind. Immediately, she heard a mockingbird singing, a young one in the mimosa tree concertizing center stage with sound so piercing and true it cut through the density of air like a laser's beam. She hadn't seen a mockingbird in ages. Her mama's favorite bird. It hopped down to the railing and changed its tune. Sung a while and then whirred away.

The sun shadowed from a stray passing cloud. It was nice to relax, taking the whole world in. A sparrow braved the distance in front of her from one terra-cotta pot to the other. Arrested its own motion, tiny breast pumping. Snapped its head, blinked its eyes, pecked something from the drainage saucer beneath a jade plant. Hop-scotched along the edge of the deck.

She breathed in with the breeze, exhaled out to the yard. Heard a baby's insistent cries. She faced her chair toward the sun as clouds rolled over it and the baby cried louder. Somebody, take care of that child. But who takes care of the children? Who took care of Daddy Riley's daughter? Who truly took care of her? She got up and started coughing. In the house, she sank onto the couch.

Daddy Riley walked in and flipped on the lights. The way he stared made her realize she must be looking awful. He slowly came and sat down, arms bent over his knees.

"Neicy, are you alright?"

"Yes, I'm..." She was about to say "fine," but then it hit her. "No, I'm not alright. What kind of alright could I be? Growing up with nobody to see after me. My daddy ran off and left me. My mama cared more about playing cards and drinking than she did about my feelings, and then she up and died. And you, you never acted like you loved me. I guess I didn't count 'cause I wasn't your precious Pearl."

"Baby, please don't say that. Your mama and me did the best we could. And Virginia couldn't help herself. She liked to have fun."

"Well, she had it at my expense. Sending me down to Miz Hedgman's. Not paying me much attention. And you? You could have kept dancing with me. You could have kept holding my hands."

"Oh, Neicy." Daddy Riley looked miserable. Tears rolled down her face.

"Why didn't you love me and take care of me, Daddy Riley? I wanted you to want me, but I was afraid of you, too."

"Oh, baby, I'm so sorry. I was doing my best."

"I'm so tired of having to take care of me, all by myself."

"I tried to love you, Neicy, but you wouldn't let me."

"Why did you let me stop you? I was a girl, you were the grownup. Why didn't you make me let you?"

"Do you remember what you told me the night you came in from your sweet sixteen party?"

"I never had a sweet sixteen party."

"That's what you called it. But I didn't think it was a party, either. I think you just went out with some of those older kids you knew and got drunk."

It was dimly coming back. She remembered rum and coke, drinking a lot of 7-Up to supposedly get sober, throwing up.

"You shouldn't have let me go out with them. I had no business doing all those things I was into. Drinking. Boys and men. Sex."

"You had started to be bad like that even before Virginia died. That night when you turned sixteen, I couldn't do a thing with you. You were mad and mean as a pit bull. Your mama was dead, you told me, and I wasn't your daddy. So don't pretend to be acting like one. I tried to tell you I wasn't out to boss you or nothing. I just didn't want to see you do harm to yourself. You just got madder. Told me you were going where your real daddy was. When I told you your father had passed away, you started yelling and screaming, throwing everything you could get your hands on, tearing up the house."

"I don't remember any of that."

"You must've been drunker than I thought. I kept trying to talk to you, but you wouldn't listen. You told me I was lying about your father and you were going to find him and for me to just leave you alone..."

"Oh, Daddy Riley..."

"It's alright. You were having a real rough time. There was nobody to see after you, just me. And we never had all that much to do with one another directly. I let your mother deal with you. Beingst as how I was your stepfather, I was extra careful to stay in my place."

"Oh, Daddy Riley..."

"You were having a hard go of it, Neicy."

"Oh, Daddy Riley, we were a pitiful pair."

Daddy Riley's birthday! Whenever she glanced over at the present she brought him, she couldn't help but smile, warm with anticipation and with the memory of how they'd talked late into the night. The wounded girl hurt and anger that finally spilled out of her had cleared her system for good. When she apologized to Daddy Riley for erupting like an adolescent volcano, he'd just patted her on the shoulder and gave her a hug. The note he left on the breakfast table didn't say when he'd be back, just that he was running an errand for himself and picking up charcoal for the barbecue. Finishing the newspaper, she heard him come into the house and rushed up to greet him.

"Happy birthday to you, happy birthday to you, happy birthday, dear Daddy Riley." She giggled, trying to fit his long name into the two-syllable rhythm. "Happy birthday to you! And many more." She bass'ed that out as she reached him in the center of the big, open room and flung her arms wide, Broadway musical style.

"I don't know how many more I got coming, but thank you." He dropped a pharmacy bag on one of the living room chairs. "79 on 9. I wasn't sure I would make it this far." His khakis and plaid shirt jacket were rough, but he'd closely shaved, his moustache was trimmed, a blue Oilers cap hid his receding hairline. He looked great.

"Do you want to open your present now or save it for later?"

"You got me a present? You didn't have to do that. You coming down here is all the present I need."

"I know. But there's a little lagniappe, too." She handed him the oblong box, shining in metallic colors. "It's not much, but I wanted to get you something. And when I saw these..."

"It's a tie." He was hefting the box, turning it from corner to corner, giving it a shake. "Naw," he said, "too heavy for that. Must be a belt." He shook again. "That's what it is, it's a belt." He looked at her like he had solved the puzzle and was waiting for her to validate his answer.

She couldn't recall that anybody receiving a gift that she'd given them had ever brought her this much pleasure. She gently pushed him into a chair at the table. "Open it, and you'll find out."

He took off the ribbon, managing to preserve its swirled bow, but gave up on the paper, which was folded back and forth into itself and taped in too many places. He ripped it off, balanced the silver box against his midriff, and lifted up the top with his fingers. He had to set the box on the table and open the tissue before he could reach the suspenders inside.

"Jalousies!" he cried, letting them lengthen in front of him. "I've never had such a fancy set of suspenders."

"Do you like them?" she asked.

"I love 'em." He was rubbing the tips of his fingers over the satiny black material, examining the intricate trim. They really were gorgeous, the classiest pair she had ever seen. That's why she had bought them.

"I'm going to have to wear these to the party tomorrow."

"That's what I was hoping."

He was delicately handling the crosspiece at their back, figuring out how to adjust them. He let that go, stood up, held them again in front of his body, turned halfway around. Just like a woman who has put on a new dress and searches unconsciously for a mirror. He walked to the one in the vestibule. "The cat better find a new pair of pajamas to go with these guys." He was grinning like a cat.

"Those are really gonna look good on you, I can tell."

The twinkle on his face said he could see it, too. He walked back to the table, sat down in his chair. Started resettling the suspenders in their box.

"Where did you get these?"

"At a haberdashery on the upper east side. A boyfriend I had when I first moved to New York used to take me there with him."

"He must've had good taste."

"You mean me – or the store?"

"Both," Daddy Riley shot back.

"His taste was better than mine."

"You trying to say he wasn't worth all that much?"

"No, he was okay, just stuck on himself. His name was Trevor. He was from England and thought he brought royalty with him. The two of us didn't make it very far."

"Not like that nice fellow you were with, what was his name?"

"Curtis."

"For a while, I thought you two were gonna get married."

She shook her head, no. "Curtis wasn't into marriage."

"Oh, one of those playboy types?"

"Not exactly. He just didn't think he was meant to be with one woman." She sat down in the dinette chair, pulled it closer in. "Curtis wasn't a playboy, he was actually a very serious man. But he fell in love with women and women fell in love with him and, like, well, when I was with him, he had two other girlfriends at the same time."

"Hot stuff, huh?"

Self-conscious heat rose at the back of her neck. She tried to douse it, but the blush overtook her. "Well, maybe that, too. But I didn't want to get married, so it was alright with me." Her flushed body fluttered, leaned over and kissed him on one cheek under the bill of his cap. "I wish I could find me somebody like you."

Daddy Riley ducked his head. "So, what happened to you and Curtis?"

"We broke up when he let Cynthia have a baby. She was a pharmacist who thought the best life for her was rearing her children. After that, things between me and Curtis started to get dicey."

Daddy Riley pulled his handkerchief from his pocket, wiped it across the hairs at his nostrils. "Seems like he didn't know you ain't meant to be with everybody you fall in love with. The way your generation wants it all can make life too complicated."

"But look at your generation. How could you and my mother be together and not talk about anything? Not about her ex, my daddy, sneaking around our house. Not about why she was letting me mis-raise myself and how you felt about it. I don't think that's what I would call keeping things nice and simple."

"Neicy, you're making a good point. But what you need to know is that men and women who were together didn't get into each other's business. I think because life was so hard for us black folks in those days that everybody had had to do things they didn't feel proud of and didn't want to talk about them. I'm not saying it was right, and it did cause suffering. But slavery and jim crow laid down the roots for a whole lot of misery amongst us and keeping silent is one way we coped with it."

"I never thought of it like that." That was a lot to think on.

"See, baby, everything was fragile. Couldn't take any more stress, any more pressure. But, since you've been down here and you and me been talking, I see I could've done more than I did. Husbands and wives do need to communicate with each another. One husband, one wife," he emphasized, index fingers shooting up in the air, one at a time. "That's complicated enough."

"I got it. Two people, one couple. But we were trying, though. Now, I believe that the only way something like what we were doing could work is for everybody involved to be healthy, intact individuals who have important connections with each other."

"Well, maybe the next generation after you and Curtis can faffle that out."

"But I really wasn't ready for a real, deep relationship even though that was what I said I wanted."

Daddy Riley was listening hard. "Why not?"

"Letting someone close in, being vulnerable, commitment. I really get shaky whenever I think about giving somebody my hand and saying, 'Look, here's me. I'm bringing who I am and going all the way with you.'" She could feel her chest thumping. "Just saying the words is making my heart race."

"Your heart's supposed to be pumping like crazy when you say those words to somebody. It's more than a play thing to yoke up with another person like that."

Her heart was still thumping. "Suppose I can't stick it out, that I don't have it in me? Suppose I'm really not enough to hold someone for that many years?"

"Baby, you're wiggling your finger on the problem. You got to know who you are and be comfortable with that. If you don't, every one of them things you're fretting about could happen. But if you do, you and the next person might have a chance." He set his cap midway his head and scratched a slick spot. "The main thing about making a go of it with somebody is you can't be indecisive. You got to shit or get off the pot. Get yourself together. Make your choice. When you say this is it, let it be that." He stood up. "Come on, let's get over to the restaurant. You gon make us sit here 'til I turn eighty on my seventy-ninth birthday?!"

Daddy Riley got his steel drum smoking back behind the restaurant. He stood in a paved corner with his pit, grilling utensils, white-ragged sop spoons, and a large pot of barbecue sauce. "I doped this up myself," he bragged, running his finger across his tongue and licking it. "The real McCoy." His buddies sat near him around a picnic and a patio table. The scene was worth at least a million dollars.

"Can I help do anything, Daddy Riley?" She hovered around him.

"Run in the kitchen, look in the little refrigerator behind the door, and bring me that last pan of ribs."

When she returned, two more guests were getting out of their car. The man was unloading a stereo system while the woman held the rear door open. "I'm the music man," he shouted. "Can't have no celebration like this without the right oldies but goodies."

This elder she liked immediately. He was squat, dark-skinned and shiny with some serious liver splotches. As he stepped away from the car door with the receiver in his arms, she saw that one leg was shorter than the other and he walked with a noticeable limp. He set the receiver on the picnic table as Daddy Riley came over.

"Neicy, I want you to meet these two people. This is Swank's aunt, Aunt Maxine, and her husband, Willie. They helped talk me into moving down here."

"Pleased to meet you, Aunt Maxine, Mr. Willie."

"Drop that Mister stuff and just call me Willie. I ain't as old as I look." He started laughing, flashing a gold crown on his left dog tooth, and didn't stop until she joined in with him. It must be nice to spend your days with somebody who can make you laugh about nothing. Aunt Maxine smiled and took her hands. She had on a purple pants suit with a long-sleeved purple and beige print blouse.

Willie got the music going. And Daddy Riley served up barbecue. Aunt Maxine put herself in charge of the drinks cooler, handing out beer or sodas or wine spritzers like she knew who should have what or whose meds put a "no-no" on them.

She accepted a second spritzer from Aunt Maxine and moved to the table nearest the grill. The warmth felt good. This was like being at those places in California where people sit outside running patio heaters in denial about the cold. But everybody else seemed fine in the winter sunlight with their summer jackets, fall sweaters, and shawls.

Too late she saw she was sitting down next to Mr. Dinkins. He methodically wiped sauce from his fingers with a crumpled paper napkin. The two other old folks at the table – another gent, and a tall, thin woman – were still concentrating on their plates and barely glanced up at her. "The Honey Dripper" was bouncing in the background.

"You know, I really had a good wife." Mr. Dinkins twisted his thumb in the napkin, finished his cleaning, and gave her a roguish look. "I walked past her house everyday. You know how it is, we were living in the country. One evening she called me over. 'Come here,' she said. So we got to talking. She was fourteen, I was going on twenty. 'I see you come by here everyday. I think I like you.' 'I like you, too,' I told her. I'd had my eye on her, you know, knew who she was and everything. 'What you want?' she asked me. I said, 'I'm looking for a nice person to marry.' 'That's the same thing I want, too.' We stayed together, raised all of our chirren. Fifty-eight years it'd been when she died."

"They need to turn that music up. Nobody can hear what he's playing." It was the woman across the table, cutting her eyes in the direction of the sound, her long shoulders haunching like a turtle. "My name is Donzell."

"Pleased to meet you, Miss Donzell. I'm Mr. Riley's stepdaughter from New York, Neicy."

"You always complaining you can't hear nothing," the gentleman next to her spoke up.

"Neicy," Miss Donzell inquired, "is that music loud enough?"

"I can hear it just fine." Mr. Dinkins threw in his two cents.

I'm going to Kansas City, Kansas City here I come. The bass keys were walking. *They got some crazy little wimmen there and I'm gonna get me one.*

I'm gonna be stand' on the corner, Twelfth Street and Vine. Gonna be stand' on the corner, Twelfth Street and Vine. With my Kansas City baby and a bottle of Kansas City wine.

The honky-tonk beat had caught everybody and heads were bopping. She was humming under her breath. The gent next to Miss Donzell was really taking it out, jooking side to side and snapping his fingers, then exaggerating on the refrain, *THEY GOT SOME CRAZY LITTLE WIMMEN THERE AND I'M GONNA GET ME ONE.*

"And after you get her, what you gon do with her?" Miss Donzell goaded.

He kept jooking and bopping.

"Robinson ain't nothing but a old ass, always talking 'bout women." Miss Donzell looked at her for support. She didn't know what to say, but before she had to say anything, Robinson fired back.

"Older the bee, sweeter the honey."

"When a man gets old, his car gets cold. Has that ever happened to you?" Miss Donzell was not about to be outdone.

Robinson ignored her.

"Well, I'm with Moms Mabley. The only thing a old man can do for me is show me the way to a young man."

"Moms Mabley hadn't met the right old ram."

"Older the buck, the stiffer the horn." Mr. Dinkins cried out, authoritatively, with a snigger and more spunk in his voice than she'd heard before.

She couldn't believe these old people. Riffing like this about sex.

"No more hock-ey, though, for the old field lark-ey." Miss Donzell put another cap on it.

Robinson came back. "I'm born'ed, like my mammy used to say, but I ain't dead yet!"

Beulah used to say that, too, but she never thought Beulah was talking about sex.

"You know sometime," Mr. Dinkins kicked in, "you have a horse, and you just love to ride that horse. Don't want nobody else to ride him, just want to keep him to yourself..."

"Excuse me." She got up from the table.

"Baby," Mr. Robinson asked, "could you tell Maxine to send me another one of them Budweiser's?"

Daddy Riley's eyes lit up when he noticed her coming toward him, making her way past two men setting up for dominoes. "Baby, how you doing?"

"I had to take a break from that table. They were out of control."

He laughed, glancing over at Mr. Dinkins, Miss Donzell, and Robinson who were still going at it. "I saw you sitting down with them and thought to myself, Neicy is going to have to hold her hat with that bunch." He kept laughing. "What were they jawing about?"

"Sex."

Daddy Riley really cracked up, then stopped abruptly, peering at her. Her face felt tense. Those elders being so out there had bothered her.

"Sex, huh? Nothing wrong with that, is it?"

"Naw, I like sex. Sex is fine. But why does everybody have to spend so much time worrying about it? Sometimes I wish it would just go away!" She heard herself sounding like a pre-adolescent beseiged by boys and budding desire. Those elders weren't worrying, they were having fun. "Bah, sex. Bah, men. They need to just keep their pants zippered up."

"Sweetheart, you don't mean that." Daddy Riley looked alarmed.

"Why don't I mean it? That would save everybody a world of trouble. Oh, I'm sorry, Daddy Riley." He didn't look relieved. "I'm just being ignorant – and regressed."

"What's regressed, Neicy?"

"When a grown person under psychological stress is acting stupid like a child, which is probably what's been happening most of the time I've been here. Look, over there. Aunt Maxine is trying to get your attention. Go 'head on. I'll dig you later."

"Sweet potato." Still perplexed at the brow, he set off toward Maxine and the cold drinks cooler.

He was the one who found her after the barbecue disbanded, stretching her tired legs on the picnic table bench after walking further away from the restaurant than she should have and then hurrying back. She'd set out cold, now she was sweating. From one extreme to the next.

"Neicy." Daddy Riley eased onto the bench. "Sit down and let's finish our conversation. We were talking about sex." He said the word sounding embarrassed but determined to be forthright.

She sat down.

"Neicy, don't be afraid of it, even though people misuse and abuse it. I don't know why that's been such a hard hill for you. I wouldn't be surprised if somewhere along the line, before I took up with you and your mother, some lowlife molested you. But all men aren't like that. Some of us you can trust."

In a dark corner of her mind, she saw herself pushed over and lying on her back, panties down and swinging around one ankle, dress up over her head, belly exposed, legs spread open. She was being done to. Against her will, was it? She hadn't said yes, somebody had made her. Was she or was she not helpless? But the whole thing felt good.

Her high yellow face reddened with shame. "I'm a bad girl, Daddy Riley."

"What's that word you just learned me?"

"Regressed."

"Appears to me you're being it again. You're a grown woman now, Neicy. You don't have to trust us men if you don't want to. Trust yourself. You know yourself well enough now to understand what to look for, who to stay away from, where not to go. You want to be with somebody. You told me that the other night. That's the clue. If your whole self, your body and soul wants a relationship, that's the Master letting you know it's right. Hew to that, trust that."

"I don't know if I can." Transform or die. Two options, one choice, if choice you could call it.

"Yes, you can." He stood up slowly, looked down at her. "By the way, Jonai has been asking about you. I think he wants to see you again."

"Jonai's too young for me."

"Well, some people might say that. But just so you know. Age ain't got nothing to do with love — and vice-versa. It may say what we do with the love, since we have to have ways to try to live with each other. But that ain't about the love." One of his pauses. "Why don't you just take it easy for a while? Then, if you feel like it, you can go to the Raffers meeting tonight like you said you wanted. Jonai extended you a special invitation."

CHAPTER 16

She walked into an argument that must have begun as soon as the Raffers meeting kicked off, since it was only 7:15 when she slipped through the back room door.

"... you all forever talking about white people. White people this, white people that. I come to Recovering From Slavery because I'm sick and tired of white people. And then I get here and have more of them crammed down my throat."

"Wait a minute..."

"That's not true."

"You're exaggerating..."

Everybody was responding at once. There were at least three or four times as many people present as when she'd sat in night before last.

"Every time I've been here, that's been the agenda in one way or another." The sister who was speaking had the meeting in an uproar and wasn't budging.

"Let's hear Alexis out." Jonai asserted order, rising from his chair and gesturing in the speaker's direction.

The sister looked like an "Alexis." Slightly glamorous, African features in a mobile face, long nugget quartz earrings, pointed chin, beautifully dressed. "Can we, please, just for once, stay focused on us and talk about how we can love one another?"

"Yeah, yeah, let's do that." A man in corduroy pants snapped, an angry, impatient expression on his face, his tone bitter. "The one thing I want to say on that topic is that the worst I've ever been treated was by other black people."

Nobody expected to hear that.

"I grew up right here in this ward," he continued. "My daddy was touched in the head and my mama was too busy taking care of me and my brothers and sisters to do much of anything else. When he shot and killed her and they let him come right back home, things got worse..."

From all over the room, people interrupted – asking questions, arguing with him, making excuses, offering explanations. As he kept telling about his poverty and isolation, being put down and shunned, ostracized in the neighborhood and at school, she felt herself identifying more and more strongly with him until, when a slightly older woman dismissively said, "Oh, it couldn't have been that bad," she heard herself speaking out before she realized she had decided to do so, sitting upright and pissed off in her seat.

"It could have been that bad." She projected forcefully and then turned directly toward the man. "My life wasn't exactly like yours, but I was made to feel inferior because I was poor, too. Stuck-up principals' daughters thumbed their noses at me. Nobody invited me to the Jack and Jill's or the debutante ball. The teacher who was supposed to be my champion worked me like a maid at her home on Saturdays, then gave me books to read and her grown daughter's hand-me-down clothes. Because I was self-conscious and didn't know how to mix, I got called 'stuck up' and 'funny.' Sometimes that still happens." She was remembering how Vivian and Margo had to defend her to some regulars at the Philly community center. It still rankled. But somewhere within herself she was aghast that she was dredging up this mucky old shit to a room full of strangers!

When she finished her outburst and fell silent, no one argued any more about how much pain black people could cause one another. Jonai broke the stillness.

"Where we're at reminds me of one of our early Raffers discussions. We talked about how hurting each other as black people cuts to the core in ways white prejudice and institutional racism don't even begin to match. Your own is supposed to accept you and love you, and when that doesn't happen, it's devastating."

Somebody in the back affirmed softly. "You can say that again. And beingst as how we're human, we can't really love ourselves until someone has loved us. And you can't love and accept anybody else 'til you've loved and accepted yourself. It's a circle."

"Too true." Jonai re-crossed his knees. "So it becomes doubly important for us not to confuse what we do to each other with what white power does to us."

"I don't mean to be disrespectful." The female college student from the night before sounded really earnest. "But at a certain point, aren't we talking about the kind of self-love and self-esteem issues that everybody has to deal with no matter what color they are?"

That young woman is missing the connection. Resigned to the fact that she was dredging up muck and deep feelings, she sat up in her seat and spoke out again. "Self-esteem and loving each other are really tied together. I'm just learning how I didn't feel like a loveable human being because the people I grew up with weren't able to show that to me. And the reason they couldn't is that it hadn't been shown to them, and so on and so on, handed down from generation to generation. That's part of the legacy of slavery and it makes this a racial issue."

"Right on," Alexis's seatmate jumped in. "Being black in this white-dominated country puts us in the position of having to deal with those issues twenty four-seven. We have to get it from God, Spirit, Life, Somewhere how divinely worthwhile we are if we're going to survive."

"Absolutely." Thinking about her conversation with Daddy Riley, she cut back in, not yet ready to yield the floor. "I was about to say it's a shame that at this late date I'm struggling to esteem myself."

"Well, for what it's worth," Alexis's seatmate offered, "you're definitely taking care of yourself in this exchange – but in a nice way. I don't know how you are everywhere else, but you seem pretty hooked up to me."

Yes. Inside, she did feel sturdier.

"Yeah," the college young woman said, "I have to second that."

"Me too's" and "True's" sounded out from around the room.

"The Lord works in mysterious ways his wonders to perform." The smaller of the two Methodist ladies from the night before intoned, then added, "It looks like we're going under, but in the long run, we're just getting better and stronger."

Jonai spoke up. "Well, what I want to say at this point is that white people need to stop being bullies, and that the more we people of color love ourselves, we can give up the victim role."

"And loving black doesn't mean hating white." Someone she couldn't see added. "I think loving and being loved is our true nature as human beings."

"That sounds good. But there's some white people – and a few black ones – that even J.C. himself couldn't love." The man who spoke could have been L.P. Barnett's twin brother.

"Don't say that." "Man, it's true." "Tsk-tsk." Another chorus of response and chuckles. "Recovering from slavery does make some of us hard to get along with."

After the laughter died down, an imposing brother she hadn't homed in on said in a bass voice that could have been flooring the beat on a 1950s rhythm and blues record, "I just hope all this talk about loving and being loved doesn't mean we're condoning interracial relationships."

"Condone?! Wait a minute! Who said interracial relationships were a crime and who appointed you judge jury and prosecutor?"

Uh-oh, sex in the picture. This handsome, light-skinned guy was royally ticked off. He was designer slick from crown to toe, one tasseled loafer angled on his knee.

"You can't do nothing about that. Period. If we're about to start dictating who to be attracted to, well, it's time for me to get up and go home."

"Well, get up and go, nigger." She couldn't tell which man made that remark under his breath somewhere to her right. A couple of nearby people snickered.

"I can only speak for myself" – a man behind her started talking – "but what I learned is that who you think you're attracted to can't always be trusted. If you really want to know what's driving your desire and are willing to do the hard, hurting work, you can figure it out."

She turned and spotted the very unassuming brother as he continued.

"After I broke up with this sister who wanted to marry me – which is a whole other story – and began yet another relationship with one of my white female colleagues, I started to take stock of myself. And I tell you, it was not a picnic. Oh, we shouldn't be using that word, pick-a-nigger. What I realized is that I lusted after white women and didn't like or really love my own black ass self." His half-snort, half-laugh sounded pained. "I still can't regulate the lust that rises, but I understand it now and I don't act on it. It's about choice, and I'm going out of my way to exclusively be with black women."

A gaggle of folks had their hands raised, bodies forward. A matronly woman captured the floor.

"It troubles me to hear you speak about interracial relationships as if all they're about is sex." She pinned the guy who had just finished with her cool, bullet points voice. "In the sixties, I did voter registration down in Mississippi. While I was there, one of the other students I found myself on teams with was a Jewish boy from Brown University. To make a long story short, we fell in love, moved to California and got married, raised two wonderful children, and continued to work in civil rights. And I know it doesn't make sense, but I have to confess that I would like my kids to marry black. That's inconsistent..." She trailed off, looking embarrassed. "But the point I wanted to make was that when you get close to people as allies, you can't always draw a line and say, stop here." She drew the line with her right index finger, then made the stop sign with her whole hand.

"Ma'am, I'm not trying to be smart or nothing," a young man in wire rims who looked youthful enough to be in high school began. Like most everyone, he spoke with a southern accent that her ears were becoming so accustomed to they did their own automatic translation. "But why couldn't you find one of the black brothers who was down in Mississippi to marry and do good work with?"

The male professor rose to answer. In a hounds-tooth sports jacket and dark brown pants, his salt-and-pepper bush oiled and picked, he resembled Ossie Davis. "Son, it's hard enough finding somebody you're compatible with, whose mind and education match yours, whose values and ethics are congruent, whose personal habits don't drive you nuts." People laughed.

One woman called out, "Yeah, I can't stand men who wear so much strong cologne that when I give them a friendly hug, I smell like them for two days and have to send my outfit to the cleaners."

A brother from the other side of the room yelled back. "And deliver me from ladies I bring home who leave so much makeup on my pillowcase it looks like half of their face came off."

"And don't come near me with fungus feet," another sister joined in.

"Or a lying mouth."

"Or a spitty one."

Women and men from all over the room were getting in their licks. She was cracking up and then saying, loud enough to be heard by everyone, "And stuff like age is an issue. Who are you going to find to partner with when you're not in your twenties or thirties?"

"I'd like to discuss that with you one-on-one after the meeting," Jonai's voice rang out. The men whooped. He was looking sincere, wicked, macho, shy, and sheepish all at the same time. "But, wait," he quickly got back to his chairing and waved toward the professor, "weren't you about to make a point?"

"All I wanted to say was that I don't think it's prudent to add in restrictions that render finding somebody you're compatible with harder than it already is."

"Being the same race ought to be something that helps two people be more compatible," the boy defended, not retreating even from an authoritative elder.

Madame Professor said, supportively, "In a way, it does, and sometimes it doesn't. But even if you decide to be with someone of the same race who appears to be compatible, you'll still have to work at making the relationship work."

"That's precisely the point." Alexis jumped in like she'd been waiting for this opportunity. "So why not choose to put that commitment and energy into another black person. Since you're going to be struggling, why not have it benefit us?"

All the in's and out's, all the ways of trying to think about this were crazy-making. And sex was always in the mix. We are the race we are because of who had sex with whom, under what conditions and why.

She sat back in her seat. At this juncture in her life, who could give her fiery, committed, affectionate partnership? Another Curtis? Someone like Jonai? Would she get that with Richard? When she talked about him with Erma Jean and Daddy Riley before coming to the meeting, Daddy Riley couldn't quite fathom who Richard was. He ended up saying he trusted her to make the right decision and bring the fellow down for a visit. Coming to visit wouldn't be a problem for Richard, she knew that. He could fit in anywhere.

But, still, if she wanted to make a statement to the world about loving her black self and black partner, she'd need to pin a sign on his back that said, I'm actually a brother, like those bumper stickers that read, My other car is a Jaguar, or those plaques that say, My real house is in the south of France. Why was it so important to her that she have a mate who mirrored her in this way? Was it some atavistic yearning or outmoded ideal, some misplaced allegiance to race politics? Or, as Virginia might have said, only her yellow custard self wanting something black to stir her pudding! The true yardstick should be, "what serviceable thing can I use this loving to co-create?" As she'd done all her life, she could benefit black people from many sites of struggle.

"May I please say a couple of things?" The heavy-set woman two seats away from Mr. Professor invaded her runaway thoughts. The lady was dressed in flowing pink and purple, had a round, inviting face, and rings on practically every finger. She looked like the proprietor of a beauty shop who watched her favorite story every day and, between her few longtime customers and supervising the girls in the shop, read spiritual pamphlets.

"Humans have race, souls are colorless," she gently emphasized. "Our souls are on a journey and we don't have a clue about what experiences they need to get to the next stage. It's an individual thing, peculiar to each person. Laying out any kind of one-size-fits-all rule doesn't allow us leeway and freedom." Her eyes rested respectfully on Alexis. "But at the same time, I know we should heed your call to love and be true to our own."

"Maedeen, you and your fancy hoo-doo books! Like I keep telling you, we all got to get straight with the black nation. That comes first and foremost."

This was a new voice asserting itself from a group she hadn't paid attention to sitting at one side of the room. The man was about Maedeen's age and looked like he could have owned the barbershop right next to her hair salon.

"Henry's right," another one of them seconded. "If the question we're asking is how can we love and take care of ourselves and each other, then the answer is, by loving and taking care of ourselves and each other. It's as simple as that. Give your primary energies to other black people — your squeeze, your family, your close friends. And give your support to causes that benefit and uplift the race."

"But what about those white people we get exceptionally close to, who are special and helpful to us?" Whoever said that said it so fast she couldn't see who he was.

Before anybody else could respond, Alexis leaped on the question. "I think you have to back up and ask, can white people actually be our allies? The answer is only if they can do it without requiring that we bestow on them what we need to keep for ourselves. Would they give us their money, or legal savvy, or the loan of their boats and mansions, all the benefits of their white identities and experience if all they got from us was a genuine thank you? Not our time, or our love, or our music, our warmth or rhythm, our souls or our style. No hootchie-kootchie, no worship or adulation. No sitting on our platforms at Juneteenth celebrations as honorary brothers and sisters, no special invites to our down-home house parties. Under the guise of being benefactors, white people can sap out our essence."

"The gospel truth," a voice muttered.

"I'm going to say this again," Jonai reiterated. "I believe that white people need to stop being aggressive bullies, and people of color need to stop playing the victim. Sometime soon, I hope we put this on the table."

"I vote for that." Henry backed up Jonai. "We can blame whites for a lot of things, but what we need to focus on is our response. That ties in with what I was about to say. We have to get a hold on ourselves as black people first, then we can spread out from there. I say, run the black race first and win that."

"That's what we got to teach the young ones. They don't know that any more. These days, they just go mix-up mix-up and pretty soon they naa find themselves, oona, none a we." The other little Methodist lady was vociferous as she spoke, surprisingly sliding into a cascading Caribbean accent.

The elder next to Henry spoke out again. "The race is in a crisis. We're the foundational generation." He gestured around his cohorts. "And you all are the transition." He waved in the direction of the two professors. "As we die out, the network of roots is weakening, the deep well is running dry."

Miss Maedeen used the pause after his remark to thrust herself back into the conversation. "No doubt about it, we're in crisis. We don't have to argue about that. Even if race as we know it is disappearing, I want it to fade without our destruction. I can't stand what I see everyday in the neighborhood. But at every turn, we have to be careful where and how we focus our attention. Where you put your attention is where your energy goes. It's extremely complex. As we move from one stage to the next on our journey, many kinds of things happen to us and many types of people enter our world. An experience that seemed to be wrong can turn out teaching us the biggest lesson. The gravest mistake or misfortune can lead us to the greatest blessings. We can't know beforehand, can't blame ourselves, have to forgive. Each thing we encounter is grist for the mill..."

Deep. Deep. Yes, where she was now was exactly where she should be. And everything that happened to her was how she got here – from the mother God gave her to her basest sexual encounter. If it could have happened differently, it might have. If it should have been easier, it would have. But this is how it went down. She accepted that. And she couldn't have any resentments or regrets...

"Sister? Sister?" Jonai's voice entered her consciousness.

"Me?" she startled.

"I believe you're our one out-of-town visitor tonight. I was wondering if you wanted to introduce yourself or bring greetings before we closed."

Every eye in the place was focused on her. But it didn't feel like being on stage.

"My name is Neicy. I'm from New York visiting my step... visiting my father, Mr. Riley Washington."

In unison, like at the twelve step meeting she'd attended with Myrna, "Welcome, Neicy," "Hi, Neicy," "Hello, Neicy" came back at her from around the room. Having who she was returned to her like that was overwhelming. They're waiting on you to say something, girl, she prompted herself. Without a script, cue or clue, words rose like lava from her tight diaphragm.

"I'm down here visiting my father, whom I haven't seen in twenty years. This is a homecoming for me. I'm trying to figure out a lot of things in my life – who to be with, how to belong, what I need to be happy. Being at this meeting has helped me so much. I really thank you."

They heard what she said. She could see it in their open bodies, in their unhooded, accepting eyes, in the way every one of them had exchanged their seat for hers. The appreciation she had begun to feel for herself welled up and glorified them.

His unswerving gaze on her, Jonai started talking. "We always end our meetings by having anyone who wants come sit in the center of our circle. There we send to them as vitally as we can our highest collective energy. Sisters and brothers" – he swept the room – "what say we put Neicy in the center of our being and show her some love?"

To her surprise, the whole room started applauding. Maybe because Jonai made his suggestion with the flourish and intonation of an m.c. at the Apollo. Maybe because she herself caught her breath sharply, hand to her heart, when he did so, like the contest winner who had just been starrily announced. They were clapping their hands and beaming delightedly upon her. And she hadn't performed a miracle, hadn't worked any wonders. Wasn't done up beautiful, wasn't sexy. Had been nothing but her unadorned self.

At the center of the circle, in the eye of their attention, she sat in the battered brown chair without a role to play and nobody to be but Neicy. Sister. Daughter. Kin. Friend. A tiny part of her wanted to duck and run. But, now, she was big enough to sit there and receive the waves of love rolling toward her. They hit like a hurricane in the Bahamas, but transformed into green and blue laving every residual dry spot that needed the water. Her breasts expanded with an icy-warm tingle all the way to her fingertips. So this is what the sanctification around the word "family" that she heard in other people's voices was about. So, then, the place where you could lie down safely and experience human touch was "home" – no longer alien, no longer suffering from the false and unholy sense of separateness and isolation.

At some point, the Raffers started, one by one, two and one together, leaving. But they all, to a person, to a black and beautiful person, passed by and laid a hand on her. Some leaned over and squeezed her shoulder. A few whispered softly, "Take care, Neicy," "God bless you, Neicy," "Spirit guide." "Remember, we love you."

Jonai extended his hand, helped lift her up, gave her the final hug. She passed it all on, to the smiling ancestors behind her and the luminous children ahead.

She was still floating nearly twenty-four hours later as she walked up and down the stairs getting dressed for Daddy Riley's big bash. In the middle of the landing, she stopped for a heated sneeze.

"Neicy, I think we're going to take you to the doctor's on Monday if you're not out of this bug thing by then. One of the produce guys told me there's some kind of funny fever traveling up from the coast." Coming from her room with the ironing board under her arm, Erma Jean threw her a solicitous look.

"I'm alright." She kept climbing the stairs.

Daddy Riley stepped out of his room as she made it to the top. "Hey, Neicy," he said and started smiling like a man who hadn't done enough of it in his youth and was making up for lost time.

"Daddy Riley, how does this look?" Arms extended, she spun around lightly, toward one side and then reversed to the other, on the return revolution, jutting out her chest and lifting her chin, 1950's model style. Nowadays, she thought, they keep everything tight and swagger. Not how she was feeling at all.

"Yeah, wear this one, baby." He stood back, appraising. Took her by the elbow and slightly turned her. Stood back and looked some more.

She caught herself actually holding her breath. Felt the soft weight of the two pieces on her body, the top resting lightly on her neck and bosom, hugging down to her waist, the slim matching skirt contouring her hips. Winter white, simple. Something she had bought for no reason, packed on a whim, had never worn before.

"Yeah, it lays down on you just like your mama's garbadine suits used to lay on her." True, with the wide red belt and her red patent heels, this outfit was making a statement. "You look like a million dollars."

"Thank you. Are you ready, Daddy Riley? Or am I the only monkey holding up this show?"

"Two of us pooping off in the cage. I'm having a little trouble getting these fancy jalousies adjusted."

"Wait, let me see... oh, it's a little snap buckle... turn around..." She was fiddling and fixing, in charge, handling him, buttoning the splendid suspenders into the waist of his pants. "There," she faced him around, smoothed the front lines, "you're all straight." She plucked a ravel of black thread off the white sleeve of his shirt. They passed muster, each of them approving what they saw.

Erma Jean cut through the admiration, yelling from below. "If you guys don't get down here, we really are going to be late."

The way heads turned when the three of them walked into the party gave her another boost.

"Hey, hey, let the celebration begin!" Erma Jean called out, arranging things from the bags in her arms onto the decorated counter. Her call to party kicked festivities to a higher gear.

People wanted to know everything they could find out from this stepdaughter visiting Daddy Riley – older ladies interested in him inquiring about her history, sisters asking how had she done her hair and was it fun to live in New York, guys of various sizes, shapes, and come-on's chatting her up and asking her to dance. Willie, the music man, was set up at the back room side of the restaurant, dance floor in front of him, only now with professional equipment. The drop-dead gorgeous young man responsible for the upgrade introduced himself. "Maurice. I'm Uncle Willie's godson. I do dances. He let me help him out on this one, long as I promised not to mess with his groove. No 70's disco, no hip-hop."

"I'm digging it."

"It's kind of funny to me."

She looked at him harder. "How old are you, Maurice?"

"Fifteen."

"You shouldn't even be in here."

"I know. But Uncle Willie lets me come to his gigs long as I dress up to look older. I can pass for twenty-one. He says anything I see that I shouldn't will just make me wise."

"I bet you like your godfather."

"He's a cool old dude. You wanna dance?" A Sam Cooke cha-cha had started. *Don't know much about history, don't know much geography.* Before she could say yes, or no, Daddy Riley came up, insisting that she eat some food.

"Excuse me, Maurice."

"Check you later."

She found half of a booth and was getting into her catfish and potato salad when Mr. Dinkins appeared and sat down next to her.

"You enjoying yourself?" he asked. "Me and my wife went to every dance they had in the country when we were young. You know, we got a whole family of chirren after that. Six boys and a girl. We had seven of 'em. One died young, I buried my middle son last year. He was fifty-four."

Those six boys and a girl.

"That potato salad any good?" A little juice collected in the corner of his mouth. He swiveled like a rusty hinge, looking back over his shoulder. "Did you get that off the counter?"

"No, sir. Over at that other table." She pointed and he got up, headed dimly in the general direction, weaving around clumps of people.

Before she had swallowed another full bite, a man with a snaggle-toothed smile reactivated the place Mr. Dinkins had just vacated. She should have fixed her plate and gone in the back room. Now with food in front of her, she realized she was hungry.

"That father of mine." The man grinned.

She took a sip of her drink to assist the swallow. "You're one of Mr. Dinkins's sons?"

"That's right. I'm the knee baby. Me and my oldest brother still live here in Houston. One of my sisters is in Galveston, and I got another sister and brother out in California."

How could that be? "Your daddy said there was only one girl, that he had six boys and a girl."

"Oh, that's all he had with my mama. But he got two girls and another boy with this other lady. I call 'em all my brothers and sisters."

She whooped. That sleazy old devil. All that talk about his good wife and family, with this whole other thing going on outside. Men were a trip. It's like how they could have sex with somebody and put it in some part of their brain that had nothing to do with the rest of their lives. If a health worker, or counselor, or their wife or girlfriend asked if they were screwing around, they'd answer no and not feel like they were telling a lie.

"You got any kids?" That was all she could think of to say.

"Naw. What about you?"

"Me neither."

"Raising even one of them, especially these days, is more than just a notion." He said it like he had some good secondhand experience.

"That's what I thought, too. But I've been thinking lately that children always change your life, but you just go ahead and have 'em. Some of us, though, I guess, weren't meant to be parents." But what a life story she would have to tell her daughter if that long-gone baby had been born! And the journey wasn't over yet.

Mr. Dinkins's son gave her another snaggled smile and stood up. "There's still enough of them to go around. ---I'm gon let you finish eating. I just wanted to say hi."

"Hi. Thank you for stopping by."

She had to practically yell her last sentence because somebody had cranked up the music. Must have been Maurice since the speakers were blasting "Disco Inferno." *Burn, baby, burn.*

"That's my jam!" She was out of her seat, both arms up, shoulders pumping, feet stomping toward the dance floor, with nary a protest from her hip or leg. *Burn that mother down!* People were getting juiced. Talking loud, laughing louder. A sign on the front door for over a week had been warning patrons that Swanky Jean's would be closed after 5 p.m., Saturday, December 10 for a private affair. But Erma Jean and Daddy Riley were letting in their favorite customers, so the crowd was growing. She was bumping into them, they were backing into her. Jonai waved from the door.

Burn, baby, burn. Disco inferno. Burn, baby, burn. Burn that mother down!

Stuck in traffic, she stopped where she was, halfway to the sound and began jamming right there, connecting with a tall, dark dude in front of her who moved like he was good to go, too. He tipped her upraised arm and spun her. She came back around, sucking in her stomach, gracefully working her butt as they re-settled into the pounding rhythm. She would have started that pogo spring they used to do, even in her high heels, but couldn't find a clear enough space to jump. *I guess I got a little buzz on, too.* Vodka and orange juice. She hadn't drunk hard liquor since who knew when.

Somebody dimmed the lights. Uncle Willie reasserted himself, but with a perfect seque, one of her old favorites, Bill Doggett's "Honky Tonk," the driving beat both relentless and mellow. She kept bopping up toward the dance floor, slightly out of breath.

Daddy Riley caught her and began a soft-shoe shuffle, head dipping from side to side, alternating that with a light speakeasy swing. Dancing together, the two of them were smooth as butter. And she didn't even know that Daddy Riley could dance. He was bowing to her, about to ask her something, when Erma Jean walked up and dragged her away to the wall behind the counter.

"Be careful with Dar." Erma Jean's caution sounded angry.

She didn't get it. "All I was doing was..."

"You know he has that pacemaker and the doctors don't know why he's still losing weight."

She was bewildered. Although she wanted to hear it, this didn't seem like the time or place to have a conversation about Daddy Riley's health. "I'm sorry. I didn't know. But all we were doing was..."

"Just be careful, okay?" Erma Jean's eyes were flashing.

"Okay." She felt assaulted and leaned against the wall, recuperating, as Erma Jean walked away.

Around again at the front of the counter, she ran into Maurice. "Is that a drink in your hand?"

He responded with a dimpled smile. "Wanna dance?" he asked, reaching for her hand and leading them to a corner of the crowded dance floor.

They started off doing something betwixt and between to a song with that kind of nondescript vibe, picked up on another oldies cha-cha, then the pop reggae beat of "All Night Long." After that, Uncle Willie went way back for "C.C. Rider" and, as she and Maurice were figuring how to work it, Daddy Riley cut in. "Let me have a go on this one, young fellow."

She moved into his arms, both of them swaying. Found the fit of breasts to chest, where hands rest within palms and on long pliable backs. Stayed there through that song and the next one. Willie was stringing together a roll of slow golden oldies. She had been a little bitty girl when this music was hot.

Forever, my darling, my love will be true. Always and forever, I'll love just you. Just promise me darling, your love in return. Make this fire in my soul, dear, forever burn.

As whoever was singing this haunting commitment glided into the change, *My heart's at your command, dear,* Daddy Riley's arm tightened around her waist and she felt her body responding with pleasure. Pleasure with a thrill of danger, the charge beneath the surface of all the sexual feelings she generally let herself know. But, then fear, overwhelming. Such feelings weren't safe, weren't safe. She couldn't trust herself, trust him, wanted to pull away. Panic started running, chattering, audible in her pulse.

"It's alright, baby. It's alright," Daddy Riley said. The strength and tenderness with which he held her intensified. She kept her arms around him as he continued to gently, firmly rock her, not letting her go, until she relaxed with all the energy in her body. Her blood calmed. Half-timid, half-bold, she stayed with him. This, finally, was the father-daughter dance she'd never had – her own unique debutante outing.

"I'm at the end of my life, baby, feeling backwards in time. But you, Neicy, you're young. You have a world of brightness ahead. It's good, what you're feeling. That's you, being yourself. It's your womanhood, your glory. And you can choose what to do with it."

Something dark and shut down, something scared and uncertain opened up to the light. Sexual force, once aroused, wasn't uncontrollable. What she or what others did with it didn't have to hurt her bad. This was good, what she was feeling. Her being herself, her womanhood, power and glory. She rested her cheek on his shoulder, her arms, his arms keeping them close. She deserved this sweet affection, she was worthy of such love.

"Hey, wild turkey! You, birthday boy!" She lifted her head and looked to see who was calling Daddy Riley. Another one of Swank's old buddies.

Daddy Riley pulled his handkerchief out of his pocket, raised his arm and waved toward the crowd on the sidelines playing with him.

"You, wild turkey, let me see you strut!" the man called again.

Daddy Riley released her with a farewell whisper. "Whatever you do, baby, make sure love is at the front end of it."

Willie swung again into "Honky Tonk" as Daddy Riley took over the floor, stepping stiffly with his legs, flapping his shoulder blades, puffed out, claiming the space, thumbs hooked through his fancy suspenders — strutting for all the world like a wild turkey — while the guitar, sax, and organ kept up with him and everybody watching roared. He was so beautiful. He didn't know how to care for her when she was growing up with him, but he was sure loving her now. And, now, she could let him.

She was actually crying, her brain hopscotching in giddy sentences. She was drunk. No, feverish and sick. No, emotionally moved. She felt sexual current still running through all her female and nascent male parts. Whatever came into her, whatever she went into, there would be love on both of the sides. She could stop obsessing about sex and just let it be. Unsteady on her feet, she lifted both arms, trying for a spin, loving every moment, loving herself, every inch and ounce.

"Don't you all go nowhere, now." It was Erma Jean, raising her voice to the crowd. "Eat some more. There's plenty food left. Have another cocktail. Enjoy Willie's music. Isn't he great? We're going to cut the cake in a few minutes."

Erma Jean rushed over to her. "Neicy, are you alright?"

"I'm feeling a little funny." She was woozy and giggling, wiping away tears. Actually, what she felt was that she was about to throw up any minute.

"I think I'd better run you home and get you to bed."

"No..." But she really didn't have what it took to refuse.

Erma Jean was sweet with her, looking worried and sisterly. She whisked her out the rear door, letting her stop to give Daddy Riley a kiss on the cheek.

Doubled under the blanket back at the house, the flannel downy against her clear naked skin, she fell into a feverish sleep. When she woke during the night, the lamp had been turned off, so Erma Jean must have looked in on her. She instantly dropped back off, a current of heat down one side of her body and pings of liquid cold on the other. Somewhere after that, she awakened again, but not really. It was more like she came to some kind of consciousness in her sleep, still asleep but awake and at the same time dreaming. The reel that had roused her continued to roll, scenes and images moving fast.

At a large conference, she missed the excellent presenter, who delivered the best speech anybody had ever seen. But she reunited with all of her old husbands, sons, and lovers and in a blip of time, had marvelous sex with the special smooth-pubed one. It was like magical self-love, both receptive and bestowing, like breathing skillfully in harmonious wholeness on both halves of her meditatively knowing mind. Cunnilingus, coitus, her in the middle, the top, the bottom, all over the show, a rainbow medley of bodies. Finally, a finger and her ass. Phallus in her pussy. Reverent mouth mounding her clitoris. Her own hand twirling her nipples. Sex was life, and yet there was more to living than sex.

The flying in the sky after that was sheer magnificence, airy floating and zooming, overseeing the numberless days and nights of her seamless life. This must be the kind of heavenly dream visit Richard had been telling her about. But this one felt less like a teaching and more like an awesome confirmation. She'd been doing the work for a very long time. Directed to look around for her legs, to find her body, she turned like an eel or a leaf, in the torque of a supple dancer. Saw her levitating limbs miraculously up there in the wind. Laughed and tumbled down. So much for the physical form! She knew she was free. To be spirit in the body, making body matter – or not. Her choice the adventure. No longer afraid to go all the way.

Still not fully herself, she came up for the next procedure, to the soothing attendant who prepared her senses for what was to come. At the center of an arena of helpful attention, she lay down like a baby, flanked by three women, who became the two, who became the one who gently pressed her into correct and desired position, her body as boneless and pliable as the builder's fabled and slippered thumb, who folded her right hand across her breast, then doubled it back for the second, the emotional sign. Such peace, pure peace. There was nothing to ask for, no reason to move in the charged and sonorous glow of the minded air. The woman smiled, "Now you can repose in blissful contemplation of your soul." Given that permission, she began to quiver, clang, quake, shudder and then vibrate in an ecstasy of heavenly motion, to cry out her longing for eternity of this moment in a dry and sobbing release, the contemplating-crying-knocking and the cascading joy all of a piece. She felt like she was either dying or being born.

It was interrupted by the sound of music – loud country church wailing – and a woman she thought she knew coming lopsided into the picture. "Velma!" Her grandmother. Black dress and skinny hips still pumping. "Daughter, daughter," she was shouting, hands wringing in fury and anguish. "Some one of us, some one of us, some one of us has got to find happiness. Where's our sweetness?" She cried and beat and wrung and stomped, furious on the back of the bench. "Daughter, daughter," she shouted out again, shaking both head and fists at her. "Some one of us has got to find happiness." She was definitely getting her panties in a wad.

"Take it easy, please take it easy, grandmother." Becalmed, she smiled lovingly at the agitated and crackling woman, the sound of feathers clouding around her head.

Everything's gonna be alright, everything's gonna be alright. The chant was soft and the beat steady, as three little birds flew brightly off the corner of her eye and three ancient elders around a big pot beckoned her to come take a bath in the mud. She saw herself waltzing back on stage, her light face glowing, bowing gracefully over and over to outrageously prolonged applause. Saw the shape of someone she couldn't yet recognize waiting for her in the wings.

EPILOGUE

(June, 2008 – Playa Anita, Costa Rica)

Well, she was hanging on the Caribbean side of another tropical spit of land – but below the hurricane line or she definitely wouldn't have her behind here in the middle of June!

What a treat to find all these roots people, this rich brown and black history. She could thank expatriate gentrification for the upscale restaurants of delicious food and the eco-friendly bungalow she was staying in, howler monkeys baying overhead at night and the tantalizing promise of a sloth sighting. !Espanol hablado por todas partes! Bless her mentees, Twi and Dwayne, for making her learn the language.

A shift of breeze from the blue-green ocean whipped open her beach cover-up, the flimsy white fabric an easy mark for the wind. Except for a dress outfit and some bright print scarves, everything she packed was white. Not only was it cool, but the absence of color was supposed to repel mosquitoes.

The sun was taking its time sliding down the sky. The tide wasn't in any hurry either to head away from the shore. She was waiting for it to recede and flatten the lively little waves so she could jump into calmer water.

"Here you go, Deneice." Ben closed the sliding door behind him and handed her the pineapple and ginger ale mix she'd chosen from the drinks he offered.

This house of his was as fancy as her tourist bungalow, and its location on a sweeping beach curve with almond trees and an unspoiled view made it spectacular real estate. So far, since he stopped her as she passed three days ago, this tall, thin, handsome, older black man had done all the right things. He'd even asked the right questions and knew that she had found Playa Anita through her close friend, Chris, who came in the spring on a yoga break for editors and recommended it profusely. Knew that her Stepdaddy Riley had died in June twelve years ago, six months before his eightieth birthday. That she was down here trying to decide whether she wanted to star in a film version of the raunchy cult play that had made her famous.

"So, why are you having such a hard time making up your mind about the movie?" That part of their conversation obviously stayed with him. "Everything you said sounded great."

"That's because I told you all the good stuff. Yesterday was one of my pro days."

"Pretend this is a con day and tell me why you don't want to do it." With the tip of one long finger, Ben stirred the drink he was sipping.

"I don't know that I'm still interested enough in the part to keep on working with it. I'm actually tired of being a smart, sexy African American bitch named Joyce – even if she is a fresh generation role model. And I'm not sure I want the challenge of trying to succeed in a brand new medium. Being a stage actress is one thing, doing a film is something else."

She also didn't know if she felt like straining up, as Virginia used to say, to keep looking as young as she would need to, even with the aid of makeup, lighting, camera tricks, and high-tech editing. People always told her she didn't appear to be her age, but did she want her ongoing sense of self and well-being to depend on that? She'd been contemplating carrying a bit more weight and letting some silver show through her thick, glossy hair. Letting herself stop sucking in her stomach.

She released it now, sitting in this canvas sling chair, and glanced down at her midriff, the roll of softening muscle, the fine cracks developing in her deep creamy skin. She accepted it all much, much better if she didn't have to pretend it wasn't there. Wonder what Ben would say if she shared this piece with him. But if she did, every time he looked at her from this point until forever, that would be what he saw. For now, his mind was still on what she'd said about not wanting to do the film.

"That kind of uninspired is exactly how I felt when I quit my job. I was bored with juggling executives and clients and no amount of bonuses could get me fired up. I'd been in and out of Costa Rica and when I stumbled on this wayside beach town, I knew instantly it would work for me." He eyed the water. "Are you ready to swim?"

"Not yet. I'm waiting for the waves to calm down."

"You sure must like to wait."

She couldn't read his tone, jerked up her head. "What makes you say that?"

"Nothing. Just what you said. Hey, is that somebody out there hailing you?"

It was Carlos, her favorite taxi driver, arms high and waving.

"Hola, senorita!"

"Buenos!! ---Carlos drove me today. He said he might have to take his grandmother to the hospital in Limon, but if he didn't, he'd be chilling at the beach."

"I think I know him. Before I learned how to navigate that series of ruts they call a road, I flatted both tires on my bicycle coming from town. He helped me dismantle it and brought me and the bike home. He's a nice guy. Would you like some more juice and soda?"

"Yes, thank you." She trailed him inside. What made him say she liked waiting? Besides her swim, the only thing she was deferring was judgment about him – whether he was the gem he seemed to be or just another aging gigolo proving to himself that he hasn't lost it all. Once she'd gotten it that, regardless of what society or anybody messaged, her worth wasn't just sexual, it was a short step to realizing that she didn't need to legitimate herself in any external way. She still couldn't see being with somebody whose only purpose in life was to party – any more than she could imagine partnering with a man who didn't like making love. The erotic and the spiritual, she had learned with Richard, could be united with another person in service to the world. Would he, could he understand that? Photographs of him perennially smiling among different groups of people punctuated the walls.

"Ben, where is this?" She angled over to the picture that jumped out at her. Ben dominated the center in a turtleneck sweater and jacket, his arms around two women who appeared to be his wife and daughter. Another woman and three men ringed them. The clock tower in the background suggested London, but the adjacent skyscraper didn't fit.

"You would ask about the most complicated picture here. That photo was taken in Frankfurt year before last." He joined her in front of it.

"This is my youngest daughter," he pointed. The woman on his right arm. "She'd just presented a paper at a conference on translation. And this is my oldest daughter."

"Oh, really?" The woman on his left arm that she thought was his wife.

"There're twenty-four years between them. And this beauty here is my middle daughter with her husband." He touched the image of the third woman, who was waisted together with one of the men. She looked as white as her moustached mate. The other two daughters were darker than Ben with definitely Afro features. When she told him she'd been divorced for a couple of years, no children, he said he was, too, with three grown daughters. She had thought that meant one wife.

"I made damn sure my girls all kept in touch with me and got to know each other. Come, let's go back outside. I want to tell you everything."

He'd had not one wife, but three wives. The first one, his high school sweetheart, was killed in a car accident six weeks before their baby was due. The infant girl survived. Wife number two was a white woman from Barbados. They fought about everything, including how to raise their daughter, until they finally broke up.

"My third wife was named Myrna." Ben slid his chair back, evading the slanting sun. "We were project managers at the same company. I really thought I'd gotten it right when I hooked up with her. We had a daughter almost immediately and I wanted another child, hoped for a son, but she didn't. Long story short is that fourteen years into the marriage, I caught her groping one of her assistants in the stairwell at work. He was the latest in a string of affairs she'd been having since our wedding day. It took me two years to stop shaking my head in disbelief..."

"Man, do I get it! That's pretty much what happened to me." He looked at her. "No, not the lengthy deception, but the way you think you know somebody you love and the devastation when the bottom drops out. Why do you think some people get the mate they yearn for and the rest of us don't? Take my friend, Margo, for example. After running around for years, she married Otis and, of all things, got pregnant when she was forty-four and had twins, a boy and a girl. They're ten years old now. What brings that kind of luck? How do you get a future like that?"

"See, there you go again, with your what's next instead of what's now." Ben was chiding her, but gently and with good humor.

"You think you're so smart, Mr. Know-it-all!" Wait 'til she told him her story.

She stripped off her beach cover-up and threw it at him, enjoying the surprised smile on his face. He pelted it back in her direction, missing her, of course, as she ran from his patio to the chop on the sparkling green water.

ACKNOWLEDGMENTS

This is a drum roll of gratitude for all the people who have given me their literary advice, personal support, and professional service during my writing and publishing of this book. If I have forgotten to mention anyone here, the omission is inadvertent, for everybody who said anything to me, however small, helped bring this book to life.

I am thankful for:

The super-talented sisterfriend who read my first attempt and pronounced, "Yes, you have a novel."

My writing groups – beloved feministas in Santa Cruz, California and the discontinued eclectic group in Little Rock, Arkansas that I still miss. I never will forget the male corporate writer of philosophical fiction who characterized Curtis as morally "all gray."

The Women's Studies colleague who left me elated when she singled out a gale-force scene of Neicy on stage (that is no longer in this final version of the book).

The agent – an old friend and colleague – who knew early on I hadn't yet found my full story.

The attendees at a lovely Sunday afternoon tea who unawares encouraged me by choosing to listen attentively to how Neicy met Erma Jean rather than refilling their plates with hors d'oeuvres.

The two amazing male psychologists – one black, one white – who persisted in helping me to find my own clarity and honesty for Daddy Riley's dance.

Those dear ones who never tired of reading drafts and assisting me with all the things I couldn't do.

The professional editor whose work taught me how to really cut non-essentials.

The very special family member who presciently urged me to step out and publish on my own.

The goddaughter who, when she finally understood what I was doing in the novel, spontaneously called me "courageous."

The marketing consultant whose savvy eye found the last few places that might throw off a popular reader.

The scrabble whiz who fed me a better word for a questionable one; the native Arkansan whose uncensored comment reminded me to be ever more sensitive to reader responses different from my own.

But this is just the beginning of my gratitude. If I detailed every gift, that would be another book.

I feel honored and blessed by each contribution, each person. May the generosity and love you have shown me return lavishly to you —

Amy Adams
Adjoa Aiyetoro
Autumn Amberbridge
Bettina Aptheker
MK Asante
Hunter Beaumont
Denise Borel Billups
Irene Borger
Ruby Bland

Ebony Blevins
S. Diane Bogus
Carleen Brice
Erna Brodber
Shakir Brown
Deb Busman
Marcia Camp
Kent Carroll
Isabelle Constant

Faith Curry
Sandy Dijkstra
John Downing
Maxine Duruisseau
Gareth Esersky
Ann Fears
Audrey Ferber
Michele Gibbs
Molly Giles
Lawrence Hamilton
Mary Margaret Hansen
Estella Hayes
Garbo Hearne

Geraldine McIntosh
Jacquelyn Marie
Konda Mason
E. Ethelbert Miller
Kate Miller
Tom Neale
Richard Nunez
Adrienne Oliver
Patrick M. Oliver
Celine-Marie Pascale
Randolph A. Polk, III
Yasmina Porter
Elinor Pryor

David Henbest
Deni Hodges
James D. Houston
Adrian Prentice Hull
Rula Abudalo Hull
Tom Hutchison
Ralph Hyman
Joshua Jackson
Catherine John
Susan Johnson
Benee Knauer
e. jean lanyon
Kaye Lundgren
Donna McConnell

Faith Queman
Helen Resneck-Sannes
Victoria Sanders
Mercedes Santos
The "Stuff-Strutters"
Byron Taylor
Alvin Turner
Deborah Turner
Carol Whitehill
Cheryl Williams
Janna Winchester
Hal Wofford-Hutchison
Martha T. Zingo